C000138380

Caliphate

by

Grant Bayliss

An environmentally friendly book printed and bound in England by
www.printondemand-worldwide.com

This book is made entirely of chain-of-custody materials

http://www.fast-print.net/bookshop

CALIPHATE
Copyright © Grant Bayliss 2015

Cover layout deign: www.spiffingcovers.com

This novel is entirely a work of fiction.
The names, characters and incidents portrayed in
it are the work of the author's imagination

The right of Grant Bayliss to be identified as the author of this work has
been asserted by him in accordance with the Copyright, Designs and
Patents Act 1988 and any subsequent amendments thereto.

A catalogue record for this book is available from the British Library

ISBN 978-1-78456-279-3

www.facebook.com/Grant-Bayliss-395665047269707

First published 2015 by
FASTPRINT PUBLISHING
Peterborough, England.

For Jed.

My little brother.

The martyrs go hand in hand into the arena; they are crucified alone.

Aldous Huxley

The Doors of Perception

1

He is lying on the west side of a small baked mud slope, looking over the crest to the east, out into the vast desert landscape. Camouflage net draped over him, he must remain hidden. It is unusually cloudy, but still about twenty degrees. He studies the flat desert broken up by the scarring ditches and wadis with dry mud mounds. Dying scarce shrubbery is all that dots the landscape as far as the eye can see, save for a can or wrapper carried from some distant town or road by the wind. He briefly watches a small transient whirlwind get conjured up from nothing, carrying dust and dirt. It dances around the endless wasteland before tiring and petering out, scattering its cargo across the cracked surface. Then all is silent again. He widens his eyes, shuffles the rangefinder so that it's more flush on his eye sockets and focuses, placing the cross-hairs on the filthy jeep in the distance. There is slight heat shimmer but not enough to completely distort the image. The vehicle has a four-seat cab and a bed. In the bed are dual mounted DShK, heavy machine guns, and various packs and ammo boxes strapped in. He counts five packs in total. At the front of the vehicle are five men squatting around a small fire and cooking pot. They look to be sat in silence wearing loose black overalls, some with AK-47s slung over their backs. He and the group are the only ones who seem to be out here in the wasteland for hundreds of miles, but that is not true. He half expects the wind to change and carry some of the group's noise towards him. It doesn't and from this distance there is no sound apart from the wind and the hard squashing and swelling of his heart.

He presses the 'RANGE' button on the top of the rangefinder and the screen reads '1656m GR ES 23390 56023'. He notes the distance along with the grid reference on the white panel on his left sleeve then plots the grid on the folded map, assessing his location in relation to it. He slowly pulls the cam net off his head, rolls on to his side and takes a look behind at the motorbike, noting the X-wing antenna protruding out of the cam net on the front of the bike, pointing north-west. He rolls back over slowly and pulls the net back over his head, turning on the radio control unit display on his left arm. The green screen flicks to life displaying 'Harris', the manufacturer of the radio, and after a few seconds the menu shows the options 'FIRES, ADMIN, EMERGENCY, EPURGE, FILL'. He scrolls down using the directional keys, highlights 'FIRES' and selects frequency two, then presses the button on the left of the unit to tune the radio. 'TUNING', the small screen displays.

The riders are not equipped to deal with attacks. Any closer and he would risk compromise, and in this coverless landscape keeping distance is of utmost importance. Out on the rallies, there is no help. In these lands patrolled by those who will destroy everything they could ever learn from, if he were compromised off the bike by a substantial group that he could not handle, he would be wise to kill himself. Looking towards the jeep, squinting his eyes against the wind and dust and relaxing them again when the wind passes, he thinks about taking a drink of water and decides against it. He takes another panoramic look across the cracked mud desert and pulls the rangefinder back to his eyes. The jeep has not moved and neither have four of the men. One of the men is walking towards a ditch not too far away. It would be ideal for them all to be as a collective. He puts down the rangefinder and adjusts his earpiece then his throat mic so it sits more central to his larynx, and returns his eyes to the display on his wrist. It says 'TUNED'. He holds down the button on the side of the display.

Caliphate

'Hello Onslaught, this is Witchcraft One Delta, radio check, over,' he says.

He releases the button and after a short pause a clean robotic voice with a hint of white noise replies, 'Hello Witchcraft One Delta, this is Onslaught, you are loud and clear to me, over.'

A feeling of relief washes over him; without Onslaught he was useless.

'Witchcraft One Delta, fire mission one launcher, over,' he says.

'Fire mission one launcher,' Onslaught replies.

'Grid, Echo Sierra, two, three, three, nine, zero… five, six, zero, two, three… height sixteen metres, over,' he says quietly, eyes dreamily locked on the group.

'Grid, Echo Sierra, two, three, three, nine, zero… five, six, zero, two, three, height sixteen metres,' Onslaught repeats back.

'One four-wheeled vehicle with dual anti-aircraft heavy machine guns, five armed PAX, in open, over.'

'Roger, over,' Onslaught replies.

'One rocket, point detonating, vertical, will adjust, at my command, over.'

Caliphate

'One rocket, point detonating, vertical, will adjust, at your command, over,' Onslaught acknowledges.

The cold ground on his thighs, his eyes look down only once for a second and then return to the dusty jeep and the men. Death will harvest us all in the end – he made no special consideration for himself, age and careful analysis of cause and effect are the gauges to predict when it will come. Long ago he came to terms with the fact that, as time goes on, the stopwatch of our lives becomes more and more visible through the mist of the illusion that we will live forever. All we can do is shun the thought and hide behind the illusion and maybe it will forget to take us. But death is not the opposite of life; it is part of life. The final hour, he thinks, the hour of reckoning when the clock is clearest and divine convictions are tested – this terrifying hour of reflection has been deprived of these men. The hour that, without acknowledgement and acceptance early on in life, leaves life a broken compass without direction. Their conclusions of their personal stories they will never read, for the book will be closed on the page of today. Slammed shut and tossed into the furnace of time. He thinks that they do not deserve this luxury. If they knew today was the day of their departure, how many of them would elect to live their lives differently, years previous of this day? The road ends here and they saw the signs all along, but they didn't see them.

Caliphate

'Ready, over,' his earpiece confirms after a few moments.

'Ready, fire, over,' he instantly acknowledges. Heartless, he thinks, but that thought dissolves before he could care. His eyes never leave the group, his cruel empty gaze only interested in the group's future movements.

A small pause, a whirlwind somewhere in the distance. A bush rustles in the breeze. He looks at his watch and follows the second hand, paying attention to its denotation.

'Shot, six zero, over,' Onslaught advises.

'Shot, six zero, out,' he replies, making a note of the time as 09.44.55, and then all is silent.

The fifth man returns from the ditch and joins the others in squatting. A final word and thought. His eyes flick between the watch and the group. A gentle gust of wind and rustle of the limited shrubbery. The only life within five kilometres, soon to be less. At 09.45.45 he picks up the rangefinder, focusing the cross-hairs on the middle of the group.

'Splash, over,' in his earpiece.

'Splash, out.'

Caliphate

The clouds move slowly overhead, uncaring, while the ground remains inanimate. The whirlwind collapses, releasing its captive dirt, and all is still. He draws in a breath and holds it. His heart thumps with each second passing. As if time was paused, a terrifying shriek screams from the sky as the rocket breaks from its journey and plants itself into its prescribed final destination. The silence that his distance gives means the ferocious impact of the rocket briefly jolts some confusion in him with its absurd unnaturalness in contrast to its surroundings. But at the other end, where the group is, there is neither time nor cognition to meddle with such wonder as they instantly transform into a black and grey fireball the size of a four-storey house, without the slightest warning or apprehension.

There is no noise for the first second and he takes this brief moment to grip the rangefinder harder, then the muffled wet crack hits him, echoing for miles around in a slow deep rumble like a yawning giant, shortly followed by a large tremor that shakes his organs while they press into the dirt. The whole world must have heard such a breach in the flat tone of the empty land. Debris flies off in every direction, slowly arcing in journey before being reclaimed by gravity. The black cloud ascends, developing a mushroom shape, and is carried off slowly by the wind. His eyes remain on the newly reformed group until the debris has settled. He stays in the prone position for a few minutes, observing. There is no movement and there is never going to be. He stands up with the cam net draped over his shoulders, looks towards the strike and presses the button on the side of the wrist display.

'End of mission, all PAX neutralised, good effect, mark as red point, over,' he says.

'End of mission, all PAX neutralised, mark as red point. Stay safe, out,' Onslaught closes the transmission.

Some scattered clouds with the December sun far beyond them beating down. He conducts a panoramic again, checking for any sign of movement. He switches off the display unit and with his hand wipes clean the small white writing panel on his arm then drops the cam net to the floor and lays it out flat. He starts rolling from one end, keeping it tight as he does so, reducing the size of the net to that of a two-litre bottle, and places it to one side. He packs the rangefinder into a pouch on his belt kit then folds away the map. He attaches the cam net to his daysack and throws the straps over his shoulders, kneels down and picks up the short barrel M4 rifle. After a few moments he checks the ground where he has been lying for any sign, takes one last look at the mushroom cloud that has now been shifted and stretched into a long plume by the wind. Transfixed for a few moments, the awesomeness of the accuracy and

Caliphate

devastation plagues his thoughts. But behind that is the senselessness of it all – it was always in the background looming over his mind: is this what it takes? Is there no other way? But the initial thought quickly ushers it away and circles back to the initial conclusion; yes.

He heads down the rear side of the slope to the bike. He slings the rifle over his shoulder and begins to remove the cam net off the motorbike, unsnagging it from the protruding parts, and packs it away in the small stowage bag hanging over the back of the bike in-between the exhausts. He slides the rifle into the valise on the front fork suspension while he climbs on. He turns the key two clicks to the right and the dash lights up with all warning lights illuminating but extinguishing after a few seconds. He turns on the sat nav screen on the right of the dash, bringing up a small map with his position denoted by a picture of a bike. He turns the key one more click to the right, the fuel pump priming with a short whirring sound and lights illuminating and extinguishing. He presses the ignition button on the controls on the right of the handlebars, the V-twin engine cranks sluggishly a few times and then fires to life with slow sporadic thumping. Each cylinder cranks, firing idly in their huge pots, releasing deep, bass-filled thumps from the twin exhausts. He kicks up the side stand, puts the bike into first gear and pulls away, heading east across the desert using what dead ground he can, towards the impact area.

Caliphate

He crosses the open ground slowly and stops the bike about 200 metres before the impact site and removes the rifle. He uses the ACOG sight on the rifle to have a more detailed look at the situation. The cloud in the final stages of its short life. Debris everywhere, remains of packs and engine parts, a leg, a shredded torso, the remains of a tyre and a bonnet, a blackened prayer mat. The unrecognisable, twisted remains of the Toyota, so mangled there is no way to tell which side it rests on. The rocket must have hit the vehicle directly. He replaces the rifle in the valise and removes the pistol from its holster on the right side of his belt kit, holding it in his hand while controlling the throttle and creeping forward. The huge knobbly tyres make easy work of the rough, dry terrain. Around a hundred metres short of the carnage he passes the first piece of debris, half a front axle with part of the wheel still attached. Further on, the twisted remains of one of the heavy machine guns poke out of the ground by the barrel, still smoking, ticking and snapping like a cooling engine. The crater is larger than he expected, the edges curled up with large lumps of mud scattered around and the remains of the Toyota half in the crater on the eastern edge. He does a slow loop of the extremities of the scene on the bike, giving it a relatively wide berth, pistol in hand, looking for anything that represents life. Everything mangled beyond repair and recognition. The mystery of what are human body parts and what are not will be solved by whatever animals sniff out the scene. A spare wheel, tyre shredded, is on fire with the internal wire mesh exposed. Half a hand. Part of the exhaust. A sandal, oddly intact. A snapped AK-47 butt with a small picture of a religious prophet taped on the side. Everything is sprayed in burnt oil and soot and the strong smell of carbon swims through his nostrils. A short distance to the north, maybe 200 metres, a crumpled black pile, like a dustbin bag full of small odd-shaped objects, sits silently in the featureless ground, the clothing rippling and flicking in the small gusts of wind. He takes a slow ride over, checking to the east every once in a while over his shoulder. The bike slows to a stop and sits thumping. He puts both feet on the floor and holsters his pistol, looking at the pile. He looks for a long time. He never forgets a face. The colour of the face on the ground and its expression and disfigurement in death, is one that does not need to be seen twice; he will remember it. A haunting deep enough to keep him awake in the lonely desert nights. Any trauma to the body other than the face and head is tolerable, but when the body's main point of social expression is as the man's on the ground, it stirs something vulnerable in him. He takes a good look to the east, and then west. He pulls his dust mask from around his neck over his mouth and nose, and heads west, along the flat cracked desert, leaving everything in its final resting position as the explosion intended.

Caliphate

2

The cat whose fur was pure white gently trotted across the top of the fence at the back of the garden, jumped down on to the empty chicken hutch with precision and galloped along the short grass past the conifer hedge. The cat startled him as it sprung on to his lap while he lay on the hammock reading. The cat stood for a moment contemplating him as if it was studying important information and slowly began to knead his lower chest, his big green eyes welded to his face. His little claws hurt as they massaged him, stretching them to their limit and clasping into fists plucking his shirt. His purring bubbled like a scuba diver, warm paws with small pads underneath like hot beans. The purity of the day in this moment is the goal in life, he thought. All of the conditions he welcomed graciously and they rooted themselves in his standard of perfection. At any moment of his choosing he could become colder or warmer, he could drink or eat whatever he wanted within a few metres of his position. Every opportunity for happiness laid around him as if life had planted the banquet at his fingertips. He put the book down next to the glass of beer on the grass and watched the cat make himself comfortable on his chest. He raised his hand and touched the end of his rough wet nose with his thumb, and the cat closed his eyes. The sun beamed down on them both through the crystal blue sky and the odour of freshly cut grass complemented the fresh air. An electric lawnmower a few gardens down relaxed him with its unin-terrupted hum as its controller methodically traced lines in the grass. He listened to the chirping of some chicks in a bird box he'd nailed to the side of the shed at the back of the garden a few years ago. Someone shouted out of a back door and the lawnmower stopped. A whining siren zoomed past the house and careened off up the road, and he paid it no attention; the spell of peace just too unconquerable. It was a moment later that the trance was rattled when his wife shouted for him from inside the house. The cat jumped off his chest and went charging into the conservatory where the kitchen was.

Caliphate

She never shouted and this turned him to the sinister mystery that lay waiting for him. He thought maybe she had cut herself slicing some vegetables or was after his attention to share something interesting that was briefly available. He swung his legs off the hammock and before his feet touched the floor she shouted again. This time he knew it was neither of his prophecies and preparation cogs began to turn in anticipation. He went into the kitchen and saw her, hands on head, staring at the TV on the wall and saw what she was looking at. The phone rang but they didn't hear it over the hypnosis of the news. His skin shrank around his guts and the sight on the screen branded itself on to his retinas, his visual cortex and then his future. This was the emergency the world had neatly avoided all along, the kind of emergency that twisted his throat, tore out his heart and buckled his stomach. Any normal conversation within a thousand miles of him and his wife stopped in that very moment.

'Oh my God,' she whispered as she squeezed his hand. 'Oh my God.'

He rides, stopping on high features often to conduct a deep scan of the land. The route back was the same as the route to the red point, a long zigzag motion moving north-west, a turn point then heading south-west

Caliphate

using the highest ground. This patrolling method of the riders is to cover as much ground as possible, overlapping slightly with the adjacent runways. If anyone were to be moving down the runway, they would come across them either in front or behind, picking up their dust trail, tracks or heat signature. If there were points which were unable to be patrolled, there is nothing they could do.

Following his previous route this way, he knows it is clear of mines and his choice of ground during daylight would add ease to navigation if he runs into night riding, something which he is reluctant to do. The night is where the surprises wait. He also knows that using the same route is potentially dangerous in case of ambushes, but risking a different route may involve detours and unfamiliar ground, and with the bike's fuel supply against him, every journey is carefully managed and fuel is considered down to the drop, every journey down to the metre. No unnecessary throttle use and every feature of the ground accessed using the most fuel-efficient route. A discipline hard learnt.

Designated resupply points are established every week, after the red points have been established, with a grid reference allocated to each rider behind their last red point. This is issued to two of the six deep fire patrols who are in most need of resupply during the evening communication schedule, leaving four holding the red point line. The riders due resupply are given a period of one hour's notice to clear and mark their individual resupply grid. Resupplies are tight and weather dependent and, within the deep operating grounds of the riders, they are likely to be shot down. If the sky is clear, they risk detection; if the sky is thick with cloud and mist, they are blind. Resupply depends on certain conditions and, with the shoestring budget of the operation, air platforms are few and far between. In an emergency the rider can proceed, with clearance, to the emergency resupply cache at the insertion point. Otherwise he is to hold his last red point for the duration of the rally until a resupply opportunity arises. Riders who are killed or injured and unable to continue on the rally have their runways merged with adjacent runways and the other riders pick up the geographical slack. In these December months, the riders are now into winter, but the desert, with the ferocious climate change in the past few years, has become a terrain to be avoided in all seasons. The conditions of the winter rallies turn the desert into a cruel testing ground. They require the most experienced riders, with rain transforming the baked mud of the desert into a perilous plain of wax, leaving the bikes sliding and slipping at every turn. The blind, unforgiving, bitter winds torture the extremities, splitting the skin like whips striking, almost hearing the crack as it hits the face and hands with every gust, shrinking the skin and holding open the lacerations with frost forceps. Snowstorms leave the

Caliphate

ground unreadable and tracks are visible for miles, leaving the riders open to stalker patrols. A cloudless night on the wet ground is to be feared. The sun is dragged away and the night has its way with the world, becoming lonelier and infinitely more austere than the cold of day. The ice winds shake the body, violently throttling every limb, as if all signals from the brain are trapped between joints, repeating the same message 300 times a minute. Without the cloud blanket insulating the desert from the cold of space, the Godless universe stares down without expression, into the eyes of whoever is caught out of cover. The cold caresses the mind, misleading consciousness into a still sleep, switching it off and watching it drown, and then the heart.

Just before twilight, he arrives at his last communications schedule point where he stops and writes his grid on the white panel on his arm. He spent last night here behind a small dune. Should anyone be looking from the east it would provide enough cover from view for him and the bike. A short distance from the dune is a small wadi that runs for many miles west, a scar in the landscape, small, but deep enough to hold a fairly substantial river. He made sure to find an accessible point into its bed – should he need to move quickly, he can descend the bank into the dry river bed and use the flanking banks as cover as he rides west undetect-

Caliphate

ed. Staying in the wadis is dangerous, however, with flash floods common during these months when the rainstorms sweep over the land.

He kicks down the stand and dismounts. The machine sits stable in the cracked mud. A KTM 990 adventurer, four stroke, liquid cooled tourer bike. Brembo piston calliper brakes and a wet, multi disc, hydraulically operated clutch and a duel fuel tank with isolation taps should a tank become damaged. The bike was a particular favourite of famous Dakar Rally and most riders preferred the KTM to the BMW GS, its rival. With its superior WP suspension making easy work of the desert only just relegating the BMW's telelever system to second place during the trials before the operation. The whole bike is painted in multi-pattern terrain camouflage, a light brown base colour and flicks of brown, light green and cream disrupting the likely hood of any pattern. Lacerations in the paint-work all over from drops and falls all over both sides of the bike, tatty and weathered but unstoppable. From a distance it is effectively invisible. The high wind shield in front of the dash made the bike look like a greyhound sat on its hind legs, prepared, proud and ready for speed. The trellis cage around the engine allowed the bike to be dropped without engine damage and there are scars and scuffs along it from the riders tiredness and clum-siness. He would sometimes sit and look at the bike in the orange hum of dusk surround by empty desert, his horse that carried him through those

Caliphate

long rallies. He would secretly thank it for its stubbornness, resilience and its courage. The bike would look back, straight past him. Sometimes in the silence he wished it would say something back.

The rear of the seat has been removed and replaced with an accessible, water-tight housing for the ECU, radio and radio batteries. On the back right of the bike is a twenty-litre reserve fuel tank the size of a jerry can and on the left is a large metal pannier box, water tight and clipped shut with two thick latches on either end. Inside the box are rations and water, spare radio batteries, a small tool kit, four pairs of spare socks, one pair of trousers, thermal undertrousers, a heavy wool jumper, spare X-wing antenna, a jetboil cooker and gas, nuts and bolts in a small box, maps, a battery-powered soldering iron and spare radio wires looped in coils held with a small zip tie. Everything in the box is stacked in order of most common usage: rations, water and jetboil on top, and everything else underneath. If something is not being used it is stowed away. On top of the radio housing is a waterproof canoe grip. Inside is his sleeping bag, Gore-Tex sleeping bag cover, roll mat, and extra food and water. Every-thing has an order of packing to make sure the minimum amount of kit is unpacked at any one time in order for a quick extraction, leaving nothing behind. All critical kit is kept on his person or in his daysack just in case he has to leave the bike in an emergency. This includes a small radio with a spare battery, night vision goggles, a warm jacket, hat and thick scarf, twenty-four hours' worth of rations, two litres of water in a plastic bladder, a survival blanket, purification tablets, a flare, luminous marker panel and poncho. His small helmet on the front of his daysack is held on by an elastic net. He didn't wear it as often as he should as the leather padding on the inside coupled with sweat made the thin skin on his forehead head itch as if from nettle stings.

Using the bike as an anchor, he takes the small bungees attached to the corners of the poncho and ties one corner to the reserve tank side of the bike and one corner to the top of the front fork. He pulls it over the seat and yanks it tight away from the bike pinning down the opposite corners to the ground with two pegs, creating a sloping shelter enough for two peo-ple. He steps back to inspect the poncho, making sure it is tight and at a flat angle. He opens the X-wing antenna and aims it north-west, then walks to the top of the dune and looks in every direction for movement, checking potential approach routes or any dust clouds. Looking up at the sky, he does a visual weather check: some thick clouds to the north, wind direction is from the south-east. There will be no clouds tonight and it will be cold. He takes another quick look to the east and moves back to the bike, switching on his wrist display on the way, selecting from the menu the 'ADMIN' net. He checks his watch, 04.58. Inserting his earpiece, he sits up against the dune and takes out a non-permanent marker pen, thin tip. He removes the map and places it in his lap, checks his throat mic and presses the button on the side of the display.

'Hello Zero, this is Witchcraft One Delta, radio check, over.'

A short burst of white noise in his ear then silence. The evening wind smuggles itself down the nape of his neck causing a chill. He zips up his jacket a little more and pushes it up, rolling it forward to create more of a seal around his neck using his shoulders. He lies down on the slope and looks at the sky. The orange glow of the sun, slowly fading. The handover of the light to the dark. The sun will keep you warm, but the cloudless night will show you the truth of the universe, that one day the sun will have its last set and there will be no more warmth coming.

He looks at his watch, 05.00.

'Hello Witchcraft One Delta, this is Zero, send locstat, over,' the robotic voice replies at last.

He replies, sending his ten-figure grid reference.

'Zero, send last red point location, over.'

'Witchcraft One Delta, last engagement point from Onslaught on runway Delta, over,' he says as he sits up.

'Zero, roger, send conditions, over.'

Caliphate

'Witchcraft One Delta, bike five, radios five, batteries four, rations two, water two, fuel three, ammunition five.'

He replies slowly, still looking at the sky. 'Zero, bike five, radios five, batteries three, rations two, water two, fuel three, ammunition five, roger, wait out.'

Zero repeats back his message in case there is confusion or something missed. There is a pause in transmission, which he expects as they cross-reference his status with his adjacent call signs' statuses in order to cue up joint resupplies. Zero comes back. 'How are you, over?'

He rubs the corners of his eyes with his thumb and forefinger. 'Getting cold… over,' he replies after a moment, looking vacantly at the wadi.

'You are to proceed back on the original task to the last red point and clear the ground to the south, as your engagement is the most extreme eastern red point on the eastern flank – roger so far,' the emotionless voice replies.

'Roger, over.'

'Thirteen-point-three-zero kilometres east of that red point is Route 77, roger so far, over.'

He had studied the map earlier today and was familiar with the location. He stares at the darkening sky. 'Roger, over,' he says.

Caliphate

'You are to establish eyes on Route 77, by no later than 14.00 hours tomorrow, over.'

'Route 77, NLT 14.00 hours, roger, over.' He wanted to ask why but Zero controlled tasks and he was in no position to see or understand the bigger picture of the operation with its various moving parts.

'Witchcraft One Charlie will roam your northern flank until a joint resupply is given on your next comms schedule. Acknowledge all, over.'

'Happy targets, over.'

'Message from your wife, over.'

His heart flutters like a startled butterfly. He sits up and looks at the bike, studying the engine, the precise engineering of every part, looking for something.

'Send it, over.'

'I think of you every waking second, keep me in your heart, I will keep you warm,' the robotic voice replies.

It hurt every time. His eyes begin to flood, a lump shoots to his throat like a trapped apple. He looks at the darkening sky again and lets the words run their course, through his throat, his eyes, his hands and heart. The monotone, emotionless voice only added to the drama of the words. That's not how she said it, he thought as he tightened his lips, she said it with the heart of a benevolent God and the earnest plea of an inno-

Caliphate

cent man in his last moments on death row. He wipes his nose with the back of his glove and sniffs, taking a moment to gather himself.

'Roger… over,' he says.

The darkness falling over the world from the east and closing the deal in the west. Our sun is a star in someone else's sky. This moon is making someone cry. She would see the sun while he saw the moon and vice versa. The sun and moon were a common axiom to them both, something immovable that they both knew at some point each would glance at, a mirror on a blind corner.

'Zero, next comms schedule, tomorrow 17.00 hours, out.' The transmission ends, cold as ice.

Morale messages are usually given once a week, always no more than a few words. The loneliness and constant danger out in the desert can send a man insane. Some riders don't return, dying in some ditch in the desert, others return, but their minds are dead in the desert. The messages keep him in touch with the other world, letting him know that the horrors have their opposites, otherwise he would be just like them.

Remember who you are.

Caliphate

He returns to the bike removing the M4 rifle from the valise and puts down the daysack, laying the rifle on top. From his pannier he selects one of the boil-in-the-bag meals, beef stew and dumplings, and puts it in his pocket. He removes the jetboil and takes off the lid from the vessel and puts that in his pocket too. Like a Russian doll, he pulls the burner out from inside the vessel and twists it on to the bottom, shakes out the small gas canister from inside, screws that on to the bottom of the burner and sniffs for gas. He kicks a small hole under the poncho and places the jetboil inside and removes the meal from his pocket, squeezing its contents evenly through-out the bag and folding it in half, placing it inside the boiling vessel. He half fills the vessel with water from a bottle, removes the lid from his pocket and seals the top of the cooker, placing the bottle in his pocket. He turns on the gas, listening for the hiss, cocking his head towards it, presses the ignition button igniting the gas instantly with a small whoosh and places it in the hole out of the wind. Leaving the water to boil he returns to the pan-nier, removing a small half-litre flask and a sachet of instant tea. Unscrew-ing the flask, he rips off the top of the sachet with his teeth, pours the con-tents into the flask and screws the lid back, putting the empty sachet in his pocket. He takes the roll mat out from the canoe grip and unrolls it, un-screws the valve on the corner and begins to blow. Once inflated he places it under the poncho and sits with his back against the still warm engine of the bike and takes out the map, the quiet roar of the stove and the occasional rustle of the poncho catching the wind keeping him company from the silence. Tomorrow he'll head back to the red point using an alternative route, covering more of the southern side of his runway, approaching it from the south-east. He clicks on a single LED torch attached to a string round his neck, holding it between his teeth. He studies the map carefully, paying attention to the few features that the land provides to aid navigation. He picks out some key landmarks, a wadi, a large dune denoted by the tight spacing of the map contours, a large stretch of plateau, a group of crags, taking a mental note of them all on his selected path. He takes out his compass and plots the direction heading south-east from his position, and then a bearing from his turn point at the edge of his runway to the red point and writes them on his panel. The jetboil starts a little dance, shaking with the boiling water, vapour coming out of the small hole in the lid like an old steam train. He pays no attention to it. He notes the easting and northing lines he will cross in their order and measures the distance with the edge of his compass. He writes 22.56km leg 1, 28.33km leg 2 on his panel, puts the lid back on the pen and folds the map, putting them in his pocket. He calculates his fuel and the mileage of the task; he has plenty. He reaches over and switches off the gas and the jetboil slows down its dance until it sits still, the steam making a gentle hiss. He re-

Caliphate

moves the lid and pulls out the steaming bag letting it drip on the ground. Torch still in his mouth, he places the bag of stew on the roll mat and picks up the flask unscrewing the lid and pouring the hot water into it. He re-places the flask lid and shakes it for a moment, mixing the tea, and places the flask in his pocket. He checks the inside of the jetboil for any water, watches the thin layer on the sides transform into steam and disperse, dryness spreading across the walls. After dismantling the cooker, he re-places it in the pannier and re-opens the canoe grip, removing the sleep-ing bag and bivvy bag. He lays these on the roll mat, spreading them out evenly, and switches off the torch, reaching under the sleeping bag to pick up his stew. The stars are out and the desert is well lit. He can't see for miles but he can see far enough. He rips the top off the bag, the steam and hot smell of stew warming his face. He takes out his spoon and, sit-ting on the floor cross-legged next to his rifle and looking out over the wadi, eats his stew slowly and drinks his tea.

'I will keep you warm,' he imagines her saying. And she is right, she bonds him to her out here in the loneliness and the macabre. Every message from her hits hard and deep, but the cold cruelty that the world is capable of will prevail again and again. Her words keep the lighthouse on the horizon, in the sea of madness. The cold wind creeps down the nape of his neck. Some sail together quietly with the lighthouse in view, others close their eyes and float, led by deranged books, crashing into each other like blindfolded geriatrics, arms extended like the living dead, screaming in their millions. For what?

He puts the tea sachet and the empty stew bag in the hole and brushes his teeth. He spits the excess toothpaste in the hole and rinses his mouth with water and swallows, kicking the excavated mud back into the hole and flattening it with his foot. He replaces the water, toothbrush and toothpaste in their respective compartments in the pannier and climbs under the poncho. Then he just stands in the darkening desert, the wind coming in long bellows against his face, growing colder every minute. He unclips his buckle on the belt kit and places it next to his daysack under the poncho. He takes off the remote display unit and puts it in the hood of the sleeping bag for now. He undoes the heavy jacket, shaking it off over his shoulders, folding it the best he can around the protective plates and places it under the hood of the sleeping bag as a pillow. He replaces the remote display unit on his wrist and climbs into the sleeping bag, in his thermal shirt and trousers, his boots left on. Always left on.

Out in the desert during these months, his sleeping bag is perhaps the only luxury. Surrounding him, head and all, with its thick down, he is encapsulated in its warmth. Warm enough to dream, but the depth of dreaming, he thinks, is somewhere he shouldn't go when he is alone like this. He knows he is vulnerable, but the sleeping bag drugs him with its comfort, pacifying him into a carefree state and all he can do is succumb. Cocooned like this is where he can finally see her as his senses lose touch with the waking world and allow him the freedom to choose his thoughts, even if only for a few minutes before he is carried off into the abyss.

She sits on the sofa wearing a vest and some small shorts, legs tucked under with his head in her warm lap. The window is open and the gentle warm breeze tangoes with the curtain. His ear on her stomach looking up at her, he can hear her heart beat slowly in little thumps. Her small hand gently ruffles his short hair then combs it back and she looks down at him. She leans over, flicking her hair over her shoulder, she moves her head down and rests her smooth, warm lips on his and gently puts her hand behind his head. Consciousness loses focus on the moment and time and thoughts wobble, and like watching an old TV being shut down, the picture flicks and collapses into a pinhole into the centre taking the mind with it, then nothing. He is the TV and he is the viewer.

Just before dawn he wakes in the morning chill. Each morning colder than the one before. He packs away his things and cooks himself some breakfast, sausage and beans, makes tea and gets dressed, the cold air puffs

Caliphate

from his mouth and his nose is blocked. He checks the oil level unscrew-

ing the small dipstick, the tyre pressure with a gauge from the small tool kit

and then the front fork seals for any leakage. Everything as it should be.

After squeezing some warmth into his hands and stamping his feet, he

gears up and switches everything on, puts the strap of his goggles over

his head, centres them air tight on his eyes and heads out along the open

desert south-east on his first leg, leaving everything as he found it.

The open desert stretching for miles in every direction passes

by and the cold breeze finds its way through gaps in his jacket. The

ground transforms back and forth from sand to baked mud. There are

small cracks everywhere in the mud, like an endless jigsaw. The sun in its

early axis on his flank, warming the cold desert air, makes the icy wind

resistance at speed more bearable. He approaches a long ditch, whittled

out by some long ago river, and carefully eases the bike down into it, con-

trolling everything with the front brake and winding the throttle at the bot-

tom, accelerating up the opposite bank and speeding back into the open

ground. Small bushes and rocks zip past, no trail to follow, meandering

around what he doesn't need to unnecessarily ford and anything that may

cause damage to the suspension if hit too hard. He checks his mirror often

to assess his dust signature. The bike kicks up a fairly visible dust trail like

a long cone, stretching back the way he came, but with the large dune on his left, he is covered to the east so he relaxes slightly and can make good speed riding alongside the dune he identified the night before on the map. He stands up as he hits small mounds, with his knees bending like suspension as he mounts and descends them, constantly shifting up and down the gears, and sitting back down as he speeds off on the flat straights. He checks the map and bearing on the dash display every once in a while with a quick glance as the wind and dust beat his face, making sure he is riding true to the bearing. Small stones flicked up by the tyres bounce off the mudguards and scatter, like factory line workers inspecting small parts and tossing them over their shoulders. The dust gets everywhere and he pulls the mask over his mouth and nose, controlling the bike with one hand, his hair thick with it. He passes objects he has lost touch with from weeks in the desert that normally wouldn't stir him. An old cigarette packet, a chocolate bar wrapper faded by the sun, a broken toy. Old objects exhuming buried memories associated with phantom smells and tastes that still dangle the sensation of sweetness or relaxation over his nose and tongue. But no sooner than they arrive, they quickly trace their steps back to the darkness where they live; only to leave him with the blurred distortion of an echo of old sentiments that foster the melancholy of his situation. A child's crushed skull quickly snatches him back to reality. The litter of the deep desert. The breadcrumb trails left by the old pilgrims,

Caliphate

fleeing west from the rot of the Caliphate during the Great Capitulations. Chasing them from their homes back east armed with the paraphernalia of abattoirs.

He drives up and down small dunes, the back tyre spraying mud and sand everywhere as it finds grip, controlling the balance with his feet and then cresting the knife edge of the apex and rolling down the other side, suspension collapsing on impact with the returning flat ground and pushing back up into its neutral position as he accelerates off. The rough terrain requires him to study the ground more diligently, keeping his eyes on his route but the flat runs give him a good opportunity to look at the landscape for movement. He checks his map screen, dust and wind sending his hair in all directions, and sees he is approaching his boundary line, a red line that runs straight through the map, splitting the landscape, signifying the edge of his runway. He approaches a large hill, the size of a two-storey house, around a kilometre short of his boundary. He tears up the hill on the bike and stops on the flat top facing east and lets his feet down on the cracked ground. He pulls his goggles on top of his head and with his rangefinder takes a good look across the first part of his next leg north-east, watching for any movement and dust clouds. He sees nothing apart from more of the same and puts the rangefinder back in his belt kit. He removes one of the daysack straps, swinging the pack into his lap,

Caliphate

takes out the flask and drinks the tea he made at breakfast while looking out over the wasteland, the tea warming all the way down to his gut. The wind blowing his hair, he stares, squinting his eyes. Out there in the desert, men with chainsaws and machetes wait in their lines, repeating collectively and endlessly the prayers of doom, chorused by the loboto-mised mullahs. Roaming mindlessly, destroying everything, children and all.

With the bearing set, he shoulders his pack, replaces his goggles and rolls down the hill heading east. The landscape holds no surprises and is easy work, some small dunes and ditches and the wind now warm courtesy of the sun. The mid-morning heat shimmer develops, distorting the horizon. Stretched in the distortion, the blurred, distant shrubs look like people of all sizes in their hundreds all watching him silently. He has long learnt not to be deceived by the illusion, but he knows he can't make a habit of this ignorance as one day they won't be shrubs. After an hour of riding, he begins to pick up familiar sights, a pair of dunes, ancient, deep tracks laid by a heavy vehicle in the sodden desert in some long ago rain. Checking his sat nav he sees that he is five and a half kilometres short of the red point. He brings the bike to a stop and unclips the two buckles on the valise on the forks exposing the stock of the M4 and pulls away. He is soon in line of sight of the mud slope from the previous day

Caliphate

and creeps towards it, keeping the bike as quiet as possible, accelerating gently only when he has to, rolling most of the way. He switches off the engine and rolls the last fifty metres, eventually stopping in the same spot behind the mound. He kicks down the stand and gently gets off the bike, removing the M4 from the valise as he does so. He makes his way up the hill, carefully avoiding silhouetting himself and crawls on his belly the last two metres to the top. He peers over with the rangefinder.

Three men wearing military chest rigs over black overalls are standing around looking at the crater, rifles in hands and a dilapidated truck parked to one side. His gut squeezes and neck tightens. He shuffles back slightly in order to make himself less visible. He looks at his wrist and switches on the remote display, selects 'FIRES' and adjusts the throat mic. He presses the button on the side. 'TUNING.'

He looks back to the site and the three men are climbing into the truck, two in the front and one in the bed. The man in the bed is looking his way, but from this distance there is no way he could see him. The truck wheel spins off, kicking up a plume of dust, leaving it invisible, like a magician vanishing in a puff of smoke. A swell of nausea throbs in his stomach at the thought of the truck turning his way. He continues to watch. The dust begins to settle and he can make out the truck heading east, the

Caliphate

man in the bed holding on to the roll bars on the roof. Everything silent, his brain flicks a few alert switches off.

He watches for a while until the dust trailing the truck is barely recognisable and slides down the hill back to the bike, switching off the radio as he goes. He returns the rifle to the valise and takes a quick drink of water. He pulls away the bottle form his mouth and thinks. The men would be heading back to Route 77 and from there, who knows. Route 77 was a heavily used route by them and getting too close was dangerous. He quickly takes out his map and checks the ground to the north. A deep wadi, quite out of his way, would provide concealment en route to the observation point, and with Witchcraft One Charlie roaming the north of his runway he feels a little more at ease. He plots a bearing to the wadi and updates his sat nav. He has two hours, plenty of time to travel fourteen kilometres, including the distance to the wadi. He folds away the map and mounts the bike, kicking up the stand while looking north-east roughly on his bearing, and starts up. The engine confidently thumps to life, ready for anything. He sets off north, speeding on the flats and taking it slow behind cover. Keeping his eye on the east for any potential movement. They know someone is in the neighbourhood now.

He rolls into the large wadi that runs north for a short while then a long bend directs it east. The entrance is steeper than he was comfortable with and he takes care down the slope. At one point the bike is close to being vertical and any braking would throw him over the handlebars, but before any disaster, he makes it to the bed of the dry river and speeds off on the gravel plateau with the back end flicking out but quickly realigning itself, the bike rattling over the lumpy surface. The walls of the wadi are like stacked giant biscuits, layered with green lines running straight, some greener than others, each one marking the stages of the river's demise. These huge, deep valleys scraped into the crust of the desert floor once housed huge rivers, but are now only dry, redundant features. He meanders around large rocks and deep-looking shale, mainly sticking to the edges but not close in case of rock fall. He was a long time in the wadi – it was more hard going than he anticipated –and he was now pushing his luck with time. He counts down each kilometre so he doesn't overshoot the road. A prominent bend in the wadi marks the point where he will leave and he starts looking for any gradual slopes the bike could handle. At a steep slope a little further on, on the right, perhaps used by shepherds back when the wadi had shallow water, he comes to a stop and dismounts, leaving the engine on as he makes his way up the slope with the rifle. The wadi is deep and he can't see over the sides – he doesn't want any surprises when he exits on the bike. He creeps over the top and checks. The road is about two kilometres away. He checks his grid and

Caliphate

looks for any features that can provide cover on the map, but there's nothing but flat land to the road. The rushing around at the red point caused him to overlook the gradual bend in the wadi and he is now a fair distance away from the cover he initially nominated for the observation post the night before. Riding in the open ground in this light and this close to the road is out of the question. He sits down below the lip of the wadi to gather his thoughts, looking at the rifle next to him, running his hands through his long matted hair. He takes out his rangefinder and crawls back to the top, slowly scanning the flat land from the edge of the wadi round to the south. He sees a black spot on the floor in the heat shimmer and sits studying it. He fires the laser at the middle of the shadow and the screen reads 873m and a grid. An old tank trench maybe. Deep enough for a tank to be completely concealed from hull to turret, dug during one of the many wars some years back. There was no way he was moving there in the daylight and even less of a way of achieving eyes on by 14.00. He slings the rifle and climbs down the slope back to the bike, switches off the engine and pops the pannier lid. He takes out a thin brown packet of six crackers and a sachet of jalapeno cheese spread and walks back to the top of the wadi. He takes off his daysack and places it on the mud and sits down, tearing open the packet of crackers and laying them on the back of the sweat-stained pack. He rips off the corner of the cheese sachet and squeezes an

Caliphate

equal amount of cheese on to each cracker and puts both empty packets in his pocket. He takes two of the crackers and sandwiches them together, squeezing them until the cheese protrudes from the edges, and takes a bite out of the corner. He sits looking out east to the road, thinking about his life, eating cheese and crackers with his rifle, the grinding and crunching of the crackers in his teeth. Everything silent, everything still.

He sits on the lip of the wadi for a few hours scanning the road and ground. The road was invisible from where he was as the heat shimmer distorts everything. As the sun moved west and the gradual cooling of the desert reduced the heat shimmer, the tank trench became clearer and he was more confident that it would afford him and the bike good cover, and 873 metres was not far on the bike. He checks his watch, 16.56. He goes back to the bike, opens the X-wing, switches on the display panel, selects 'ADMIN' and tunes the radio. He checks his fuel, primary and reserve tank, his water, rations and radio batteries. The bike is running smoothly. No need to check ammunition, yet.

'Hello Zero, this is Witchcraft one Delta, radio check, over.'

'Zero, send locstat, over,' Zero replies. He registers a slight urgency in the speed of the transmission and he slows down.

He sends his grid and Zero reads it back.

'Zero, send conditions, over.'

Caliphate

'Witchcraft One Delta, bike five, radios five, batteries two, rations two, water one, fuel two, ammunition five, over.'

'Zero, bike five, radios five, batteries two, rations two, water one, fuel two, ammunition five, roger, wait out.' A pause. 'Zero, do you have eyes on the road? Over.'

He drops his call sign and replies, 'Negative, I have identified a position at grid three, six, two, eight, four… five, seven, zero, four, four, roger so far.'

'Roger, over.'

'I will move to that location tonight and should have eyes on target before 20.00, over.'

'Negative. Witchcraft One Charlie has nominated a resupply grid west of your location, grid to follow, wait out.'

He looks at his watch, 17.06, then looks at the sky, clouds coming in, and gets out his pen. The darkness makes its way over the landscape swallowing up distant sights. Here comes tomorrow eating up today. He can feel his old enemy the cold creeping in. Maybe thirty minutes of daylight left. Even with the pending problems, he was looking forward to speaking to another rider. He hadn't spoken to anyone other than Zero, Onslaught and the resupply helicopter door gunner for nine and a half weeks.

Caliphate

'Grid three, four, one, one, one… five, three, two, four, three. Roger so far, over.'

He notes down the grid on the white panel and reads it back.

'Witchcraft One Charlie is clearing the location, you are to be there no later than 19.00 for landing at 19.20. Roger so far.'

He notes the time. 'Roger, over.'

'You are then to proceed to your nominated OP grid and be in position with eyes on the road by no later than 22.30, over.'

'NLT 22.30, roger, over.'

'Next comms schedule, 08.00. Out.'

He writes down the time, pulls the map from his pocket and folds it out on the seat. The resupply grid was two kilometres back down the wadi in a large clearing. He has never had a resupply grid so close. Relieved at the distance, he puts the map away and switches on the sat nav. He inputs the resupply grid along with the direction, marking a way-point on the screen of the wadi exit. He takes off his daysack, unclips the two buckles on the helmet net on the front of the pack and removes the helmet. He puts it on the seat and unzips the top of the daysack, taking out his night vision goggles and down jacket. He zips up the pack, putting it to one side. He clips the small recess on top of the NVG onto the mount on the front of the helmet with a prominent click. He gives the goggles a

Caliphate

small tug to make sure they sit true then folds them up and down a few times, checking their function. He takes off his belt kit then the leather jacket, feeling the chill instantly, to put on the warm jacket, then replaces the heavier jacket and belt kit. He dons the helmet then pulls down the infra-red filter over the headlight and mounts the bike, kicks up the stand and starts the engine, turning on the heated grips on the handlebars as he does so. He tests the headlight to make sure no white light was leaking through and it isn't. Tonight was going to be cold.

He U-turns the bike facing west down the wadi and heads off back the way he came. He remembers where to ride and where not to, keeping away from deep shale and large rocks. It is now dark and with enough cloud cover to reduce the visibility to perhaps fifty metres. He snaps down his night vision goggles and twists the small dial on the left side one click and the night turns luminous green. He wiggles the rubber eye grips more central to his eyes and is able to see clearly. The universe comes to life in the empty sky with the black beyond freckled with infinite stars.

He arrives about 200 metres short of the large open clearing in the wadi and stops the bike. He looks at his watch through the NVG, 18.43. He reaches behind and puts his cold hands on the hot exhaust while he looks

Caliphate

around the area, the heat unites him with his sense of touch again. Under the rock edge of the north-western side, he sees a large infra-red light blink twice. Witchcraft One Charlie on his bike flashing his headlight. He rides the bike slowly over to the edge of the clearing and stops a short distance away from him, switches off the engine and climbs off.

He draws his pistol and holds it in one hand to his side while the other man climbs off his bike. As he does he glances a flash of the infra-red Union Jack patch on the arm of the man's jacket and holsters his pistol. They walk towards each other. With the NVG on, the other man, a little taller than himself, looks like some kind of Martian.

'Cabin,' he says.

'Fever,' the man responds quietly.

They close the gap and immediately hug each other, saying nothing. It now dawns on him how much he really needed to be in contact with somebody, anybody. He couldn't feel the man's warmth through his jacket but he knew it was there. That warm surge of human love and friendship cascades through him like an avalanche as the feeling resurfaces through the deep, impenetrable oil on the surface of loneliness his mind has been drowning in for so many weeks, just to hear a voice that was real and not filtered through a series of radios, just to hear a cough or a hello, anything. Immediately he knew that the transience of the en-

Caliphate

counter would only leave him vulnerable when it was time to tune himself back into loneliness, but he ignored this, it was the only option.

He once rode off the back of the Hercules some rallies ago with his friend, Matty. They were the same age, he had a wife at home with a young daughter. They met for the first time at Heathrow airport when the first expedition was being mounted.

The patrol was stacked up behind each other in sets of twos, six riders in total. When the plane touched down, he was next to him. They put on their goggles and helmets and undid the straps that held the bike to the aircraft, he looked over to him. They said nothing to each other, just a smile and a nod behind the goggles and masks, the aircraft engine would allow no talking over its crushing volume. That aircraft, he still recalls, as he grits his teeth. They rode off in separate directions into their individual runways. He saw his dust trail disappear into the distance.

It was Witchcraft One Foxtrot who was sent to Matty's distress call during that rally. After no contact with Matty and Witchcraft One Foxtrot, another rider was sent in a last-ditch effort to ascertain what was happening.

He found them both.

Caliphate

'It's a human spider' were the last words he said before he was sectioned.

Some riders go insane from the loneliness and never deploy again. He used to believe that long stretches in isolation rekindled a love for someone. Not any more – there isn't enough time in one's life for such stretches of loneliness. This world has surely seen enough horror by now to know how important love is.

'Good to see you, mate,' the man says quietly in his ear, squeezing him tight.

'You too, brother.'

They step back and remove their NVGs and look each other over in the dark, unable to recognise each other's faces. He can see the man's white teeth where he is smiling.

'Have you eaten yet?' the man says.

'Not yet, no. You better have beer'

He laughs, 'I wish, but I got the next best thing. Give me your dinner, I'll stick it in with mine. We don't have a lot of time, the heli will be here shortly.'

He brings his bike over next to the other and gets his dinner from his pannier while the other man sets up the cooker. They sit opposite each other, both leaning against the warm engines, the cooker in the middle with both dinners squeezed in, flasks prepped with coffee. The slow, quiet roar of the cooker gave off just enough light to see each other's faces in the flicker of the flames. The man's face is powdered with dust and streaked with sweat and he has a dusty, semi-grey beard. His lips are split all over and his eyes are sunken in their filthy sockets. His hair is long and grey and matted into thin dreadlocks. He has not seen him looking so exhausted and considers his own appearance in comparison. At around 5'9, he is a fraction shorter than the man. He has lost a lot of muscle from such a long period in the desert, but years of gymnastics keep the strength ingrained in his tired body. His brown hair too is long and down to the jaw, and it tangles in the wind and flicks across his hazel eyes as they desperately try and muster the form of the man in the darkness in their lonely dark holes, but they long to rest. His cracked lips remain together in his long, dirty beard and his prominent cheekbones are red raw from windburn. But he can see enough of the man to know that the constant hammering of the wind and sand and the poor nourishment has aged the man a hundred years since they rode off the aircraft into the desert all those weeks ago.

'How you been?' he says, pulling his legs underneath him into a cross-legged position.

Caliphate

'Well…the same as you really, I'd rather be with the coalition in Syria or Jordan. I need a new job…bloody…postman or summink. You picked up any ideas why this re-sup has been suddenly slammed on us? I fuckin 'ate it when its all sudden' the man says in an old, smokey, cockney accent where every letter that has a U is replaced with an accentuated A.

'Na, just a grid and then told me you was bouncin' down'

'I dunno mate…I dunno' He said as he exhaled 'I didn't know you was this far east, bin busy 'int ya? I'm miles back' the man said with a small hint of a smile that quickly faded. He leant back out of the light and stroked his beard down 'My body aint what it used to be. Every rock I hit 'urts my joints n' my 'ands are cold all the time, my feet are like wood. I'm not a young pup like you. What are you, twenny seven?' the man says rubbing warmth into his thighs.

'Thirty in January, the eleventh, what we in now? Dates just merge into each other out here, y'know, like one long day' he says with a smile, he looked around over the black crest of the Wadi, 'From G squadron to postman aye?'

'I just aint got the fire he used to 'ave…fuckin place takes years from ya. Sayin that, Konrad's avin' a rough time to the north of me poor sod. Saw him couple a weeks back, like this, he was going further east. Said he keeps findin' square cages in the middle of nowhere' Glenn says,

Caliphate

looking vacantly at the cooker. He pauses, knitting his brows. Then as if he has just made a remarkable discovery: 'Seventeen days' He whispers to himself then looks up 'Your twenny eight in seventeen days'

'Thirty' He corrects.

'Thirty' Glenn says under his breath

They both stare at each other, their minds cranking out the dates and then smile.

'Well, its jesus's birthday today' shaking his head slowly.

Glenn shifts his weight, quietly laughs and reaches into a side pocket on his daysack next to him, pulls out a small hip flask and un-screws the lid. He sniffs the top and reaches over the cooker and hands it to him, his hand shaking. He looks at Glenn's hand and then looks at his face. Glenn's smile dies slowly away. Part of him wishes the cooker wasn't on so he couldn't see him like this through the flames. Look away and plug your ears, what you can't see can't hurt.

'Merry Christmas, Tom,' Glenn says quietly with a shaky voice.

He takes the flask and brings it to his nose. Glenmorangie. He holds it out and studies the flask in the flickers of light. An engraving on the side in italic. *I know of one duty and that is to love you.*

'What was in the cages' Tom says

'Burnt kids'

Caliphate

Tom took his eyes off Glen, focusing on the flames for a few seconds, his brain building the picture. He puts the flask to his lips and tips a small tipple of the whisky into his mouth with his lips pursed, letting his tongue swim in the thick, fine craftsmanship. He pulls the flask away and looks once more at the engraving and then moves his eyes to Glenn's, he raises the flask and swallows, a single nod to each other, eyes fixed. The nod of honour. A silent movement sighing an unspoken disclaimer of insurance, the whisky the ink, their hearts the paper. A declaration that is adhered to the grave. An adherence of the highest magnitude, that, no matter what, I will get to you before they do.

He hands the flask back and Glenn takes a sparing swig and closes his eyes as he swallows, letting the taste take him far away, if only for a couple of seconds. But he has to open them again, everyone does. He screws on the lid and leans back over and puts the flask away. Glenn reaches over and switches off the gas and lets the boiling water settle for a moment.

'I dunno man' Glenn said with a sigh as if finally giving up to a question that has long tormented him. He took a long look around into the wide wadi, the faintest moonlight giving silhouette to the edges of the high rock walls.

Caliphate

'Maybe people need to come to places like this in times like these to appreciate such things' says Tom.

'You reckon?'

'Are you going to be all right?'

'I ope' so. I'm forgetting things more and more. I'm sure we're gettin' a dose from the fallout in Tehran or summin', maybe the wind's carryin' it over.' He coughs a single cough and continues. 'Two days ago, I slept through the night until midday. I woke up, flappin' around, not knowing where I was or what the fuckin ell was going on, sheer panic. I packed everything away and started up the bike and rode east for half a kilometre without my rifle. I didn't even know where I was going, just riding with an empty head. Fuckin' east of all directions.'

Tom stares silently, the danger of riding east unknowingly causing him to worry about Glenn.

There was a silence for a few seconds, both of them knew what sort of behaviour that meant.

'Stay with it, mate, only a few weeks left, we can ride together for a while if you like? On the down low, of course. It would probably do us both some good' Tom says, brushing his hair back with his fingers.

He thought Glenn hadn't heard him but a small flicker of flame shows him nodding, looking down. Glenn leans forward and takes the lid off the cooker, removing a steaming bag and handing it to him. Then he takes out the other and places it in his lap while he pours the water into the flasks and twists shut the lids. He puts the cooker back on the floor and then sits holding the bag, warming his hands.

'I usually get a bit like this before the end of a rally, I've got nine years on you!' His brief smile fades as soon as it starts. Then Glenn looks at him, his face transformed into an expression of deep contempt as if it were the last smile on earth.

'What the fuck is going on Tom, I mean, what the fuck is this all about' His head gesturing towards the empty land beyond Tom with a single flick of the chin 'Who are them people out there waitin' for us? Their eyes, their dreams. They want us to live like them, I get that, but then what? There is no path for humanity, we're just wandering from century to century, getting smarter and hoovering up all the mysteries of the world and churning out facts' He was lost now in his own mind and Tom could see it in his eyes 'Well…at least thats what we *were* doing. Now its all fucked, all down the swanny'

Tom looks at him across the flames. He wasn't really talking to Tom. Something in Glenn had been stirred in remembering. Something that looked as though it would never settle, what had he seen. Memories are sometimes hidden behind other memories that you forgot were there,

Caliphate

she said to him long ago after Matty was found. What is seen cannot be unseen, the picture is painted and then hung on the wall of your mind. All you can do is hang the bad in one room and the good in another. But you have to go into the rooms to put the pictures up, and that's when you have to look.

'We can't let them have the freedom they want on this earth, we can't let this happen on earth. This doesn't belong 'ere, not in this day and age. I fuckin' ate it but what kind of people would we be if we let it continue? Maniacs driving into schools and forcing children to rape their teachers. Toddlers beheading toddlers. Who are we to patrol these lands? Who the hell do we think we are?' Glenn said, lips taut and the fire in his eyes. Tom was listening intently.

'Who the bloody 'ell are we *not* to do these things? Who are we to pretend we know so little about fuckin' well being that we cannot ride in and shut them down, shut this fucking mayhem down,' He paused and his passion escalated 'No! Open your fucking eyes, there is a line…thats all we do, we make sure those with medieval ideas can see that line because if we don't, well, we haven't and now look. Liberalism is what sent those into mass graves, doused them in petrol and burnt them alive, those in the quarantine zones in them lovely little countries like France n' Switzerland n' all them other poor souls…I don't think we are all ready to live together, not until we recognise which of us are living right and living wrong and admitting it. Doing nothing brings death as well'

Glenn rips off the top of his bag and puts it in his jacket pocket, takes out his spoon and sits looking at him again. 'This world was once vacant, ya know! An empty house. Now we have all moved in and are all sleepin' in the different rooms, like a pissin' hotel, listening to each other through the walls pretending we don't know what's going on. I'll tell ya, Tom, I don't know how much blood needs to seep through the ceiling before we all realise you can't call the landlord. There is no landlord to call. The room that has the happiest tenants and all that, the tidiest room makes the house rules and everyone else should follow.' Glenn looks into his bag in the darkness and begins to eat the steaming pulp. The musings of a lonely exhausted traveller.

They sit in the darkness, the warm bike engines keeping them from the cold. Tom tears open his bag and starts to eat.

'Who appoints us landlords, then? We've made some mess in other people's rooms in the past…' Tom says, looking at Glenn in the darkness, mixing up his dinner with the spoon.

'No one appointed us, we just tidied up the fastest while others sat in the mess trying to read how to tidy. But they don't know that they already know how to.'

Caliphate

Tom looks into the dark figure. A veteran of untidy rooms.

They finish their meals and bury the bags next to the stove and sit with their flasks. He reaches into his jacket and pulls out a small box wrapped in a waterproof bag. He opens the bag and the box, takes out two cigarettes and puts them both in his mouth. He takes the small Clipper lighter from the bag and lights them and puffs them to life and hands one over the cooker to Glenn.

'I'm trying to bloody give up,' Glenn says, and then takes a drag, his face glowing red so Tom can see him again.

'Not the time or place, mate,' Tom says. He takes a long deep drag and lets it sit in his lungs. The poisoning a welcoming feeling. He begins to feel slightly mellower.

'In't that the truth,' Glenn says.

They sit in the dark finishing their cigarettes, absorbing the feeling of what it feels like to be around another human. Glenn checks his watch, 19.09.

'Let's get this landing zone marked, shall we' Tom says as he stands up.

He leans over and takes Glenn's hand and helps him to his feet. The cold had turned off their legs partially and their knees and thighs

Caliphate

felt gelatinous. Getting up required a few seconds of learning how to walk again. Once moving, Glenn packs away the cooker while Tom buries the bags and cigarette ends. He climbs on his bike and starts up the engine. The bike sounds incredibly loud and it concerns him. It is loud anyway and he knows the darkness amplifies the noise but then he realises he has been sat for a while with Glenn and has completely forgotten the situation of being in a desert plagued with destruction. He had drifted off point while sitting there. Being around someone else recalibrated his senses and the noise of the bike was reversing the calibration again. He pulls slowly to one of the corners of the flat patch of cracked river bed and faces the infra-red headlight of the bike into the middle and walks it backwards to the edge of the clearing, allowing enough room for the helicopter to land. He hears Glenn's bike fire to life and then the slow crunching of the dirt and stones under the tyres as he positions the bike and the headlight. He puts on his helmet and buckles up the chinstrap and snaps down the NVG. He switches them on and everything is painted luminous green once again, like the sun has instantly appeared with a light green filter. He looks at his bright headlight as it cones out in front across the flat ground, cutting the flat in half, then Glenn switches on his headlight and positions the bike headlight at such an angle so it crosses the other beam in the middle a short distance between the two bikes, perhaps twenty metres.

Caliphate

He looks at Glenn, now with his NVG on, and sees him switching on his wrist display and climbing off the bike with his rifle. Tom gets off his bike, removes the rifle from the valise and slings it over his shoulder. He unclips the two latches on the radio housing mounted on the back of the seat. He opens the thick plastic Peli case, switches off his NVG and folds them up. He takes his small torch attached to the string around his neck from under his thermal shirt and clicks it on, placing it in his teeth. He shines the light into the plastic case and sees the face of the radio, about the size of a small shoebox with the small screen as long as a stick of gum, dimly lit with a row of ten numbers. He switches the dial to 'OFF' and the screen fades to black. To the side of the screen is a thick wire, the same thickness as a pencil, screwed into a port. Next to that is a thinner wire, the thickness of a lollipop stick, also screwed into a port. He undoes these and moves them to one side. He unsnaps two latches each end of the face of the radio and slides out the radio in its entirety, disconnects the charger cable on the bottom, separating the radio from the bike completely. He places the radio on the seat, leaving the Peli case with padded sides empty and open with the three cables hanging out of the front. He opens the pannier box and takes out his spare battery and checks its charge. Five LEDs illuminate as he holds down a small button on the top. He places this to the side of the radio and takes a look around. Glenn will

Caliphate

have done this before the rendezvous, and he leans against his bike, NVG on, watching him.

He takes the radio and turns it upside down so the battery is facing up. He takes hold of the bottom of the battery and twists it anti-clockwise, separating it from the radio. He puts down the radio and presses the small button on top of the battery. Two of the five small red LEDs light up. Batteries tend to last about a month in the summer, less in the winter. The radios are dormant and are woken when he switches the display unit on. Providing he does more than five kilometres every other day, the battery should stay above two red LEDs. The batteries draw their charge from the alternator and if the bike is static for any longer than forty-eight hours, in this state and in this weather, a battery with two LEDs would die and not be rechargeable.

He places the used battery down next to the fresh one. He looks over to Glenn and can make out his outline and the bike in the low moonlight, he is quietly talking into the radio to the helicopter. He stands there listening with his free hand on the exhaust keeping it warm, concentrating on the horizon to the west, squinting as if that would help him hear better. A very faint, slow, thumping noise can be heard somewhere out there in the desert air, like two people with sticks taking turns to beat the dust out of a thick, hanging carpet in slow succession far away. If he can hear the helicopter, so can others. He looks back at Glenn and sees him walking over. He turns the torch off in his mouth so it doesn't burn out Glenn's retinas behind the NVG.

'Heli will be here in figures two. I'll stick your dead batteries in my bag,' Glenn says.

'Roger.' He picks up the used battery and hands it to Glenn who dumps it in the bag and leaves the bag on the seat.

'We need to get away from here quick time when the heli fucks off, they never resupply this deep and it's going to attract an audience. There were a couple of them looking for me today at my last red point not far from here,' Tom says.

He could see the green glow from Glenn's NVG reflecting off his eyes and saw him looking around over the sides of the wadi.

'How many?'

'Three.'

'How come you didn't drop?'

'They pushed off east before I had a chance.'

Glenn was looking at him now. 'We're gonna 'ave to work on your draw, son.' He swings round his rifle to his front and walks back to his bike.

Caliphate

Tom picks up the fresh battery and places it on to the base of the radio, aligning the locking lips with their respective holes and then houses it, twisting clockwise, the thumping getting closer, echoing across the desert and in the wadi. He attaches the charging cable to the bottom and slides the radio complete back inside the Peli case, then snaps shut the two latches and screws in the cables. He switches the dial to 'ON'. The screen blinks to life and eventually displays 'Harris' and a few seconds later the frequency. He closes the case and housing, fastens the latches sealing it all in, folds down his NVG and walks to the rear of the bike and keeps watch up the wadi to the east, scanning the edges. Weapon in both hands.

The thumping of the helicopter blades chopping the desert air is close now. He looks in the direction of the noise and then suddenly as if he was wearing earplugs all along that were quickly pulled out allowing all the noise of the world to be heard clearly, the chopping lost its bass and gained its pitch and tempo with the helicopter flying over the edge of the wadi seemingly dangerously low. He looks up and sees the black outline and a small glow from the cockpit. He watches it fly over them, bank sharply north and disappear over the other side of the wadi, and the earplugs are back in. He looks over at Glenn and sees him with his rifle in his shoulder, moving it in small circles. He looks at the cross made by the

headlights from the bikes and sees Glenn marking the cross of the headlights with the gun's infra-red laser, making large circles around it, to give
the helicopter more clarity of its landing zone. He looks back east.

      After a few seconds, the chopping grows again and he naturally
looks in the direction of the noise and the earplugs are suddenly removed
again with the emergence of the helicopter slowly, almost crawling, over
the lip of the wadi, its nose lifting slightly, with dust and dirt flying everywhere off the edge. The blades trail wavering circles of static like halos
and the whirring of the engine sounds more like a chalkboard being
scratched over and over again with a knife. The edge of the wadi is about
fifteen metres high. He looks up and sees the door gunner leaning out
holding on to the side with his safety strap taut holding him in. The door
gunner isn't looking at him, he's looking at the laser and headlights, guiding the pilot on. The helicopter moves slowly into the centre of the clearing,
staying at the height of the wadi. The down-draught of the blades kicks up
a ferocious amount of dust, forcing him to look away. He looks at Glenn
still marking the cross but looking away to escape the dust storm. He
looks back east, shielding the side of his face, but mainly his eyes with his
hand. It's stronger and stronger and throwing him off balance slightly. He
looks up as the helicopter swings its tail east and slowly begin its descent,
the nose and pilots now facing west, the door gunner still guiding them

down. He looks at the cockpit and sees the pilot looking over his left shoulder towards the cross, which is now out of view to Tom as the helicopter drops down. As it gets closer, the draught loses some of its power and the dust lets off slightly, and then there is hardly any dust at all. The helicopter had taken anything that was loose on the ground and thrown it away from the clearing, there's nothing else for it displace. At about ten metres off the ground, both he and Glenn could see the door gunner clearly, checking the tail clearance and shifting his gaze back to the floor, one hand holding on, the other shielding his microphone on his headset. The helicopter slows its descent even more and the front wheels briefly touch the ground, lift slightly and touch down again with all three sets of wheels slowly pressing into the sand. He looks at Glenn and sees he has shifted his laser to the rear rotor painting it in stripes of green for him so he doesn't run into it. He slings his rifle and looks at the door gunner who shifts his gaze from the floor to him and displays a thumb-up. He ducks his head slightly to one side and briskly walks to the door, careful not to run. He detests the stench of aviation fuel being burned, it gives him a headache, but the hot fumes being blasted out of the back of the engine whooshing against his face felt wonderful. He gets to the door and looks at the door gunner, his full-face helmet and the glow from the NVG making him look like a droid from some advanced planet, and he throws the bag of dead batteries into the door. The gunner turns and slides two half-filled bags over to him which he grabs by the knots tying them shut and drags them out. He thought he would be able to control the weight but they fall to the floor. He wonders why they are so heavy considering it's only rations and a few radio batteries, but then realises how weak he has become from weeks in the desert on little food. He turns around and carries the bags away from the helicopter a few metres, heads back to the door where the gunner is undoing some straps around jerry cans of fuel attached to the floor. Tom pokes his head in the door and looks to the rear where the seats are.

A man, filthy with oil, mud and blood sits in the chair, strapped in, rocking backwards and forwards. He cannot help but stare as the man stares back. The man's eyes are wide open as if he had been recently blinded. His face is gaunt and filthy and filled with fear and Tom knows he has seen something so terrifying he will be unable to ever understand it; mouth wide open to the point where it has partially split in the corners. His hands clutch something in the dark of his lap. The door gunner grabs Tom's head and pushes it back out of the door and shouts something he could just make out over the engine.

'Don't look.'

Caliphate

Too late. The gunner leans out with one of the jerry cans and drops it gently on the ground. He stands there staring at him, his hair dancing frantically in the draught. The hot fumes beating on his face. He is frozen. His mind empty and his body hollow, whatever relief the situation of human contact and resupply had is now a vestige on the horizon and between him and that feeling is a long and wide gulf of the potential candidates of images and actions that could turn a sane man into a shell filled with madness. The sight of a man who was previously capable of conversation, humour and love but had now made the turn to insanity took Tom's mind with the grip of a metal gauntlet and dragged it through that gulf, bumping and snagging on to everything violent, everything abhorrent and everything capable of sending sanity into reverse. The gunner places down the other jerry can and signals to Glenn to come over. Glenn slings his weapon, comes briskly over and looks at the gunner and then at him standing frozen by the jerry cans.

'What are you doing?' He shouts over the engine.

He pushes the door gunner back causing him to stumble on to his rear. Glenn looks around the door to see Witchcraft One Bravo in the seat, rocking, holding the charred remains of an infant girl, refusing to let go. He could see the small burnt foot in the minuscule light. He pushes

Caliphate

himself off the helicopter and stumbles backwards and grabs Tom by the arms.

'Come on, we need to go right now,' Glenn shouts in his ear.

Glenn scoops up both jerry cans and waddles over to the bags, head kinked to shield the draught, drops them down and comes back. Hasn't this been the way the world always is? The basic brain function started to muster response in Tom's head. Is there nothing we will not do to each other? How could they, he thought, how dare they. Someone take me far far away from here and empty my head into a well with our books of doom and fill it with cement leaving it deep in the earth and let the earth think it for me. No, he countered. There is no well and no cement. There is only this land and this sea, this bird and this tree, there is this you and there is this me. Leave it in there and let it burn a hole in your soul for you to look through. Take a peek and turn away. This is what we have done and what we will do. No. Take all this and put it in a box and burn it in the middle of the night as a signal for those alike. This is not me, and scream it across the universe, this is not what I do. Scream loud enough and those alike will scream with you.

His head sparks and jump-starts to life. Everything back in focus, the gunner, the helicopter, objectives and desires all flowing back in their normal

Caliphate

paths turning the cogs again. His wife. He watches the gunner move to the door, swing round the mini-gun in its mount and lock it into its final locking point so the barrels are facing out. The door gunner leans out over the six barrels and the motor. He remembers he has legs and starts to walk backwards then Glenn's arms grab him and spin him around nearly toppling him over and he ushers him over to the jerry cans and holds down the bags. They both watch the helicopter as it takes off, the draught getting stronger again, still looking for loose dirt to throw at them. The door gunner stares back at them and gives a small nod as he holds on to the mini-gun. The nod of an apology. They stare back, with their bikes behind them and the jerry cans next to them rattling in the down-draught. Both filthy with dust and matted hair. Their gloves and trousers patchy with oil and mud and small tears. Dirty beards hiding their expressions and the NVGs hiding their eyes. Under the clothes, their malnourished bodies crank out their movements as ordered. But the mind and the heart are busy, with all their strength desperately holding the door closed to the room with the bad paintings. But the lock is broken.

They watch, huddled next to each other, as the helicopter slowly ascends; it must have recently picked up the man. Not a single part of them wants to be on there. The minute he saw the man holding the child, they were in debt. The warm blasting fumes bathe both of them, a farewell

Caliphate

gift. The helicopter gains a little altitude and the draught reverts to more of a fast gust, then a slight wind as it dips its nose forward and moves west, up and out of the wadi. They watch the static on the blades as the chopping loses its pitch and tempo, transcending into incremental thumps. Glenn turns to him and grabs his shoulder.

'You don't have time for that. You need to shut it away somewhere because if you don't you will stay out here and die. Is that what you want?' He shakes him once, aggressively 'Is that what you fuckin' want'

He takes a deep breath and wipes his mouth and spits over his shoulder, clearing his mouth of the dirt. 'I'm sorry, I didn't think I would ever see something like that.'

'He is gone and he is going home, we are here to make sure it doesn't turn into a habit. Get your bike filled.'

They pick up a jerry can and bag each and hurry to their bikes. The jerry can is heavy on his arm and shoulder. He switches off his night vision goggles and folds them up on top of his helmet, pulls out his torch and puts it in his mouth. He clicks the torch on with his teeth and twists the cap off the reserve tank, putting it on the seat. He unscrews the lid of the jerry can and smells to make sure it's petrol. He hefts the can on to his knee and cradles it with one arm. Steadying the end with his other hand, he carefully fills the tank, spilling nothing. His mind is elsewhere.

Caliphate

Everything around them is quiet, just the sloshing of the jerry cans. He fills his reserve tank to the brim, puts down the jerry can and screws the lid back on the tank. He then opens the primary tank on top of the bike and begins filling that. The can is now a lot lighter, making it easier to handle.

He watches the petrol pour into the tank making sure to keep the flow even so as to avoid spillage. Something makes him look up and over to the south-west and sees what look like lasers flying in different directions then disappearing in the sky. Tracers.

A distant, crackling, monotone roar, a couple of seconds in length, travels down the wadi, sounding like a giant beast being abruptly awakened somewhere in the desert. Then another. He looks over to Glenn.

'The mini-gun,' he says to himself.

'Get out of here now,' Glenn shouts over.

He hurries to empty the jerry can into the tank, runs over to the edge of the wadi and dumps it under a rock ledge. He starts his engine and climbs on the bike returning the rifle to the valise. He leans down and scoops up the bag and dumps it in his lap, holding it there with his legs, and shoulders up his daysack, pulling the straps tight. He rides over to Glenn and pulls up next to his this bike. He is hurriedly putting in his petrol.

Caliphate

'I'm going back on task to the east. I've seen a position that I think we could get the bikes in for the night,' he says.

'I can't, mate,' says Glenn worriedly, putting down the jerry can and closing the lid on his primary tank.

'My left flank is now completely open with Konrad gone. I'm gonna 'ave to merge runways and I don't think I've got the fuel.' He dumps his empty jerry can next to Tom's, comes back and gets on his bike, starts the engine and puts the rifle back in the valise, and looks at him. 'Whatever happens, just think of your wife, think of home. It will end. Look after the bike. I'll see you at the extraction point,' he says, pulling his gloves on tight.

A low glow is now coming over the southern edge of the wadi. They lean over and hug with their lower halves still on the bikes.

'Stay in cover. I wish you was coming with me, Glenn,' he says. He quickly takes out the packet of cigarettes, slides out three and hands them to Glenn, then puts the box back in his jacket.

'For fuck sake, I'm trying to give up,' Glenn says, taking them and putting them in his breast pocket.

Tom watches him put them away. He can tell Glenn is too humble for his own good. He's bricks and mortar, an unshakeable unit with his foundations cemented deep in stoicism, resilience and determination.

Caliphate

There isn't anything this desert can throw at Glenn that will shake those foundations, no matter what he says.

'I'll follow you up the wadi for a bit. I'll be in touch,' Glenn says.

Tom looks at the dash and then at Glenn, a quick nod, twists the throttle and begins the journey east again back up the wadi. He can hear Glenn's bike behind him for the first few hundred metres then it disappears. He must have found an exit on the north side of the wadi. And once again, he was alone.

The ground was much more difficult than before due to his fatigue, and his eyes were getting heavy and the cold was coaxing him into laziness. He was doing his best to fight it but his riding was getting sloppy, hitting rocks and bumps harder than he should. Looking in his mirror, he could see no light. Not being pursued allows him to justify his laziness. The cold wind streams up his sleeves and down his neck, and it's a long time riding back the two kilometres but after a while he sees the slope exiting the wadi. He hasn't once checked his sat nav – the movement of putting his head down opens a floodgate of cold air down his neck and he is too interested in preserving what warmth he has left. He already misses the warm down-draught of the helicopter, and Glenn. The silence all around mocks him, just a little longer is what he wishes for, he is dreading turning off the en-

gine. He can feel the desolation of the cruel wasteland nurturing that feeling of loneliness again. That quicksand in the mind. How long before you
discover something that will irreversibly change you? His mind snaps at
him. Not now, not ever, he swallows the anxiety; not like Konrad. He pulls
up the bike and puts the stand down, takes out the rifle and makes his
way up the incline.

Nothing. The floor is luminous green, a flat plain with the horizon splitting it in two, the top half dark green, sprinkled with glowing stars.
This is the coldest night of his rally so far and he needs to put on his thermal bottoms under his trousers. His knees feel like cold wooden discs and
his hands are numb and he can't tell how many toes he has in his boots.
His hands struggle to make sense of the rifle. He looks towards the direction of the tank trench, squeezing his hands and rubbing his knees, constantly sniffing.

He walks back down the slope to the bike and loses his footing
and slams on to his rear, sliding a couple of metres before standing up
again, to cold to care, to tired to respond. The bike is as he left it. He replaces the rifle in the valise and leaves the clips undone. He moves to the
back of the bike and puts both hands on the hot exhaust, and looks down
the wadi the way he came. After his hands gain some feeling he mounts
the bike again and just as he starts the engine he hears a distant thump

Caliphate

and snatches his head in the direction of the sound. He cannot see over the northern edge of the wadi. He begins carefully up the slope, the huge rear tire propelling the bike up the gradient effortlessly. He reaches the apex and moves over the lip and moves the bike on to the flat and immediately turns his head to the direction of the thump and the long echo through the wadi. In the distance, maybe five kilometres away, a mushroom cloud is ascending. Glenn was being tracked and he had dropped. Good and bad news. Whatever he dropped on, he probably hit. Glenn must be coordinating fires while riding, a skill not many riders were capable of. He would have to give a future grid he is travelling through and his direction of travel, then give an instant 'add' correction anticipating where the pursuing vehicle would be, working out how far the vehicle was behind him and its speed. He would also need to factor in the time of flight of the rocket and calculate that into the add correction based on how far he and the vehicle will travel in the flight time of the missile. Essentially he would be riding through where the missile would hit while the missile was in the air and then the vehicle would drive into the impact location as the missile hit. All this while on his own, navigating at night in the freezing cold. But he found some relief in the strike – Glenn was still functioning and the explosion somehow closed up the vastness of the desert. For a while he wasn't alone. He watched for sometime, there was a chance that his friend would die tonight, a crushing feeling as he could only watch.

Good luck, he thought, you can do it.

He looks towards the road and sees it clear so heads for the tank trench. He rides slowly because the cold night wind is too much for him to tolerate at high speed. He approaches the eastern entrance of the trench, pulls up on the lip of the slope and visually checks it for mines and improvised explosive devices. It looks empty and it's deep, perhaps three metres, with the ends sloped to allow access from the front and back. If it could conceal a tank, he thinks, it would keep him out of the wind for the night and provide good concealment from the road. The only concealment. He takes another look to the north; no more mushroom cloud. Time would only tell whether Glenn was being crucified somewhere or his limp body being dragged through the desert, tied to a jeep, or if he was successful with his drop. He looks for a while, sitting there with his hands on the engine, the bike trembling and thumping. He wonders if he should go back and look for Glenn. Don't you dare leave him like that! You know he's in trouble. His mind snaps like a bear trap back to reason. He knows what he's doing. Does he? The retort swings back. He is old and deteriorating, he said so himself. Get a grip, don't be foolish, you're trembling with cold and you have no idea what you would be getting into, God knows what's going on

Caliphate

over there. What would God know? What in this universe would he know? He knows all, but does nothing. I'll be in touch, Glenn said. He hoped so with all his heart, not just for Glenn's sake, for his. You can't get a grip if there is nothing to hold.

He gently pulls down the slope into the flat bed of the trench. He can't see over the sides and he treats this as if no one can see him. He switches off the engine, takes the bag from his lap and places it on the floor, kicks the stand down and gets off the bike, which is facing west up the slope, for a rapid extraction. He is shaking. He can feel the frost on the mud beneath his boots. His feet feel wet, even though they aren't. He pulls his rifle from the valise, clumsily banging the muzzle against the bike's fuel tank as he does so. He shoulders off his daysack and places it down next to the rear tyre and puts the rifle on top of that. His back now feels even colder – the pack had been holding some heat in his body. With numb, icy fingers, he hunts for the buckle on his belt kit, struggling to find the teeth of the clip, unable to see properly with the NVG on. He releases it accidentally and the belt kit falls from his waist and lands on the ground, the pistol clanking against a small rock. He leans down and picks it up by the buckle, laying it over his pack. It is getting colder by the minute. He can feel the frost on his gloves beginning to crunch. He walks halfway up the slope and checks in all directions; everything is clear and cold. He comes back

Caliphate

down the slope and switches off and folds up his NVG, and begins another struggle: to find the small buckle on his helmet strap. He finds it, takes off the helmet and lays it on the dash, night vision goggles still attached. He might get a visit in the night and may need to use them again. He picks up the bag from the helicopter and swings it over by the knot next to his daysack, opens the canoe grip and pulls out his roll mat, dropping it on to the floor next to the engine and stands blowing into his hands, the air so cold it hurt to breath. He reaches back into the bag and scoops out his sleeping bag, also throwing it next to the bike. He removes the remote display off of his wrist and stows it in his jacket pocket. He unzips his leather jacket and lets the heaviness of it assist in sliding off his shoulders and he catches it, folding it in half and throwing it towards the front tyre. He can feel what little heat he has left now being claimed by the cold. He opens the pannier and pulls out his jumper, replacing its waterproof bag and closing the lid, throwing the jumper over the back of the exhaust to warm it and unzipping his down jacket and dropping it on to his pack. Standing there in only his thermal shirt, he thinks that if he were to be suddenly teleported away from the bike into some remote part of the desert, he would want to die as quickly as possible.

He starts shaking more uncontrollably and reaches over to grab the jumper, pulling it on and trying to squeeze his head into it. He can't

Caliphate

understand why it's so tight – it feels as if the jumper only has two sleeves and no neck hole. He takes it off again and holds it out in front of him, feeling for the sleeves and neck and making a plan. He would take the jumper by the base and slide one arm in and locate a sleeve, any sleeve, he didn't care, then the other. Once they were located in their respective sleeves, there would only be one hole left and that would be for his head. Foolproof. But the sleeves feel ridiculously long and he can't find the neck hole. He's beginning to lose his temper so he takes out his torch with his trembling hand, puts it in his chattering mouth and clicks it on. He studies the jumper in the light only to realise he is holding his thermal trousers.

'Fuck's sake,' he snaps at himself, throwing them at the sleeping bag and going back into the pannier, this time with the small light. He finds the jumper and pulls it out the waterproof bag and closes the pannier.

The jumper doesn't make the difference he was desperate for and it takes a few seconds before he feels some of his precious heat being grounded. He spits out the torch and blows into his hands, the cold like scalpels slowly slicing down the ends of his fingertips. The small torch dangling round his neck with the light dancing around on the floor. He looks down where the torch is spotlighting and sees three fingertips poking out of the mud. He holds the torch still and kneels down, shaking. It is definitely three fingers. All grey and the skin taut. He feels the security that he foolishly, desperately, hoped that the trench would offer crumble to dust and his already exhausted focus on the task from the constant apprehension begins to consume all hope for safety. He stares, no plan. He feels some compromising factor closing in on him with the promise of utter, hellish torture. He stands, grabs the down jacket and puts it on, zipping it up to the top. Not the hood though – he needs to be warm but also needs to be able to hear clearly. He begins a more thorough search of the trench with the torch in his hand. His shaking has died down slightly and the jacket feels alive in certain areas, catching his precious heat in little jars for him and all the jars being held like lanterns against him. At the rear of the trench, partially up the slope, half a buried face is exposed, as grey and lifeless as concrete. The skin tight and the exposed eye looking up into its head like it died trying to see its thoughts. Its mouth is half open and filled with dirt and its black ratty doll-like hair trembles in the wind. The cold, his shaking and teeth chattering take precedence over his thoughts, there is nothing he can do, he has to get warm. He goes over to the sleeping bag and picks up the thermal trousers and puts them on the seat of the bike. He switches off the torch and walks halfway up the slope, stands in the silence listening for anything that could catch him off guard. The desert surrounding the trench is as dead as the face in the ground. He comes

Caliphate

back down, switches on the torch and places it back in his mouth, sits down on the sleeping bag and unlaces his boots. He quickly checks up on his rifle, lying there on his pack, spray-painted green and brown the same as the bike. Cold and inanimate until the trigger is squeezed and the combustion takes place in the chamber sending the message down the barrel. Messages will be sent soon… and read. He slides his feet out of his boots, which he places to one side, and grabs one foot at time, squeezing and rubbing life into them. They don't feel like his own. He stands up on the roll mat and unbuckles his belt and drops his trousers, heavy with the map and belt and Kevlar lining, stepping out of them shivering. His legs are white and etiolated like some blind, albino cave salamander.

He picks up the thermal bottoms and hunts for the legs with his feet and slides into them, tucking his shirt in. He then hurriedly puts his trousers back on, shaking. The torch falls from his chattering teeth as he buckles his belt. He sits back down, convulsing, as he slides his wooden feet back into the boots and ties his laces. He doesn't blow up the roll mat tonight. He throws out the sleeping bag on to it, jacket left by the front wheel, and unzips it partially and clambers in. He would establish eyes on at sunrise; he always woke before then. He zips up the sleeping bag over his head, slips his hands between his legs and curls up into the foetal position, waiting for the warmth that he hopes is stored somewhere inside

Caliphate

him. He shuffles up to the engine, still warm. Lying in the cold desert, shaking, alone with nothing but the company of the face and fingers of the dead. Glenn out there. Witchcraft One Echo somewhere south. Hunted by the prophets of horror, propelled by honour. He thinks of his wife with the cat, in the warm house knelt down on the carpet with her hands clasped together, eyes closed, chanting. A chant to summon whatever warmth she can and channel it to him via his memories. Just remember, that's all you have to do… please.

'I'm trying,' he says to himself, as he closes his eyes.

He was sat in an old wooden chair with his limbs tied to the arms and legs, his head unable to move, only his eyes. The chair was in the middle of a white room. Everything white. He couldn't see behind him but something was there. On the floor was a drainage hole. He thought nothing of the situation and it felt as normal as being sat at home, even his lack of movement. He felt completely comfortable as if he was meditating, a re-laxing state. He felt no threat from the obscure surroundings.

Something unlocked behind him, two heavy chinks and then a gradual creaking. There was a door in the room that he couldn't see, and now it was open. He heard no further noise but two men came to either side of him, passing, holding large paintings, the painted side he couldn't

Caliphate

see. They were completely silent and were wearing smart black suits and no shoes or socks. They had blindfolds on and their feet were not touching the floor by about a foot. They levitated to the back of the room and he watched them prop the paintings against the wall with the painted side facing away from him. The two men drew out a claw hammer and a nail each from their jackets and proceeded to hammer the nails into the wall at head height. He could hear himself breathing but he could not hear the hammering, it didn't cross his mind that there should be some audio sensation coming from the hammering action. The men finished and dropped the hammers to the floor and he heard the metal collide with the floor and bounce slightly and collide again and then all was still. The men stood with their backs to him, the knots of the blindfolds in the centre of the backs of their heads. They stood there for some time. Motionless as the moon. Something behind him again and another man glided past, feet off the floor by about a foot again, and swung round in front of him over the drainage hole. The man was wrapped in a sheet that he held shut in the middle underneath, all that was visible was his head. Glenn's head. His head was just as filthy as he remembered from the resupply. He stood there staring at him in the chair. Everything as silent as stone.

The two men behind bent down and picked up the pictures and hung them on the nails so the painted side was facing the wall and then slowly turned

Caliphate

round. The two men, Glenn, the drainage hole, the paintings, the hammers on the floor and the nails in the wall.

The two men glided over to Glenn so they were at his sides. Glenn knelt down over the drainage hole, still staring at Tom in the chair. The men in suits either side of him slowly reached into their jackets and drew out medium-sized kitchen knives and held them by their sides in their hands furthest away from Glenn's head. With their free hands they each reached over and grabbed a fistful of Glenn's hair, holding his head taut. He remained in the chair expressionless and emotionless. He was neither afraid nor content, indifferent to either of their meanings. He was merely observing a situation as it was conveyed through his senses into his consciousness, completely free of judgement. His mind and thoughts lay dormant, unable to reason with situation. He watched without sensation. He stared at Glenn and saw his mouth miming something slowly, a few words, and stop.

Then the men either side took turns stabbing Glenn hard and indiscriminately and clumsily in his face at a rapid rate. One hit his forehead jarring off his skull, the next into his mouth slashing his gums and lips. His eye, his nose, under his scalp, into his cheek, slipping off the bottom of his jaw and into his throat. His face slowly becoming an unrecognisable red pulp. Bleeding all down the sheet and into the drainage

Caliphate

hole. The two men with their blindfolds facing him in the chair. They couldn't see yet they look at him. He thought nothing, no worry or care. Completely numb. He heard the rustle of the men's suits and the dull thump of the stab and withdraw over and over. He heard the punches of the knives entering Glenn's face and the blood and flesh hit the floor. But that was it.

His neck became limp like he had suddenly had his head removed from a vice and it flopped down so he could see his lap and arms. His arms and legs were not bound to the chair. They were never tied. He was free from the start, but he was none the wiser. The noise stopped and he slowly looked up. The men, Glenn, the hammers and nails are gone. No blood on the floor, not a trace of any evidence that anything went on in front of him. Only the paintings remained. He looked at the paintings and they slowly began to turn around, scraping against the wall, on their own, no nails holding them up. Everything silent but the scraping. The paintings came halfway around, still keeping their canvases hidden. He still felt nothing. They kept moving slowly round and he began to see what had been painted.

Nothing in this universe could prepare him for the paintings. Nothing in his memory had ever terrified him as much as what was on those canvases.

Caliphate

In the white room, he screamed a scream not of this world.

The door wide open.

Then black.

His eyes open and he regains consciousness. He makes out shapes and some details of the shapes and then he could see the outline of the bike. He is sat up against the opposite side of the trench in the sleeping bag with his pistol in both hands. His eyes regain their focus and the bike takes form. The long tube exhausts, the chain and uniform engine covers, the chunky wheels. He becomes aware of the light from the rising sun and the cold temperature.

He looks around the trench. Everything in its place as he left it. Rifle on the pack. The pack next to the wheel. The wheel on the bike and the bike in the trench. The pistol he is holding is cold in his hands.

He remembers nothing from the dream, but he is aware that he has seen something and that there is something displaced about him. He stands up with the sleeping bag around him and reluctantly shakes it off on to the cold floor and kicks it over to the bike. He walks halfway up the slope and peers over the edge towards the road. Always dawn. The orange glow from the sun bathing the desert and the twinkle of the light as it prisms on the frost, leaving the desert floor an endless field of jewels. He

Caliphate

blinks and squints, cleaning his eyes, and comes back down the slope. He sits and puts the pistol down next to him and stares at the ground, waiting for his brain to engage with consciousness again, searching for its motivation amongst the cold air and thoughts of the helicopter. He sits for a few moments and stands up. It is cold but he isn't shaking.

He slides the pistol back into its holster on his belt kit and reaches for his jacket folded by the front wheel and slides into the frosty sleeves and zips it up. He stamps on the floor a few times to wake up his seemingly comatose feet and looks around the trench. The face with its introspective eye. The fingers, reaching for something. He stands for a moment, looking around, aligning his thoughts and making sense of last night and where he is now. There is no sense to it all; maybe that's the point. He feels like he is waiting for something that has a fragrance of something terrible. Some intuition was pulling him somewhere dark, but he refuses to go with it. He needs to eat something warm.

He puts his sleeping bag and roll mat away in the canoe grip, tidies up the pannier, and sets up the cooker with water and breakfast inside, the slow burner quietly whooshing away. He picks up his rifle, pressing the magazine release catch, ejecting the magazine into his hand. He makes sure the first round on top is seated correctly and puts the magazine in his pocket. He holds the rifle with the handguard in his left

Caliphate

hand while with his right, he places two fingers over the charging handle hooks, and slides back the working parts to the rear, ejecting the chambered round; holding it open with the bolt catch on the left of the rifle. He inspects the chamber for cleanliness plus the bolt face and firing pin. It is surprisingly clean and wonders about this. He releases the parts forward then draws them back again to make sure the movement is free and fluid. He holds back the working parts and places the rifle on the pack. He bends down with a stiff back and picks up the ejected round, inspects it, cleans it like a diamond inspector. He takes out the magazine from his pocket and snaps the round back into the magazine and slaps the back of the magazine against his hand, making sure the rounds are all seating correctly. It hurt his hand a little with the cold and he thinks it's bruised. He bends down again and picks up the rifle, replacing the magazine and releasing the working parts with a smooth, well-functioning clunk chambering a round. Everything as it should be. He looks at the cooker doing its little, frantic dance, leans down and switches off the gas with the rifle still in his hand. He picks up his belt kit and swings it round his waist, lifting the rifle over it, clips it together and pushes it down so it is seated flush on top of his hips. He puts the rifle on his pack and preps a flask with instant tea. He eats his meal, piping hot corned beef hash, and drinks some tea, and the warmth of the food and drink add clarity to his thinking. The hunger was distracting him from the objective; watch the road. There is a different side to people when they are hungry. On a full stomach, people are more in touch with their good nature but this changes dramatically when the food is gone. Vegetarians and vegans soon gain the desire to eat meat again when thats all there is with the supermarkets empty and shelves dusty, he thought. He packs away the cooker and kicks a hole for the rubbish, near the bike and away from the fingers and face.

He rips open a Velcro pouch on his belt kit and slides out the suppressor for the rifle. He looks through it, making sure it is clean. He walks halfway up the slope, looks over the edge towards the road and the rising sun, and feels the warm food in his stomach stoking his warmth back to life. He can feel most of his toes and is no longer shaking. He looks east with an expecting gaze, and screws the suppressor on to the rifle muzzle.

He remembers the bag from the resupply; he had completely overlooked it. He climbs back down the hill and hefts the sack on to the bike seat and twists it, looking for the call sign tag. He finds it, Witchcraft One Echo. He stops for a moment to prepare for frustration at the incompetence of the resupply. He looks over the bag again as if the mistake was on his part but comes back around to the same tag. He shakes his head and squeezes his eyes shut. We are the ones out here he thought, not fucking you. He bows his head for a moment to let the thoughts of the mistake have their say until they sit still and wait for his response, which they knew; What can I do? He snaps off the zip tie, undoes the knot on the neck of the sack and opens it out.

Rations broken down. Dinners, crackers, cheese sachets, breakfasts, drink sachets, grain bars and water, all in their individual bags and bottles as usual. No radio battery. He rechecks the outside of the bag and call sign, and looks around his feet. He puts the bag on the floor and opens the pannier and looks for the spare battery. Nothing. The door gunner gave him the wrong bag. Witchcraft One Echo presumably didn't need any more batteries. But for Tom, no batteries is serious. No batteries means no Onslaught and without Onslaught it's just him and a rifle against whatever trouble he may stumble upon. He throws the bag at the floor, squats down and rests his head against the bike, the cold leather seat hard against his forehead. This hole is filled with bodies under your feet, he thinks. He has to get over the batteries and he knows it.

He stows the rations into their individual bags and boxes in the pannier and folds the sack and puts it in the canoe grip. The sun is now lighting up the desert once again. And the road. He climbs the slope with his daysack and rifle and establishes himself in a comfortable position. Now he can see the road more clearly, he notices it is a lot closer than he first realised. The road must have a bend in it that he missed on his initial scan, maybe because of the heat shimmer and the darkness. The bend comes into the desert close to the trench then bends back out to the south. He takes out his rangefinder and focuses on the piece of road closest to him, 693 metres. He puts the rangefinder down and shuffles down the slope and sits with his elbows on his knees, runs his hands through his hair and rubs his eyes.

'Moron… wake up. Wake up!' he hisses through his teeth, punching his thigh.

He looks at the face and hand with his head bowed and spits to the side still looking at them. He wipes his mouth and sits there staring at the buried face.

He is the furthest east now, the deepest into the established Caliphate out of any of the riders. Alone. This is not the time or place for mistakes and error. You get seen, you die; fall off the bike, you die; weapon jams, you die. The territory of the harbingers of death, the heart of the poison. They want him badly, his head, his entrails, everything, they want it in the dirt stamped on and shredded in every twisted and demented way. Think about that, think long and hard about it. Turn him into a statement, a message: this is inevitable for you all.

Caliphate

Squash the thought. He swallows hard and brushes the hair from his eyes. Whatever was positive about the situation had to be rationed.

Are you sure? Look at me, look, are you sure you should stay? He feels as if he's looking at himself in a mirror. For the first time all his faculties look at his rationale, waiting with baited breath for his answer. He can feel his blood in every artery, every vein as his body hunts for its courage, for a reason to stay, some crumb of it buried somewhere, some minuscule, remote crumb of reason. He blows hard through his dry mouth and cracked lips.

'Wake up,' he whispers.

He moves back up the hill and looks at his watch, 07.57. He switches on the remote display and highlights 'ADMIN'. He adjusts the throat mic and earpiece.

'Hello Zero, this is Witchcraft One Delta, radio check, over.' There is a pause for about thirty seconds. Then an intermittent transmission comes through consisting of mainly white noise. He could hear something but couldn't work it out.

'He… ions… r,' says the unknown call sign.

'Hello unknown call sign, this is Witchcraft One Delta, you are unworkable, over.' He closes his eyes slowly.

Caliphate

'…do …k.' More of the same white noise and unintelligible faint language.

'Hello unknown call sign, you are unreadable, over.'

Nothing but white noise.

There's no point wasting any more battery on bad communications. He looks at the display, selects 'FIRES' and tunes.

'Hello Onslaught, this is Witchcraft One Delta, radio check, over.'

He looks back to the road, somewhat more concentrated, caressing the barrel of the rifle with his thumb slowly in small circles. A slight mist on the desert. The clouds moving from the north. He looks towards the wadi as if to see Glenn.

'Hello Witchcraft One Delta, this is Onslaught, you are loud and clear to me, over.'

'Witchcraft One Delta, you're good to me, out.' He ends the transmission and switches off the display unit. At least he has Onslaught. He found that crumb, but for how long. He takes the cam net from the daysack, clips open the buckles and flicks the net out to one side. The sun is warming everything up, taking most of the chill out of the air.

He lays on his side looking out, he hadn't seen a road in a while and this added some minuscule interest to the view. He thinks about how

Caliphate

long he has left until he has to be at the extraction point. Eight days. Nine. Zero usually gives a 'proceed to' time and date. He thinks about all the riders at the extraction point greeting each other and swapping stories, but this was unlikely. He wonders how many are left on the rally and how many strikes had been delivered. How many had to be extracted because they turned insane or had requested medical evacuation. Some claimed to be in need of evacuation but were turned away at the helicopter door as fraudulent. He began to realise that it wasn't so much that he wanted this end, he needed it to. He always thought he would be able to contain himself and chain down his sanity and hold the key to the lock. No one has the key to the locks. The keys are held outside the mind and to be unlocked it may take one key or a thousand. Some have their locks picked and others just get flat out broken into and everything is stolen, leaving the mind plundered. All one can do is hold on to what locks one can and hope the rest hold themselves. Control, stay in control. Monitor everything, the small voice of bravery whispers behind his eyes. He nods gently. You see them first and you vaporise them, simple; the small voice says with a little more authority this time.

Vaporise them.

Caliphate

He spends the morning in the trench looking towards the road. There was no activity, which was a well-received break. He needed to stay warm and eat as well as he could today. He also needed to hydrate: he urinated outside the trench and realised he was dangerously dehydrated with his urine a light brown colour. Dehydration would only add to the torment, it would add fuel to the fire. Being on the bike most of the time and static in observation, there isn't much scope to sweat, not in the winter. The teas and coffees had been taking off the edge off the thirst but if he had to run any substantial distance, he knew his body could cramp almost immediately and his mouth would instantly remind him how thirsty he really was. He knew what this felt like and didn't want a revisit. He didn't like drinking water in the winter. Drinking water as cold as it was and the weather as cold as it is felt like it was putting out the little fire he managed to kindle in himself to keep warm. He could feel the coldness of the water travel down his throat and hit the pit of his stomach, as if the cold liquid was mapping out his organs letting him know what was where. It sometimes surprised him how long it took to reach his stomach. People often forget what's inside them, especially the heart. He had been sparing with his rations and had a fair amount before the resupply and now had more than he needed.

He climbs down the slope, and returns with the cooker and a meal, some cheese and crackers, a grain bar and water. He checks the road and sets up the cooker just below the lip of the slope, fills it with water and squeezes in the bag. He watches the road while eating cheese and cracker sandwiches and drinking water. Once the hot food is ready he takes out the steaming bag and switches off the gas. Beef cassava, thick chunks of tender beef drenched in gravy with potatoes and chopped vegetables, steaming hot. A rare delicacy among rations. He thinks that he would actually pay for this in a restaurant, but remembers he has been in the desert for over two months, and his standards of living and eating had been relegated to that of a homeless man. How we forget. He puts the bag to one side, takes some crackers and crumbles them up in the packet. Poured into the cassava, the crumbled crackers would absorb the gravy and make the meal more stodgy. He sits looking across the barren landscape towards the road, slowly eating the meal, every spoonful giving him more warmth.

He looks up from his bag towards the road and sees a small black something trotting over towards him, the wobble of heat shimmer giving it no form. He places down the bag and checks the rifle next to him. He picks up the rangefinder and centred it on the black figure. A dog. He puts down the rangefinder, takes the bag of cassava and looks inside it. Some beef left. He sucks the spoon clean and puts it in his pocket, gets out his knife and cuts down one side of the bag then places it to one side opening it up. He couldn't think of anything that has aroused such excitement in him in his time in the desert, not the resupply, not even Glenn. He hadn't even seen the dog's eyes yet or touched its fur. He didn't know if it was rabid and vicious. He didn't care. He kneels up and checks around. Everything still and silent in the cold desert air, the sun trying to penetrate and clean up the mess of the cold from the night before. He picks up the rangefinder and takes another look at the dog coming towards him, getting closer. He takes the bag and places it just over the lip of the slope, the dog now perhaps a couple of hundred metres away. He looks back through rangefinder and sees that the dog had stopped.

'No, please,' he says to himself with the rangefinder pressed into his eyes.

The dog is standing with its head held high and its nose twitching, hunting for some distant smell. He smiles. He can feel himself welling up.

The dog began to trot on its same line of march. He doesn't need the rangefinder any more and places them down. The dog stops a short distance away. He can see him, eyes and all. He doesn't know what to do.

'Look, what's this!' he says in an inviting tone, nodding to the open bag.

Caliphate

The dog's ears flick up and tune into his direction like some radar. Its mouth is open and his tongue is hanging out panting. The dog closes his mouth and looks more intently at him and pants again. It walks over with its tail wagging so hard and fast he thinks it might fall over. He draws his pistol and puts it next to the rangefinder; the pragmatic part of him still in action. It could be rabid.

The dog approaches with its wet nose twitching. It is nearly walking sideways with its head bowed low and its eyes looking at him. It flops down on its side and looks at him with its tail beating the floor. Huffing with small whines over and over, its belly rising and falling and its legs up. He doesn't want to get out of the hole so he just edges up slightly more so the dog can see more of him and see he isn't a threat. He only wanted to hurt some animals, the ones that buried the bodies in the trench. The ones who burnt the infant on the helicopter. He wants the dog to know that he would never hurt it. Ever.

He is already thinking of different ways to take the dog with him on the bike. He could put him down the front of his jacket with its head poking out. He could sit it in his lap and take it slow on the rough terrain. It isn't a large dog, maybe still a puppy less than two months old. He starts a premature commitment that he knows is childish and unsustainable. The dog is a mongrel, maybe half Labrador and half something else. It has the head of a Labrador, square, black, friendly head with droopy lips hanging over the side of its mouth and sad eyes, but he can't pin down the body. It has a muscled front half and a slender rear and it a thick coat, perhaps its winter coat. Its eyes are brown and its ears long. Its coat is pure black and dirty with sand and mud and the dirt had matted the hair on its under belly and neck into thick, short spikes. He sees its teeth were white and thinks that could be a sign of how young it may be. He pushes the bag closer to the dog. Lying on its side, he could tell it was a girl. She rolls on to her front and begins snooping forward with her head down and her legs pushing her forward with her belly rubbing the ground. She gets closer and twists her head and shows him her teeth. A gesture not of anger, but maybe a smile. He can't take his eyes off her, her wet nose inflating and deflating rapidly. She is nearly at arm's length now and he reaches out. She is still snooping forward in a prone position, pushing with her back legs. He pushes the bag with the beef towards her a little more. He takes off his gloves and puts them in his pocket. His hands are dirty with mud, the skin cracked on the fingertips from riding in the cold. He puts out his hand – not to touch her but for her to smell him. Smell that he is safe. She takes no notice of the beef, and sniffs his fingers looking at his face. She sniffs closer and he can't feel her touch him with her nose but she had; the light wind makes the spot cold. He extends his fingers and she licks them

Caliphate

once and twists her head as if requesting him to scratch behind her ear. He notices he is crying. He could touch her neck now but he gently scratches behind her dusty ear and her dark eyes close. She dips her head down and starts to sniff the beef and then licks off the gravy and gingerly eats the beef and potatoes slowly. He leaves her to eat and she licks the bag until it is silver again, her tail beating the ground. Once finished, she comes closer and he remains still as she sniffs his face and eyes. He wants to cough but doesn't want to scare her. He digs a small hole with his hand about the size he would dig for the cooker and takes the licked packet and places it in and pushes it down making a sub-surface bowl. The dog is now standing wagging its tail, watching his hand constantly. He takes the cooker with the cooling water and pours most of it into the hole where it sits on the bag. The dog sniffs the cooker and his hand and finds the hole and sniffs that too. She starts to lap up the warm water and he is glad she does. He drinks the warm water from the cooker and collapses it all down, places it to one side and puts his hand on the dog's mid back and pats it gently.

'Stay there, sweetness,' he whispers to her.

He picks up the pistol and the dog flinches. He slowly puts it in his holster and pats the dog's head for reassurance then takes the cooker and makes his way back down the slope, his eyes never leaving the dog.

Caliphate

He goes to the pannier and puts away the cooker, goes back up the slope and takes out the grain bar. He pinches the top on the seal and pulls it apart, squeezes the bottom, pushing out half of the bar. He snaps it off, offering it to the dog. She sniffs it and gently takes it out of his hand with her front teeth. She lies there awkwardly eating her bit and he sits watching, eating his.

'Please stay,' he says quietly to her.

He coaxes her down the slope to keep her from drawing attention to his position. The dog sees the buried face and the hand and looks at him. He checks around often and plays with the dog on the slope most of the afternoon. She sleeps and rolls around and puts her head in his lap and sleeps again and he watches the road all the while. All he wants to do is care for her, feeling as if whatever had been displaced in him had now been put back. He felt balanced. But he knew what the dog didn't, that he would eventually have to get on the bike and ride west and leave her here alone, as she found him. A love short lived. But he wasn't promiscuous with his love, he knew what to hold on to and what to let go. He did his best to override the thought and lived in the moment for the day, finding what happiness he could in this plight and holding it close, pretending. To the dog though, it wasn't pretend and this was breaking his heart.

Caliphate

The dog is asleep by the bike and he's on the slope. Maybe four hours of daylight left. He picks up the rifle and comes down to the bike and places the rifle on the pack. Strapped on the side of the pannier is a folding shovel, used to dig the bike out of deep mud or sand and to dig holes to bury waste. He loosens the small ratchet strap and takes off the shovel. He unscrews the neck and folds out the head and extends the handle and screws it tight again. The dog watches him with its head on its front legs. He goes to the side of the trench furthest from the bike and begins to dig a hole, a hole the size of a child's bed, a couple of feet deep. He was expecting to uncover something ghastly, but he doesn't. The dirt is soft and it doesn't take long and he makes a pile of the excavated dirt on the slope and rests often and checks around. He goes to the fingers in the ground and gently digs the dirt from around them and uncovers the full hand. The dog now has her head up watching him. He puts down the shovel and takes his gloves from his pocket and slides his hands into them then picks up the shovel. He digs some more around the hand and discovers the forearm, attached to nothing. He puts his thumb and forefinger around the palm of the cold dead arm and lifts it out with a gentle tug. It's a man's arm, he can tell by the hair on the forearm and the thickness of the palm. He carries it over to the hole and places it down gently and stands there looking at it. It has been removed from its owner by means of a machete

Caliphate

or some other crude form of surgery. The stump end lies black and decaying with no bone protruding. He walks over to the face and starts to dig around it and uncovers the buried side. The other eye looks directly at him. He pulls up his dust mask over his mouth and nose and starts to dig gently around the neck, then the shoulders. It hasn't been buried but has been left here and a sandstorm has covered it quite deep. He scrapes the soil off the naked chest and the left arm. The body is naked and there appears to be no immediate sign of an entry or exit wound in the head or chest. He continues his exhuming down the body and discovers the thighs, naked, with two tourniquets on the top of each just below the groin, tied tight enough to leave them dented in the skin, properly applied. He knows what is coming. He proceeds to scrape deeper but realises there is nothing below the tourniquets so he begins removing the dirt off the right arm stump, tourniquet around the shoulder, tight. He stands there looking at the filthy corpse. Its eye still looking at him, its left hand reaching up the hill, its legs stumps. A young man maybe, perhaps twenty by the looks of his teeth and his body size. He drops the shovel and goes and sits over next to the dog and she rests her head on his knee. He sits for a long time staring.

The man had been brought here and butchered. He had heard one of the other riders talk of this type of execution. They gave him morphine and hacked off his arm and stopped him bleeding to death with the tourniquet. They hacked off his legs. Tourniquets applied again. Then left him here and he has tried crawling up the slope with his remaining arm and died later in the cold.

He daren't open his mouth. Have we not learnt anything, he ponders as he looks over the lip of trench, expecting to see some kind of judge and jury listening to him as if he was a lawyer. Teach the children, that's it, teach them the book. Show them how and show them your truth. His eyes move back to the body, inculcate, indoctrinate and incinerate their compassion. Take all the empathy, smash it into dust, scoop it up with the pages and throw it in the desert and then send them to try and find it among the dust and dirt. He drops the shovel. The maniacs in their hordes, triumphant in their shared delusion. Holding hands and dancing in circles of death. There is no one to fix them, they must fix themselves and all we can do is throw them the tools. But the tools are thrown back covered in blood.

He looks up to the empty sky. 'Are you seeing this?'
Yes, we all say.

He gently picks up the body by its remaining arm and stump. Solid and cold. He takes it over to the hole he dug and places it down

Caliphate

gently next to the arm. He doesn't look for the legs. The small body lies in the hole. A man looks very small when he is just a torso with one arm. No religious ceremonies to be had for the body, it's already had enough of that. Its eye is now looking up at the sky as it lies flat. He takes a good look at the butchered man. Psychopath or not, how can someone do such a thing? Do they not feel the revulsion, the embarrassment, the bodies rejection of such behaviour. Can we really read ourselves unfit to serve with humanity. Do they not hear the screams, the snapping of the Ulna and Fibula, the recoil of the muscles to their tendons as they rip through with the blade. Tell me you can see the eyes, he thought, can you not see the eyes. He buries him completely and flattens out the dirt. He checks over the slope to the road. All quiet. The dog watching him.

He fills in the shallow holes where he pulled out the body and the arm and pats the soil with the reverse side of the shovel, to leave no sign of his presence. Then he scrubs the shovel in the dirt and collapses it and reattaches it to the pannier, goes back up the slope with the rifle and sits for a while watching the road. The dog comes up and joins him. He takes off his gloves and places them in his pocket and strokes the dog's warm body, her tail wagging and beating against his hip.

'Unnatural, isn't it. Would you do something like that?' he says.

The dog just looks at him and blinks. Her wet nose still.

Caliphate

He stays on the slope until the sun starts to lose the fight. He thinks perhaps there is no fight, rather the earth is the one turning its back on the sun. He thinks about this and about the earth naturally spinning on its axis and decides, actually, everything is fair. Neither has an advantage over the other and both have equal time to kill or comfort. Everything is fair. Everyone has their share of light and dark and it is just a matter of where you are when the darkness comes and how you keep each other warm. The darkness should bring us closer, that's what it is there for, otherwise we can't see each other to keep each other warm. And if we can't say that we know the difference of when it is dark or light, then we have lost all hope, we have blinded ourselves.

He rolls up the cam net, buckles it tight and throws it down to the daysack. He switches on the wrist display, selects 'ADMIN' and presses the button on the side.

'Hello Zero, this is Witchcraft One Delta, radio check, over,' he says.

The dog looks up at him thinking he is talking to her. He scratches her ear and takes his pen from his pocket.

'Zero, you are difficult but workable to me, send conditions, over.'

Caliphate

'Witchcraft One Delta, bike five, radios two, batteries one, rations five, water five, fuel five, ammunition five, over.'

He closes his eyes briefly in relief, but the thought quickly catches up with him that each transmission deteriorated the batteries further.

'Zero, bike five, radios two, batteries one, rations five, water five, fuel five, ammunition five, over.'

'Witchcraft One Delta, I am in location with good eyes on the road, I have comms with Onslaught. I have been resupplied but I have Witchcraft One Echo's supplies and I am down one battery. Roger so far.'

'Zero, roger over.'

'Witchcraft one Delta, therefore I request a resupply, over.'

'Zero, negative on resupply, you are to maintain comms with your spare battery. We have an extraction grid to follow, over.'

He lifts his head with his eyes closed, looks at the dog and smiles and shakes her chin playfully. Her tail starts chopping again against his thigh. The extraction date has been brought forward. A rare occurrence.

'Witchcraft One Delta, roger, send it, over.'

'Zero, Map six, grid, two Papa, three, nine, eight, six, one, two… Nine, four, six, six, nine, one, roger so far, over.'

He writes it on his panel and reads it back.

Caliphate

'Zero, you are to remain in position with eyes on the road for a further eighteen hours as intelligence suggests movement approaching that area. Witchcraft One Charlie will be extracting for the next twelve hours under your cover, roger so far, over.'

So Glenn was still alive and has triggered movement to the north and passed it on to Zero. For whatever reason he was unable to drop – maybe he couldn't get comms in time or maybe it wasn't enemy. He'll give him grief about that: 'we need to work on your draw, Glenn.' He loved Zero for telling him that. Whoever it was speaking on the radio he didn't care, but if he could he wanted to thank them deeply.

'Witchcraft One Delta, roger, over.'

'At twelve hundred hours tomorrow you are to switch to permanent comms and wait for the rendezvous grid. Acknowledge all, over.'

When an extraction grid is given, the riders move back three at a time, leaving three holding their last positions in order to provide some overwatch. If there is a relief rally, he would stay in position until another rider rendezvous with him and he hands over. After the first three have checked in with Zero or after a ten-hour window, the next three riders move down their runways. This will happen until a rendezvous grid is given to all call signs so they can collocate before they ride as a complete packet to the extraction grid.

Caliphate

'Witchcraft One Delta, will I have any flanking cover for the extraction? Over.'

'Zero, no, Witchcraft One Charlie has been injured and is making the full run back, there are no comms with Witchcraft One Echo, Alpha and Foxtrot, you will be moving on your own, over.'

His window of happiness was short lived. He was in effect by himself now with Glenn moving back non-stop. He pauses to think about this.

'Witchcraft One Delta, roger, over.'

'Zero, the world has changed in the last few hours. We all wish you the very best of luck, out.'

Everything has changed – Was this why the rally was finishing early? It explained why there was no relief but it explained nothing else. Maybe Glenn knew, or perhaps Zero told him nothing either. Where have they all gone, he thought. The breeze whisked up his sleeve and across his chest and tied the cold cape of his vulnerability around his neck, and, for a moment, terror blinded him as he mindlessly stared at the ground by his rifle.

He switches off the display unit and watches the light of the screen die away. He sits and looks at the road and thinks about how even more exposed he now is, but an air of excitement distracted him. Maybe

Caliphate

Witchcraft One Echo has comms problems like he did yesterday, or maybe not. He tries not to think about him out to the south. He thinks about Glenn riding back in the freezing night injured. After twelve tomorrow he would be able to speak to him, maybe find out what's going on. Everyone will be able to speak to each other because the bikes will be moving and there will be no need to conserve batteries. At least then he could check on Glenn and, if needed, ride to his grid. He looks at the dog lying down. Maybe he can take her with him, it's not completely out of the question, she's small enough to sit down the front of his jacket. 'My wife would squeeze you to death,' he says to her. She just looks up at him with her head on her paws and her tail goes again. Maybe she understood him. Maybe it was the tone in which he said it or maybe she was just happy to be with someone. He needed her more than she needed him.He picks up the rifle, puts his gloves back on and makes his way down the slope. He puts the rifle on the pack and goes into the pannier to get out the cooker, some food and some water. He would have double rations tonight and he would give the dog a full bag.

He sets up the cooker and fills it with water. The dog walks down to the bike and he could see her nose going haywire. She knew what the cooker meant. He squeezes two meals into the cooker and preps the flask with tea and ignites the cooker, the thump of the flames combust-

Caliphate

ing makes the dog jump and she looks at it with her head twisted. He glances back over the slope to the road and sees it is clear and comes back down and takes out all the maps from the pannier. He looks around, maybe an hour of daylight left, it's starting to get cold.

The maps cover areas of ground spanning some 600 kilometres to the east from the infiltration point and spanning his whole runway. Each map was one in 50:000 and was Military Grid Reference System, which meant he could plot accurate grids and call fires in an emergency without the rangefinder. He knows the extraction point would be a little closer and leafs through the stack of maps for map six. He slides it out of the pile held by an elastic band and puts the rest back. He opens it out on the seat of the bike and looks around it and finds the zone prefix 'two Papa'. He then looks for the grid, his fingers running down the grid lines, and finds that too. A plateau of desert maybe seventy kilometres east of Palmyra, near the border. Isolated and flat, a good spot to land the Hercules. He has a look at the area surrounding and is happy. He makes a visual snapshot of the grid and any key features. He does not write on the map. If he were caught, they would see the map marking and he didn't want to compromise any other riders at that grid. He looks at the cooker and sees the jet of steam shooting out the top and bends down to switch off the gas. The dog's tail is at it again. He folds that map and places it in

Caliphate

his right map pocket. He then switches on the sat nav on the bike and inputs the extraction grid. He will follow the sat nav until they give him a rendezvous grid later on in the ride. For now he will head in the direction of the extraction grid. He presses 'grid' on the unit and the screen displays 'PLEASE WAIT'. He bends down and opens the cooker and pulls out one steaming bag, rips off the top, places it on the floor and carefully cuts down the side with the knife, the dog doing some sort of tap dancing with its feet and its tail once again nearly pulling it over. He leaves the dog to eat and goes back to the navigation unit. It was set: the display is still with the picture of a motorcycle denoting his position and the mapping in a bird's eye view. He goes down to the cooker and draws out his steaming bag then puts a bag of pudding in the cooker and fires the gas up again. The dog is still eating. He gets the maps and looks through them one at a time while eating his dinner, a spoonful at a time, placing the bag down while looking back at the maps. He makes points on every prominent piece of flat ground and bearings to each of them from the one before. He wants to get there fast so he chooses the fastest route that kept him away from families of dunes and deep wadis. He turns off the gas and lets the pudding stay hot. He plots these grids and bearings into the sat nav as waypoints in order of approach. Whenever he got to one of his nominated waypoints, the sat nav would switch to the next one with a new bearing

Caliphate

and he would just follow. It takes a while to set and by the time he's fin-ished it is dark. He folds all maps away apart from the one he was current-ly riding in and the one with the extraction point in, then he puts the rest back in the waterproof bag then stows them in the pannier. He would switch maps on the way, as and when they overlapped. He switches off the sat nav and gets the sleeping bag and roll mat out of the canoe grip and lays them out next to the bike. He takes out the pudding and puts it in his pocket and pours the water into the flask then packs away the cooker.

The dog has finished her meal and is nudging the bag around with its nose and paw. He sits on the laid-out sleeping bag and finishes the rest of his meal, tuna rigatoni, and then starts to eat the treacle pudding. He sits there for a while enjoying the steaming, sweet sponge. The dog comes over and sniffs the sleeping bag and begins to walk in small circles on the bottom of it before settling down in a ball. He watches as he eats his pudding. It's not as cold as the night before but it's pitch black as there is no moon light due to clouds, he might take off his down jacket and sleep in his jumper. He finishes his pudding, takes out his torch and places it in his teeth. He picks up the bags including the dog's then kicks a hole and buries them, then goes back to the sleeping bag, takes off his display unit and puts it in his trouser pocket, leaving his throat mic on. He is far too close to the road and he shouldn't get too comfortable. He takes off his belt kit and places it next to the rifle, then his heavy leather jacket and folds it into a small bed for the dog placing it next to the mid-section of his sleeping bag. He scoops her up gently with her licking his chin and places her carefully in the jacket. She is surprisingly docile for a feral dog. Where did she come from, he wonders, wandering through the desert all alone? Did she have a family that missed her? A home? He had never met a feral dog so willing to interact with him. She just stayed in the same position as he left her while she just sniffs the pockets for traces of food. He goes into the pannier and takes out a pair of socks and a small bag with an elastic cord in the top that had been wrapped around the opening to prevent the talcum powder leaking and places both in his pocket. He unlaces one boot and takes it off then the sock. His foot is clammy and cold but he could feel it. He rubs the foot and wiggles the toes. He unwraps the cord on the bag, opens it out wide and puts his bare foot inside then rubs the talc into every nook and cranny of his foot. A wonderful sensation, his foot trapped in a boot all day and then given a talc bath. He rubs the talc between his toes and into the nails, pressing hard. It is cold on his foot but this is better than no feeling at all. He leaves his foot in the bag and unrolls the fresh socks and puts one back in his pocket. He takes his foot out of the bag and slips it into the sock. It is cold but he can feel the softness and it makes his foot feel brand new.

Caliphate

Dry feet is a luxury that is only realised when one spends any longer than a week with wet feet. To walk a long distance with wet feet requires a degree of meditation, and not just any walk, but a walk that will lead not to dry feet but to another activity prolonging the wet feet. He learnt long ago to train his mind to stop listening to the cries of the wet and loose skin on the foot; after a while they merely become a means of transport and not the body. If you stop listening to them they eventually stop hurting. But in the end they are part of you and eventually you will have to take off the boot because you need them. You just have to look and see what damage you are doing at some point.

He puts his boot back on and laces it up then does the same to the other foot. Once finished he places everything back in the pannier and takes off his down jacket and stuffs it into his daysack inside the water-proof bag, zipping it up. He checks the rifle and turns off the torch then slides into the sleeping bag. The dog has settled nicely into the jacket and he leans out and touches her head. He feels her ear flick and then her wet nose.

'I'll see you in the morning,' he says to her.

He zips up the sleeping bag fully and curls up like the dog. The both of them in the hole with the butchered man, and them out there. He thinks it was a shame there was no hell for the rot to go to. The warm food inside him, the thought of riding on to the Hercules aircraft soon and the dog next to him.

He remembered being in a pub not long ago, drinking ale. The country pub on the side of a quiet road with a pond in the back garden and a road leading into a small quiet village. Knock on any door in the village and you would be greeted by an excited dog and the smell of some late afternoon food being cooked, a man in the back garden potting plants or trimming the hedge or a woman hanging out wet washing. The warm sun and the green trees surrounding the garden in full blossom. The birds would land in the trees with their different coloured beaks carrying collections from their various journeys in fields and gardens to add to their tiny nests where their young cry with their mouths pointed up and open. Tiny little bodies fragile and big eyes still sealed. Some cows slowly wandering in a group in a lush green field. The ducks coming to land in the pond from some mission, with their flat orange feet pointed out and skimming quietly in the dark green water and there they would stay, washing and quacking to each other in some language. They would put their orange beaks under their wings and sleep, floating in the warm quiet water with the smell of trees and fresh cut grass and ale. He would sit there with his arm around her waist. She was wearing a loose dress with small sunflowers printed on

Caliphate

it. Her legs where crossed and he could see her bare feet where she had kicked off her shoes and was rubbing her feet together slowly. Tiny nails painted yellow. Her small hand in his. Some others laughing and drinking in the sun with tree shadows cast over them, moving gently in the wind. They would sit there with birds whistling and singing and watch the ducks do nothing until the sun faded, but the darkness didn't matter. Because she held his hand.

Preserve this painting, and guard it with your heart and rifle.

The sleep came and took him once again, but not to the same white room.

He wakes in the darkness, unzips the sleeping bag a fraction, pokes out his head and leans up on his arm. The jacket is empty and the dog is curled up at his feet on the roll matt. He sits there for a moment and looks at her. She is no bigger than a small toddler and doesn't take up much room at the bottom. He checks his watch, 04.32. Another hour, he thinks and zips up the sleeping bag.

Another hour

Caliphate

3

HELL

He wakes in the first few beams of light of the early sunrise, unzips the warm sleeping bag and leans up and looks down at his feet. The dog has gone. An unreasonable amount of panic washes over him. He looks around the trench and she isn't there. He climbs out of his sleeping bag and the cold air immediately cleanses him of his precious warmth. He gets his down jacket out and puts it on before the cold dawn could slay all warmth completely and puts on his heavy jacket and reattaches the display unit from his pocket. He puts the belt kit on and then packs everything away and gets out his flask that he filled the night before and makes his way to the top of the slope with the rifle. He rubs his face with both hands, rubbing his eyes with his fingertips and brushing his hair back. The dog is maybe fifty metres away sat down staring to the north-east. He calls for her but her ears simply prick up and then flop down as she continues to stare. He feels the panic subside but then he sees it.

A shaky glint off the windscreen of some vehicle in the far distance a few kilometres away. His heart starts to thump.

'Come here!' he hisses at the dog, louder than he should have.

She turns and sees him then looks back to the vehicle in the distance and turns back and comes galloping over to him. He has to keep the dog in the trench. He quickly goes over to the bike and opens up the X-wing antenna, gets his helmet and unclips the NVG and stows them back in the daysack. He puts the helmet on and clips it under his chin, takes the cam net off the side of the pack and throws it to the slope. He puts on the daysack and pulls the straps tight. He takes out a grain bar from the pannier and gives it to the dog in the packet to keep her busy and in the trench. The dog's tail chopping away, she knows what's was coming. He goes back up the slope and places down the rifle and unrolls the cam net, pulling it all the way over him so he is completely covered, then takes out the rangefinder and map and looks towards the vehicle in the distance. He was ready to leave in a second's notice.

Caliphate

The sun is now dully lighting up the open desert from the east through the thick clouds. There's no frost but it is still cold. A light wind from the south carries the cold down his neck. The glinting of the vehicle's windscreen is flicking on and off on the rough road. He can now see it is a large vehicle but he could only see it from the front from his position, it looks orange. He slowly turns to the dog, she is still lying down trying to get through the wrapper. He looks back to the truck with the rangefinder and fires the laser: 1765 metres and closing. It slows and turns east and back south on its original route, maybe to avoid a pothole. In the brief moment in its turn he can see it's a tipper, but he can't make out much else. Then there's another glint behind the tipper. From his angle at ground level it is difficult to see but another vehicle emerges through its dust cloud. It is a jeep and it does the same manoeuvre in the road to avoid whatever is there but he can't see the side of it through the dust, just the glinting of the sun reflecting off the windscreen. If the vehicles stopped near him, he wouldn't be able to ride out of the trench without them hearing the bike start, let alone not see him. He could out-ride the truck but the jeep could give a steady pursuit. He would shoot them before he rode off. You would have to, he thinks – he doesn't want them following him. His mind is strict now, no questioning. He hopes they're just some innocent vehicles and would pass him without conflict. The truck was getting closer and approaching the bend, which would draw them closer to him still. He looks through the rangefinder and tries to steady the cross-hairs on the truck and get a better look. The dust cloud is substantial from the eight wheels but a small window of visibility gives him a glimpse of the cargo in the tipper. People squatting down. How cold they must be in there. He can't count them but is sure it's over thirty. He can now vaguely hear the engine chugging, the wind carrying it in brief samples, teasing his senses. As it gets closer it no longer needs the wind – he can hear it well enough. He lowers himself a little more and slowly turns and looks at the dog. She is lying there licking the wrapper of the grain bar. He looks back to the truck and can now see the heavy machine gun poking out from the top of the jeep in the dust cloud. He selects from his wrist display 'FIRES'.

'TUNING.'

The rattle of the loose tail-gate and the slapping of it against the bottom of the tipper as the truck finds holes and bumps in the road made more noise than the engine with its sharp claps. The truck and jeep turn into the bend in the road and are heading straight for him. He lowers himself more. Any lower and he would be part of the ground. He reaches to his throat slowly and holds the throat mic closer to his larynx and with his other hand presses the button on the side of the display.

'Hello, Onslaught this is Witchcraft One Delta, radio check, over.'

'Hello Witchcraft One Delta, this… Ons…ght, you are lo… and clear to me over.'

'Witchcraft One Delta, standby, over.'

'Onsl…ght, st…by.'

He picks up the rangefinder again and looks at the truck and jeep then scans across to a piece of road further down the bend and fires the laser. 801m GR ES 45276 66362. He takes out the pen and writes the grid on the panel.

The vehicles now getting a lot closer, he lasers the truck, 943m. They are already too close. They would see him if he were to ride out of the ditch now. The truck continues around the sweeping bend drawing it closer to the trench. The ground is completely flat all around, offering no cover at all. The closest cover is where the dunes start again back west, about a kilometre away. The truck is now close enough for him to identify the Mercedes badge in the middle of the front of the cab. He wants to turn and look at the dog but he has to keep still. The cloudy sky still holds back most of the sun and a dull light is cast over everything. The truck is still rumbling closer at an angle, four people in the cab, maybe forty in the tipper, all crouched down. Some hands holding on to the side. The huge tyres kicking up swells of dust. The jeep has two people in the cab and four in the bed surrounding and holding on to the heavy machine gun. All of those who were not in the bed of the truck are wearing chest rigs and black attire. Some with black fleeces on, others with black bandanas with some sharp Arabic writing on. A slogan of death. His heart begins to beat faster and he tries to stabilise this with steady breathing, but he is out-numbered and outgunned and no steady breathing is holding that down. If they see him he will have to get on the bike and blast out of the trench west for the dunes and hope to lose them there.

What if the bike won't start? It will; it always starts. What if the cold over the last two nights has killed the batteries? The closer they get the more the paranoia creeps in. What if you get hit while riding to the dunes and fall off the bike? Then you put the pistol in your mouth and pull the trigger.

He thinks about checking the chamber of the pistol to make sure there was a round chambered and realises he should stay still. Who is asking these questions? What part of him did not know the pistol is loaded? There is no separate part of him, there is just him and his thoughts, and his thoughts came from the darkness of his consciousness and beyond that, nothing. He was walking through life reacting and had been since he was born. He loaded the pistol and put a round in the chamber days ago and he knew that and there was no other 'him' that unloaded it.

He couldn't drop because he didn't know the situation with the people in the tipper. He doesn't know who they are or whether or not they are armed. The truck approaches closer still. He fires the laser, 632m. Stay still and let them pass. But the truck creeps a further seventy metres and stops with the hiss of the brakes its final sound. He has no idea how hard a heart can beat until that truck stopped. He can hear some faint talking and then some shouting. He can hear the dog behind him start to whine. He slowly turns the rifle around and points it at the dog standing there with its ears pricked up.

The dog would have to die before it started barking.

'Shhhh,' he says very quietly, looking at the dog.

The dog looks at him, lets out a few more whines and sits down. He leaves the rifle on the ground aiming at the dog and slowly turns back to the trucks and gently brings the rangefinder to his eyes and fires the laser at truck. The dust has settled and he sees the jeep come to a stop behind and the men in the jeep dismount while the four men in the cab open the doors and climb out. The people in the tipper are still crouched down.

Caliphate

'Witchcraft One Delta, grid, echo sierra, four, five, zero, seven, nine… six, six, eight, one, two, height fifteen metres, over,' he whispers.

'Onslaught, grid, ech… sierra, fou… five, seven, …ine… six, …x, eight, one, t..o, heigh.., fift… metre, …ver.' Onslaught's reply comes over broken up. Comms were becoming difficult, he could afford no misinter-pretation in the fire mission details. One chance now.

The men are now arranging themselves around the tipper. People inside are still down.

'One heavy vehicle and one four-wheeled vehicle, ten armed PAX, in open, over,' he says.

'One heave…o………….el…, te… ar… …X, in op.., …ver,' Onslaught replies, more broken. That will have to do.

'Two rockets, danger close, point detonating, vertical, at my command, over.'

'Two ro…ets, danger cl…, point detona…, vertical, ……… mand, …ver.' Broken but workable. As long as there is no confusion in the grid and 'at my command' it will pass.

The men begin unslinging their weapons and start signing with the barrels to the people in the tipper to climb down. Some of them stand up and others are more cautious and remain down. He lies there still as a rock under the cam net. The wind picks up slightly and carries some of the

Caliphate

noise away from him but only for a split second. He thinks that maybe the people in the truck were recruits for their cause and they were training them out here. But when he sees a few women's heads among those standing he thinks this unlikely.

'Rea… ver,' in his ear.

'Ready, out.'

One of the men points his rifle in the air and fires a single round – there's a thump and a sharp, short whizz as the bullet travels up into the sky, with the short distance making the shot sound dull. The shot makes the people in the tipper flinch and most stand and begin to climb out of the back. One of the men with rifles has his weapon slung over his back and is holding a video camera, walking around capturing the scene. The men start to herd those already out on the ground into a line a few metres away from the truck. There isn't much aggression from those with the rifles, and those climbing out of the truck are compliant. The men are wearing just their underwear and the women are naked. They are all shaking violently – how long have they been on the truck like this? In this cold he has no idea how some of them didn't die on the journey. Eventually the last person climbs off the truck and falls into the crowd that is being manoeuvred into a long line. Forty was a good guess – he counts forty-one, minus the men with rifles. The people are all in a line on his side of the truck. He can see their

Caliphate

bodies. Some skinny and wretched and some well fed with smart haircuts. Some tall and others short and of all different ages. The women try to cover themselves and their hair flicks and dances in the wind, covering their faces.

He briefly sees one of the girl's faces, light brown skin with jet-black hair. Her green eyes look as though they could cut diamond. She stares at the ground as if she has seen something that she can't look away from in case she loses it forever. But there's nothing there apart from dirt. She's preparing something in her mind, maybe the realisation that all ambition and desires end here in the next few moments. How do you prepare for such a thing? He looks at her lips and sees she is reciting something, and then he realises most of them are, some have their heads held high and others hold their heads cocked to the side against the wind. There is no crying or begging or whining, just the wind. One of the men slings his rifle and climbs on the back of the jeep and swings round the DShK machine gun and aims it into the centre of the group. The other men form a line behind the naked people and bring up their weapons.

'No… NO!' he yelps.

He reaches for the rifle and grabs it by the stock, moving it back round so the barrel faces the group, twisting it on the dirt and sliding it up. He drops the rangefinder, grabs the pistol grip and flicks off the safety with

Caliphate

his thumb, but before he can get the rifle into his shoulder, he is hit by a salvo of gunfire noise. He ducks down as low as he can.

'Fire, FIRE!' he says urgently, pressing the button on the display.

The DShK machine gun thumps like some giant running across the desert and enormous orange flashes burst out of the end of the barrel, dust being kicked up from in front of the jeep. The men with rifles in their shoulders spray rounds into the line of people. There's a continuous rattle of thunder and clapping of all different pitches. Bursts of dust kick up in front of the people as the rounds travel through them and ricochet off the dirt into the desert. Most of the people fall to the ground, several crumple to their knees like some dark ballet, and others remain standing covering their heads. Those who fall to the floor look like rag dolls. Their hair shoots up on the backs of heads and blood streams from every orifice of their faces as they buckle and slam into the ground like felled trees. Those who escape the initial barrage are laced up with a hail of rifle fire, the flash of the rifles and the thump of the round striking the ground after passing through someone's liver, brain, throat – indiscriminate. One man tries running and falls face first before he can take more than five steps.

He lies there watching and blinking and shuddering with every round that strikes the floor, every flash from every barrel. The horror and

Caliphate

pointlessness of it all. The green-eyed woman on her front in a pool of dark red blood. Her face disfigured from the exit hole on her cheek. Her long, black hair blowing in the wind and dust as her body jumps slightly whenever she is hit by another stray round, like she is being electrocuted with her arms tucked underneath her. The whole scene unfolds in about ten seconds. The men walk up and down the line closing the spectacle taking single shots to heads, placing the barrel point blank. He sees everything. Every single man or woman or teenager right there by the side of the road dies in every single way a bullet can kill. The line of bodies lies there as the dust settles from the pummelling of the gunfire and the steam from the gallons of blood slowly twists and rises about the respective pools in the cold air. The men mingle, changing magazines and checking the bodies. The man with the camera films everything.

Every muscle in his body is poised for action, apart from his heart, which aches with grief. He has no thoughts of any constructive response apart from vengeance; burn them now is circulating through every emotion. Every person in that line had a family and friends somewhere. All had ambitions and desires of what they wanted to become and where they wanted to go. They all had the capacity to love and raise a child or bake a cake or hold the hand of someone they loved and now all that belonged to the dust and mud. It leaks from their eyes and mouths

Caliphate

into the ground never to be known again. The dog barked once during the whole execution.

He suddenly realises he hadn't heard 'Shot' from Onslaught and looks at the display. It flashes 'BATT'. There was something wrong with the radio battery. 'No,' he says.

He slowly slides down the slope on his belly with the rifle and pulls off the cam net. The dog is under the bike whining. No time for the dog. He goes to the radio case and quietly unsnaps the catches and opens the lid. The radio is completely dead. He stares at the blank, dark screen. Random shots from the site echo across the desert. He closes the lid and snaps shut the latches and grabs the suppresser on the end of the rifle and twists it to make sure it's tight.

He is going to have to kill them from here. Take them out one by one, starting with the man on the DShK. He has good cover and it is achievable. The fear might be seen through his skin but he has no choice. He can wait for them to move but that idea is torched before it gains any momentum because with the fear comes his anger.

Just as he turns, a monstrous heatwave and blast throws him to the floor with an earth-shattering crack and a dust storm that nearly vaporises him. Everything turns to white noise, he can actually see it, everything crackling, hissing and fuzzing for a split second with black and white blobs fizzing in his eyes. Dust and black smoke everywhere. No! That can't be Onslaught, the batteries are dead! Everywhere he looks is dust and soot, a slow roar fading all around him. He rolls on to his front, gets on to his knees and rapidly starts checking himself over patting everything, deep confusion. He pats his legs, his arms, his neck and his groin then looks all over for some idea of what just happened, his eyes straining and that taste of carbon mixed with dirt filling his mouth and nose. The dirt crunching between his teeth and his mouth dry as flour, he spits and coughs as he stands and searches for the bearing of the road.

He turns to the road and the entire cataclysm bursts to life again as the world around is shrouded by some monstrous sensory sabotage, this time even more intense. The heat and blast throws him back and he shouts some unintelligible cry. He lies there, hoping, searching for an indication that whatever was happening was in decline. Where is the ground? Which side is up? The white noise all over again. He curls into a ball – stay small. He is choked by the hurricane of dust and soot. He can't open his eyes. His ears strain with tinnitus. Something wet is running down his mouth. Do something! He snaps into focus. Do fucking what? Trapped in a cage of confusion and darkness, nailed to the floor of some crematorium incinerator. His face is stinging from the heat like a giant oven burst open. A land mine? IED? He uncurls himself as the roar dies down and checks himself once more, looking all over as if he has just figured out he has a body for the first time. Get up! Figure something out. The dust has subsided enough for him to see the bike is on its side. No thought of the dog. He couldn't hear anything apart from ringing, a high-pitched squeal. He looks frantically around the trench like a trapped animal, searching for some sign pointing towards what just happened. His thoughts begin to regain order, working around the explosion and retracing their steps backwards. Explosions, Onslaught, a jeep, the dog. The rifle! Where is it? He gets on his knees and hunts for it in the dust cloud patting everywhere, scraping around like a mole. He crawls around and touches something round and cylindrical, grasps it and drags it towards him feeling around it. The rifle. He fumbles around trying to figure out how it was meant to be held and after a few seconds holds it by the pistol grip and grabs the magazine to check it is still on. The disorientation drove him to madness for a moment. He remembers what was happening before the colossal explosions and crawls to the slope to look for the vehicles. Nothing, the dust is still thick. He looks to the right and sees the front of the bike and can see it has fallen on its side. He looks for a few seconds and realises he is facing the wrong way and shuffles down to the bottom of the trench and crawls in the other direction. When he gets to the lip of the trench he puts his hand into some shredded and blackened piece of meat.

Caliphate

He snatches it away and feels around, sliding his free hand along the ground, scanning the surface of the desert. He grabs the rangefinder. His thoughts become clearer and more aligned and he has a pretty good idea of what just happened. The pain from his face and the feeling of the dirt underneath steadies him, anchors him back to the reality of the situation; Onslaught must have heard his command 'Fire' and the radio died after. He spits the thick, gritty substance from his mouth and tastes more of the carbon-enriched air. Everything starts to make sense, apart from the massacre. He suddenly becomes able to prepare reactions to events that could transpire from what just happened. The dust starts clearing but the air is polluted with the smell of carbon and cordite, as if someone had just set off fifty tons of fireworks all around him – a sweet smell. He looks at the sky and sees two rising black clouds coming to the end of their form and melting away into the atmosphere, carried off by the parent wind like lost children. He looks back at the display and sees 'BATT'. He suddenly thinks of the dog and looks around for her. There's no time for her but the thought persisted; is she dead, a twisted carcass sprawled somewhere outside the trench? Is she under the bike?

The bike! The thought blasts to the front of his priorities. He slides down the hill and drops the rifle. With one hand he grabs the handlebar grip and, with the other, the exhaust on the same side, then adopts a squatting position and deadlifts the bike a short way up, straining so hard he thinks his eyes would burst out if he opened his eyelids. He is weaker than he thought and drops it back into the dirt. For Christ's sake, hurry up! He takes hold again and with everything he can muster pulls the bike up to waist height, repositions his hands and jerks it that last stretch until it is upright. It nearly kills him. He looks underneath and sees no dog. He eases the foot of the stand back down, letting the bike settle.

He turns around and the dog is there – it makes him jump. Show her you care, quickly. She is filthy but fine with her tongue dangling out of her mouth and shaking. He drops to his knees and grabs her head and kisses her between the eyes, stands up and climbs back up the slope. The tinnitus is beginning to subside and he starts to hear the wind again but with a monotone humming, as if his ears are packed with cotton wool. He rubs his eyes and checks himself over again and does a mental check to make sure any pain hasn't been clouded by the confusion and the sensory bombardment. He was okay. His face is on fire and he can feel it red like some horrendous sunburn. His legs are like jelly and his mouth is choked with dirt and when he coughs it sounds to him as if he is in a fish bowl; he could hear every crackle and wheeze in his throat as his ears worked overtime to retune themselves. He leans out of the slope more than usual to look over the settling dust. He can still see nothing. He stays

Caliphate

there looking as it settles and begins to see a huge crater where the truck and jeep were. He studies the ground around it and sees the truck on its side. The cab is on fire and the tipper had been thrown off to one side, everything twisted and blackened with only a few patches of orange remaining. He scans further left with the rangefinder and sees the remains of the jeep, the front half buckled and blackened. He takes away the rangefinder and sees another crater; the one from the second rocket. It is maybe 300 metres away from him – it dropped short of the target. There's debris in all directions, everything without form and indistinguishable from its former self. The rocket had transformed everything in the radius into a meat and metal jigsaw. Blackened charred remains of human beings are everywhere, some on fire. He stares for a moment at the crater and begins to feel the aches and pains setting in. No time to notice, he has to make a move. He stands and looks through the rangefinder down the road towards the north. He studies the desert around him for a few minutes. Body parts dotted around like broken toys.

His ears still ringing, he is plagued by thoughts of the people in a line. What had they done? Skull and brain flying everywhere with every round. Because they were the wrong religion? But they weren't. The fundamentalists can't even worship the same God in the same way. If only they could invest in this life instead of the nonsense of paradise. Blackness forever, that's what they deserve – he didn't care how they died, just as long as they did. Quick or painful, he didn't care, just send them away from here, far far away in whatever form. Yes, put those people in a line. People without weapons or intention to kill and stand them there and turn them all into corpses, that's what God wants. That is what he wants, and he says it clearly. He wished with every ounce of his being that there was some force behind him to stop them. But there was only him and the rockets, and now just him and a rifle. I'm so so sorry, he wanted to say to them. Futile words, embarrassing.

He rubs his eyes hard and rolls them around in their chambers to cleanse them. He coughs hard and after a few bellows that audibly rattle the lungs, he holds back the involuntary coughing that his lungs catch onto, before vomiting; that copper taste of blood now hand in hand with the phosphorus, sooty flavour lining his taste buds. He needs to buy himself a moment of steady breathing. His eyes settle with a mild haze and as they do, they pick up, maybe a kilometre away, a dust cloud.

His heart starts its song that it knows every cell in his body would listen to; the hard kick drum thumps, the call for order, the bell on the mountain that everything turned to when sounded… everything waited for the eyes' confirmation like poised lions hunting in the grass.

Caliphate

He pans to the left slowly and sees a man at the side of the road, with a set of binoculars looking straight back at him talking on a radio handset.

Every cell in him stops. He freezes with fear. Every hair on his body stands to attention and his heart plunges into the ice-cold bucket of water. They had seen him and were coming straight for him. He jumps down the hill, puts the rangefinder in the pouch quicker than he has ever put them away in his life. He slings the rifle over his neck and throws himself on to the motorcycle and kicks up the stand. He turns the key all the way to the right and fires the engine to life, pressing the button. He yanks the throttle and kicks the engine to life harder, wake up right now. He looks at the dog staring at him.

'I'm sorry, please forgive me. I'm so sorry,' he says choking back the tears and fear, the dog just staring back.

He wheel-spins out of the trench, up the slope on to the plateau and thunders away. He dips his head to reduce wind resistance and gain speed, dust kicking up everywhere. The cold air rushes down his jacket. No time to be cold. His goggles, where were they? No idea, no time to think about them, but without them it was only a matter of time before he couldn't tolerate the dust and would have to slow to a pace where they would catch him. He hears a single round snap past his head. A loud crack like someone has snapped a bamboo cane next to his ear. Don't look back, don't even think about it. You must make the dunes. He glances at his mirrors at lightning speed and sees only dust.

He never looks back at the dog. He rides dangerously fast, the engine rumbling with a high-pitched roar. He dips his head behind the screen, staying out of the wind and dust as much as possible. Dust and wind bombarding his eyes, all he can do is squint as much as he can and hope that nothing too sharp penetrates their delicate tissue. The tyres rip the cracked ground to pieces and thrash it about everywhere, like an angry dog tearing up a newspaper. Shrubbery and small mounds pass in quick succession; the rifle rattles against the tank. There's no way they could keep up with the bike, this was all the comfort that he allows himself. And he was right, they couldn't, but they wouldn't have to. He ramps up the first dune, twists the throttle and the back wheel finds its grip and slips and catches until he reaches the apex and rolls down the other side, him standing up on the foot pegs.

Another round snaps past but not as close – he could tell by how loud the snap was. A poorly fired round, maybe because the jeep was on rough terrain. He hits the flat ground and sees the wilderness of high mud mounds and dunes and another flat stretch. He gets low again and twists back the throttle, lifting the front wheel partially off the ground and then back down. The sand becomes a little finer the deeper he goes into the dunes and it wreaks havoc on his vision. The flat stretch becomes harder to see, sacrificing one eye at a time by closing one for a few seconds then switching, desperate for his goggles but he can't slow down. He stands up to get some more idea of where he is going and sees he is still on a plateau, the next set of dunes maybe 600 metres away. It's a very open area that he has to get out of, his eyes stinging and squinting making studying the terrain impossible, just a tornado of blurred features.

He stays standing and looks behind him over the dust cloud of his rear tyre and sees nothing, just the last dune. He winds forward the throttle slightly – maybe they had given up chase. There's no time to think about anything other than self-preservation. When the time comes to run with death in close pursuit, the mind becomes clear.

Anything that has nothing to do with the evasion of the pressure of death is dissolved and the mind becomes one with the situation like an advanced spiritual guru. Every thought about hunger, desire, love, hate, thirst is overridden by what needs to be achieved in order to keep your heart beating and your brain thinking. There is no wasted time in the mind and no thought of God; every thought is a precious form of navigation away from death. Where are the exits, look for cover, stay low, my rifle is by my side, is there anything that will slow me down. In them moments, in them truly abysmal moments where death squeezes in all around and you can feel it in the marrow of your bones and the certainty of demise dawns in the final precious seconds, the eyes bulge, the throat tightens and the breath is held, this is the place where the absence of God is realised, because in the end, to live in this world is the only thing of any value and we know it. An advanced form of autopilot; an emotionless, heartless survival machine. He would know when it is time to start thinking about comforts again and it is not now.

He turns his head forwards again and has maybe half a second to see the small, deep scar in the ground just in front of him.

He catapults over the handlebars, a doomed acrobat, the bike stopped by a wall of solid concrete. He closes his eyes, no thoughts. He does an entire flip and for a moment is airborne, then he crashes into the floor, landing on the back of his neck, the daysack taking most of the impact. He rolls over once and is airborne again but this time it's briefer before he smashes into the hard ground face down, scrubbing his cheek against the mud with his hands out trying to find anything. His arms loose, flapping everywhere. The rifle jabs into his lips then he goes into a rapid side roll with the daysack acting like a speed bump every time it hits the floor, throwing him into the air, his legs loose. There is nothing any part of his body could do, he has to let his body smash into the floor as many

Caliphate

times as it needs to before it slows down. Roll after roll, slam after slam. No pain, just his eyes opening and closing catching brief glimpses of the world as it rolls around, like the earth spinning a full rotation of day and night in a second. Ground, then the sky, then the ground again. Dust and dirt in every opening of his face, blinding and suffocating. In that moment he is out of control in every conceivable way. The abuse finally halts with the daysack acting as a wedge.

He lies still waiting for something further and tries to open his eyes but they sting like trapped wasps and he can feel the dirt caked around and inside them. Thoughts obliterated as the delicate tissue of his brain recovers from its beating off the inside of his skull. That awful uncertainty, that inability to conceive of what just happened left him still on the ground paralysed. He slowly leans over and rolls on to his front and presses himself on to his knees and spits blood and sand onto the floor and tries to focus on the blood. He opens and closes his eyes, pressing them together as if to squeeze out the dirt and he begins to focus on it. He lifts his right arm to wipe his eyes and his left arm buckles with deep drilling pain as the full weight of the top half of his torso is transferred on to it. The pain squeezed the contents of his stomach into his throat and he retched hard. He almost slams into the floor but catches himself with his right arm. He immediately identifies the problem with his left arm – his

Caliphate

elbow. The beginning of what he knew would be terrible pain started there. No time to check it out. He pushes himself up into a kneeling position, tucking his left arm into his abdomen and a pain shoots straight through his left knee and he yelps and bucks on to his back. He lies looking at the sky, the vision in his left eye becoming more and more blurred as he tries to figure out what to do next. A swell of nausea surges through him just as he remembers he was being followed. With his face white with shock he grimaces and rolls over on to his right side and pushes himself up on to his right knee then twists his foot so his boot sole is flat on the floor and pushes up, hopping. He delicately puts some weight on to his left knee and it takes some before shooting with pain again, it bowed out and he caught it before it dislocated.

He looks back east towards the dunes and sees a dust cloud on the other side of them. They're coming. What he felt was like no other despair, In the centre of that dust cloud was a force without rules and restrictions. If he was looking at police he would at least be assured that they wouldn't dismember him and prison he would welcome in his state, but they were lawless and untouchable, unbounded extreme torture was what was coming and his imagination ran wild with absolute terror at what they where going to do to him. Whatever it was that was hurting would have to wait. He pats around his numb body for the rifle and finds nothing.

Caliphate

His heart once again sinks deeper to the depths where nothing but panic and despair lurk. He looks down with his stiff neck and sees his belt kit has also come off. No pistol. If there's one thing he has to do in the next few minutes, it's find one of his weapons. If he found the rifle he would see if he could take them out. If he found the pistol, he would lie there with it under his chin until the moment came. He stands on his right leg and the tiptoes of his left foot with the leg bent, his left arm cradled across his abdomen. His final hour is nearly over. He has never been so terrified. This is it now, his mind turns over its cards to show the hopelessness of it all. There's no hiding the truth, there's no poker face to distract him from it, he could almost hear the knives' and machetes' blades ping with sharp- ness, and bluntness. Their mouths watering as they find him staggering as if blind drunk. Think of her, his mind offers, that's all I have for you. Make these moments count, every second. Don't pretend there's some other place after, you know there is nothing after this.

How does a man choose between death and slow death when he knows life is finite?

He frantically scans the ground around him. He has no idea what direction he is meant to be going in. He looks towards the dune, the dust cloud still approaching, maybe 500 metres away. He scans to the left and sees a fire. What is that? He must make his way to that, no reason,

Caliphate

just that it's something other than sand or mud. He has now completely lost the vision out of his left eye due to the swelling. He wipes his mouth with the back of his glove and he snatches his hand away as it stings as if a hot iron has been pressed into his lips. He could now feel his face on fire with pain, mainly the left side. His lips seem huge. He looks down and sees a steady trickle of blood dripping down his jacket and on to the ground; it must be coming from his face. Not important. His hearing is still muffled from the rocket strike but slowly returning. He has to figure out which parts of his body are working and which aren't and how they could be used and he has to do this immediately. He takes a deep shuddering breath and starts to limp towards the fire, looking everywhere for anything. The weapons can't be far, surely not, the nearly dead optimist whispers to him in its seemingly final breaths. He sees small bush shrubs and cracked dirt. He sees the dust cloud turning and making its way to the side of the dune where the ground is flat. He looks towards the fire and can make out the handlebars of the bike poking out of the flames.

'Oh God…' he cries.

He had reserved some hope of the bike being intact and operational and now this was erased in a flash from his mind. Now his thoughts are of the weapons.

Caliphate

He limps on, his head darting everywhere, blinking frantically, mouth cocked open, wheezing. With every step his optimism gets stronger. The rifle is close, it has to be, find it and prepare it. Your fingers still work, you can operate a trigger. He looks at the fire and traces a line from that to where he is and scans the line. That must have been the direction he rolled so there must be something. He studies the line carefully with his right eye, taking quick glances at the approaching dust cloud now close to the end of the dune. His wife – no time to think of her. He spots a mound through his teary eye that stands out from the flat surface, maybe twenty metres away. He blinks hard to release the tear and sends it running down his cheek into something that starts to sting again and sees it clearly. His belt kit. Option two. He doesn't take his eye off it as he starts moving faster. Maybe the rifle is somewhere near that. Every step is agonising but the pain is losing its edge slightly and he finds a way to walk that doesn't generate all of the pain that the injury was capable of. Arm still cradled, he hobbles and hobbles. Keep your eyes on the kit and do not look away, he thinks, and does just that. Now ten metres away, he drops to his good knee then to his belly and drags his smashed carcass to the belt kit and lays his right hand on it and pulls it towards him. The pistol is still in its holster. He grabs it and draws it out with his good hand, welcoming the cold feel of the metal, even if it only meant a quick death. You have

Caliphate

one good arm, but you have no hope at all to aim. Try and take them out. Fool, fifteen-round magazine, you'll miss the first five, the next five will hit the engine and miss, do the maths; by the time you get to round nine you'll be laced up from the face down. The battle waged inside him. You get hit in your good arm and you'll have no option. You know what to do, he concludes.

He looks at the dust cloud now coming around the dune and looks back at the pistol. He sits up into a cross-legged position and presses the magazine release catch and the magazine dropped into his lap. He pries his left arm from his abdomen and with his left hand takes hold of the top slide as tight as he could, the pain now permanently thumping through his elbow. He puts his right hand on the pistol grip and pulls it to his chest and with all his strength, coupled with an amplified dose of pain, yanks back the top slide of the pistol with a yelp. No round chambered. Tears stream out of his good eye, and he wipes it with his shoulder so he can see clearly and checks the chamber, the barrel and into the magazine housing. He blows it through, shaking any dirt from it. One shot. He has one chance at this and if the pistol doesn't work, he can forget about a quick death. He picks up the magazine with his left hand and looks at the top round to make sure it was seated correctly and wipes it with his thumb then slides it into the magazine housing. He looks at the dust cloud and sees the jeep with five men come through it around the corner, all looking straight at him. He presses the release catch and the top slide slides forward, chambering a round with a neat sounding metallic ching. He looks at the SIG P226 and checks the hammer is primed in its pulled-back position. He looks at the jeep, all men looking his way, three in the front and two in the bed; one holding on to the roll bars and the other bringing up his rifle. He looks at the pistol then draws it up under his chin. A round snaps past his head. Another kicks up some dust to his side and careens off into the air. He sits there, the cold barrel against his skin, finger on the trigger as he watches death approach. Time changes gear and slows its pace, a favour. He had factored this into his plans from the start and now here it was, his final moment. Take your time and they will take theirs. He couldn't grant them that. Don't worry, it's just like going to sleep, he consoles himself, weak effort. We all go to sleep every night without a single care and the world disappears into darkness, it must be the same, it must be. Another round snaps past, his body jerks and flinches every time, hiding his chin behind his shoulder. Please let one hit me, please, in the brain – take this responsibility from me. The distance now closing rapidly. You have to do it now, he desperately thinks, there is no time. They will saw you up. He can't see their faces through the dust but he knows they are ravenous for him, lips curled and teeth exposed, eyes of insomniacs, red and bulging with the fantasies of hell's most championed surgeons.

He sees her standing there watching him, her face stern and resolute but the first sign of tears trembling in her eyes. This is the only option and no training he had ever received could untie him from such a situation. He positions the barrel deeper under his chin with more pressure into the throat. A clear trajectory to the brain. He closes his eye. One last tear rolls down.

'I love you,' he says, grimacing.

And then an explosion from the jeep. He opens his eye.

Caliphate

4

He opens his eye just in time to see the jeep lift off the floor by about three

metres, nearly fold in half and the two men in the bed fly in different direc-

tions. A black cloud lifts it higher. He can't see the men inside as the vehi-

cle begins a flip forward in its descent and it's as if he's looking at it from a

bird's eye view. It crashes into the earth as it lands on its roof, windows

bursting and metal buckling. All this happens in an instant. A wheel falls

out of the sky and then one of the men, slamming into the ground without

a bounce. Then all is still apart from the sound of the fire of the bike behind

him and the echo of the explosion travelling across the desert. The wind

scooping up dust and black smoke from the vehicle in spirals. He is locked

Caliphate

into a gaze. It takes some time to recognise his fortune through the eyes of a man who was, a second ago, taking his last breath. He goes to look to the sky as if to see some kind of deity there turning knobs and switches in his favour, but he doesn't because he knows better than that and sees the situation for what it is, unfortunate. If this is what we call luck then we need to redefine luck, he thinks. He double and triple checks all around him – is there someone out there? Why did that happen? The childish questions begin in his mind as it wanders in its maze of speculation. He was leaning into the mist of the unknown, the cusp on the horizon of death. Eventually the hundreds of lights flickered back on individually in the warehouse of his mind until it glowed again. A cocktail of absolute terror and salvation, the rarest of all feelings.

And then his focus turns from an empty gaze, vacantly skimming the surroundings until it arrives back at the smoking wreck and becomes a stare of intent. His pupil dilates and contracts and then still, his grip tightens on the pistol as the hunter in him that he was a few days ago reanimates. For a brief moment there is no wind as if nature itself is flabbergasted at the scene.

He grabs the belt kit and swings it around his waist and, with his left hand, pulls the buckles closer to his front, carefully mitigating movements around the pain. He manages to buckle the belt kit up and picks up

Caliphate

the pistol with his right hand. The wreckage is hissing and smoking and creaking. He looks back at the bike then at the dune he needs to get to and back at the wreckage.

He was in a legacy minefield. That was an anti-tank mine; maybe deep enough not to be triggered by a man of his weight but only by something as heavy as a vehicle. There was no respite from the turmoil but he took comfort from that fact that the minefield had gave him another chance at life. Tread carefully, he thinks, that's all you can do.

There were people at that wreckage he had to deal with. He reaches around to a small pouch around the size of a harmonica and draws out a small coffin object. He opens the small coffin and inside is a morphine autoinjector. He takes it out and places the red cap end in his mouth and bites, pulling the injector away from his face and the red cap off the needle end. He feels his right thigh to make sure that there was noth-ing between the trouser and the skin and places the needle end on the side of his thigh, takes a few breaths and presses the blue plunger on the top, firing the needle deep into his thigh. He winces with the pain and draws out the needle quickly, drops it on the floor and lets the red cap drop from his mouth then climbs on to his good foot. He looks at the wreckage and begins to hobble over, his body jerking out its steps. He walks slowly and checks the ground and around the wreckage as he approaches. No

Caliphate

sign of movement, just the smell of burning oil. His leg kicks something hard in a shrub and he looks down. The dusty rifle is lying half in the small shrub. He drops to one knee and holsters the pistol, reaches down and grabs the rifle. Standing it upright, he presses the barrel into the hard dirt and uses it to push himself up. As he gets closer he can see the crushed windscreen and a man half hanging out with his face in the dirt. He looks around more closely and sees one of the men maybe twenty metres away whining, rolling on to his back and looking at him. He changes his axis and makes his way to him. His left leg is becoming more operational and his left arm more manageable with the morphine.

He can see the man is badly injured, and it becomes clear as he gets closer that his legs had compound fractures. The black loose trousers spiking out under the knee from the protrusion of the bone, no shoes on. He gets closer and the man is looking at him with the expression of a war between fear and vomit-inducing pain, his eyes darting from Tom's bloody face to the rifle.

The man is wearing an American woodland camouflage shirt with a woollen jumper underneath. His long ginger beard and his hair shaved short, maybe number two, stained with traces of blood. White in colour and skinny, he thinks perhaps Chechen and he is right when he hears the man speak. The man's scarf sprawled around his neck and his trousers dirty with oil and dust and ripped down one side with blood pooling around his snapped tibia. One of his hands cleaved down the middle all the way to his wrist and he holds it high on his chest with the other hand.

'Pozhaluysta!' the ginger man says, his face twisted with pain.

He stands and looks at him, staring through his good eye.

'Pozhaluysta pomogi mne,' the ginger man says.

'Ostanovit,' he interrupts. 'Angliyskiy.'

'Yes…' the ginger man says.

He looks at the sky for a moment and then back down at the man. 'Look at the sky,' he says, his swollen lips hindering his speech slightly.

The ginger man does so, his eyes flicking to the sky and the rifle.

'What do you see?' he says as he takes the rifle in both hands.

'Nyet, nothing… please…'

He shoulders the rifle in pain and aims the sights at the man's head, looking over the top of the sights.

'That's right,' he says.

He has not spoken to such a person before and there is nothing the man on the ground can do to convince Tom that he doesn't deserve to die right where he lies. Nothing. He watches him with an expression of determined rage, lips taut and teeth clenched, then squeezes the trigger and shoots him in the side of the forehead, two rounds in quick succession. The rifle makes a loud, dull hiss with a crack as the rounds leave the barrel, like a thick whip striking. The rounds strike his head and it jerks and blood instantly streams out of his nose and down the side of his face. His eyes roll back and his mouth opens and closes four or five times with a few twitches and then is still. Just the pooling of blood next to his head. No speeches, he always said, just as long as they die. He turns to the wreckage and starts to walk over, still limping. Rifle in both hands and blood no longer dripping from his face. He feels nothing for the man.

He approaches the passenger window and sees one of men crushed into the driver's seat by the engine, still ticking and contracting into its new shape, the stench of diesel. He kneels down to take a better look inside, holding on to the edge of the door. One of the men is upside down, sprawled on the inside of the roof and one is hanging out of the windscreen. He pulls the rifle in his shoulder and steadies his aim and fires a round into each of their heads. Unless they were mangled beyond any scope of survival, he would make sure this is where they rot. He stands up and walks around the back of the vehicle. He finds the last man on his back with his legs in the splits position; he had completely smashed his

Caliphate

pelvis but was still conscious. He has brown skin but is white from shock. His ratty beard is patchy around his lower face and his hair long and dark and caked in dust. He is wearing a black dishdasha with a brown trench coat over the top. His breathing was laboured, perhaps from tension haemothorax. He is babbling some incoherent nonsense, maybe a prayer; he doesn't much care.

He looks down at the whitening face looking back at him.

'Inshallah, huh,' he says with an air of casual greeting, slowly nodding his head.

The man stares back, his flail lung sucking and flapping in its cave and his mouth gasping. His massive internal haemorrhage in his pelvis, like a stretched bag of blood, is slowly filling up from his severed femoral arteries. His head rolls side to side in the dirt. His chest is rapidly rising and falling on the left and his arms are flat by his side; he may have a broken his spine somewhere.

'Are you ready for paradise sir?!' He says with a smile that stings every part of his face. Tom limps to the man's pelvis and squats down using the rifle for support, placing his knee on his groin, crushing what's left of his pelvis. The man tries to scream but wails a bubbling gasp, drowning in his own blood from his lung cavity filling up.

Caliphate

He kneels there, pushing his weight on to his groin and stares at his face. No pity, not a dot of remorse, razor-sharp pain until death was the only deal the man was going to get. He dealt him the same emotion he shows towards rocks.

'All that wasted time. All that nodding and kneeling, banging your head on the floor and kissing that book.' He said as he shifted weight forward, leaning right into the mans face, he wouldn't let the mans eyes escape him. Blood was dripping from his lips again because of the smile and he let it drip around the mans mouth. The man trapped in a cosmos of pain.

'Feel it, feel all of it' Drips of his blood falling into the mans open mouth as he gasped with shallow breaths, he could feel the broken pieces of the mans pelvis on his knee.

'Go now…' He scowled, the rage caught up with him once again and placed his elbow onto the mans collapsing lung in its shattered cage

'You fuckin' cocksucker get out… go on, fuck off' He pressed harder and could feel the pulses of the mans shaking lung.

'Go and suck his cock for eternity'

He kneels there and watches the man's breaths grow more and more shallow and bubbling, his skin grow more and more white. The man

Caliphate

now in his final few breaths and his eyes roll down and look at him, a brown bloody froth foaming from his mouth.

He kneels there and stares back and pushes in closer, the ends of their noses touching and watches him pass into Gods desperate retreat from knowledge. The little girl and Konrad on the helicopter, the people sprawled out at the side of the road. Everything we have to lose in the world.

He plunders the vehicle for anything salvageable and comes away with two bottles of water and a roll of black duct tape, a piece of snapped-off roll bar about a metre in length and a shard of mirror. The weapons were a different calibre so he left them and any more weapons would just weigh him down. He didn't want to move too much around the area surrounding the wreckage so he retraced his steps back the way he came.

He sits by the burning bike for a long time, the ground stained with burnt oil and bits of engine and ashes of items from the pannier. The fire is now small and mainly just burning around the rear tyre and reserve tank. The sat nav and spare antenna are nowhere to be seen. The radio is hanging out the back, snapped and twisted wires, black and melted, and the pannier is emptied around the bike. Rations, maps, clothes – everything burnt. The tyres are just blackened wire mesh hanging over the forks and swing arm and the cam net is half in the bag smoking. The exhaust is bent out with Akrapovic stamped on the stainless steel, the only thing he recognises. Most of it black.

It's lying on its side with the front forks bent in towards the engine from the impact and one end of the handlebars bent into the tank, puncturing the side and the wires from the dash and headlight were dried drips of plastic, frozen in their fall. He sits and studies it. The headlight staring back, unflinching and stoic in the fire. An old friend that kept him warm for all those nights and carried him for all those miles now in its open grave, broken and bent but just as alive as the day it was molten metal. And then the shock of the situation finally overwhelms him and he buries his head in his hands, tears rolling down his cheeks. When someone who believes in no God confronts the precursors of death, they become even more desperate to live, his brain still and numb, old thoughts of death once pondered in comfort now truly contested. No slipping away into the abyss and carried into some fairy-tale, he thinks. Just his broken body and his nearly broken mind. Be resourceful, there is always a motive to live, even if it is in one's head. But God is not it, it is the opposite and a false investment of hope. You have everything to live for, you just need to remember.

He doesn't bother looking around because he doesn't care, he just sits and weeps for everything that matters to him. The carnage all

Caliphate

around him, his state and everything he wasn't going to see again. Stripped bare and dropped here crippled, like a drop of rain in the sun, just a matter of time before he dries up and is forgotten. His pains were now being soothed by the morphine and then he just sits in a dreamland. The cold wind blows his hair with the dust rustling and sprinkling around, the shrubs rattling and then just the crackling of the fire. They will catch up with him and they will have their way with him, the thought was alone and heartless.

'That's what will happen, okay.' His internal dialogue now warning him out loud. 'If that's what you want then sit here waiting to join the rest of them by the wreckage.' His voice was hoarse and speaking felt like swallowing sandpaper.

His lip throbs with every flex of movement no matter how minor – a sharp precise pain that accurately mapped every aspect of the damage. The heat from the flames licks his face and he closes his eyes. Think about what they will do to you, the cancer of the earth is coming and you're going to sit here and wait for it. He thinks about his wife and how much he wants her to take him away. He thinks about another rider stumbling upon him, drawn by the explosions. Part of him keeps a lid on this because this was irrational. There was a plan, he just couldn't confront it yet. He had to come to terms with the fact that there was nothing coming

Caliphate

to get him and this is what was ultimately feeding the despair. His eyes are stinging from the dirt and tears and the blast. He is alone and on foot with enough food for perhaps four days at a push, enough water for maybe two. His maps were gone and he only had the last and first one he needed in his pockets. Lay everything out in the mind and start from the beginning. You can't walk two hundred kilometres like this, he thought as his hair gently waved past his eyes but they stayed firmly on the bike; he wasn't ready to look away from it. You have done it before, not like this, but you have done it, it's possible. His eye glistened like dew beads in the morning sun. You don't have enough water or food to make it; the thoughts an endless list of problems he just didn't have the answers for.

He leans over and pulls map six out of his pocket and unfolds it to find his location. He couldn't have come far since the trench, maybe a few kilometres. He looks at his position and traces the map south with his shaking finger and one eye. There's a road running west maybe ten kilometres away – that was into Witchcraft One Echo's runway. Taking his chances in the deep desert without maps or features was dangerous. He could push to the road and handrail it, keeping his distance and follow it to Ar Rutba. At least by the road there is a chance of finding water or food. He takes a bearing in a south-west direction and knows that he would

Caliphate

eventually come into contact with the road so he wouldn't be wandering around forever.

He has a look at the damage to his face using the shard of mirror – the pain burnt, the kind of pain that is manageable as long as he didn't look at it. The left side he doesn't recognise from the blood and scratches, like rare steak marinated in dirt. A four-inch laceration running down his forehead towards the left eyebrow represents all of the pain on his face. His eye is sealed shut from the swelling and both of his lips are spilt on the right side – it felt like a thousand wasp stings throbbing with every beat of his heart. He slowly opens his mouth, clenching his teeth, and sees his lateral incisor and canine on the right had been chipped in half forming a V shaped gap. He tosses the mirror and looks at the bike as he folds the map and puts it away. He takes out his laminated map of the extraction point and opens it out and folds it lengthways. He lifts his left trouser leg above the knee and straightens it out. No pain yet. He takes the duct tape and finds the edge with his thumbnail and rips off a strip and sticks it to his other leg. He takes the map and wraps it around his knee twice, pulling it tight, then sticks the ripped piece of tape over the edge to keep it from unfolding. He begins to wrap duct tape around tight, making sure it overlaps on to the skin. He places the tape and the water from the jeep in his daysack, zips it up and shoulders it onto his back then gently

Caliphate

stands up, swinging his left leg out, using the length of roll bar as a crutch, pushing himself to his feet. He puts a fresh magazine on his rifle and places the part-used one in the magazine pouch he was likely to use last then slings the rifle over his head. He has to make a move from here while the morphine lets him. He looks around the area from where he is standing. The five men dead, his bike smouldering and the mine struck wreckage. It doesn't have to be like this he muses, looking though his hair, but these people insist this is the answer before they even know what the question is. He stabs the bar into the ground and puts the end under his armpit and places the left side of his bodyweight on it while hopping his right leg forward, carefully looking for anything abnormal on the ground, and slowly makes his way to the next dunes.

It takes a few hundred metres to get to grips with his new method of walking but it begins to become manageable. He thinks maybe his leg isn't broken, rather he just badly hit it. There was no crunching or unusual shape to it, but he was wary of the morphine. He makes the dunes and looked towards the south. Mud mounds and flats for miles which could afford him some cover should he see any trouble. He looks back east and sees no movement, just the graveyard of vehicles and bodies. He descends the dune awkwardly and reaches the bottom. A chapter done, he cannot see over the dune and he uses it to subtract

Caliphate

himself from the last situation and keep it out of his mind. The next major mound is maybe 200 metres away and he makes a point of breaking the journey down to 200-metre legs as a way of alleviating the seemingly impossible task of getting to the extraction point. He hobbles quite quickly and makes the mound where he sits down for a moment catching his breath and looks to where he is going next. His laceration is bleeding again and a trickle of blood constantly drips off his swollen eye and chin; he looks down and can see the crimson drips splash into the dirt. Another set of small mounds is maybe 150 metres away. He catches his breath and stands back up and pushes on in the wind and dust. The dry cracked mud makes it easier for the bar to dig in and the shrubbery gives him something to look at. As he approaches bushes, he looks for insects or lizards; he is desperate for some company. He passes the shrubs and looks to the next one, looking for tiny eyes and little legs, all the while keeping the next mud mounds in his mind. Think of nothing else, salvation lies at the next mounds.

He repeats this for about two kilometres and it takes him maybe four hours. He has to stop and rest for a while. He drops the pipe and looks to the sky. The clouds look greyer and he thinks that would make the night less cold, a small gift, and he even considers walking into the night and through to the next day but suddenly becomes staggeringly tired. He shouldn't have sat down. He is losing control of his eyelids as they desperately try to seal themselves. He can't get up, the urge to sleep just sweeps over him with such power, and before he knows what is happening he has unslung the rifle and laid it by his side and taken off his pack. He looks around with his good eye and lies down and eases his head on to his pack without even checking his watch. The day has sapped the life completely out of him, all the shock of what had happened now gently relaxed and his body needs to shut down to manage what is wrong with him. He responds without the slightest fight, the silence of the deep desert surrounding him, waiting for his next move.

Caliphate

5

He was in the white room, standing. Everything was white and he couldn't

make out the corners and it made the room appear endless. The only way

he could tell that he was in a room was that there were two paintings on

the wall in front of him. There was no light in the room; it seemed as if the

brightness of the white walls themselves were enough to illuminate every-

thing. As far as his memory was concerned, he had never been here be-

fore and he recognised nothing, but a mysterious part of him was expect-

ing to be somewhere like this all the time, the thought flicked on and off for

a moment and then vanished. He felt completely normal and completely

unsurprised about where he was but there was nothing to hear, everything was silent, apart from the tinnitus, a very slight monotone squealing drilling in his eardrum. He could look around but he couldn't turn around and there was nothing to the left and right of him but white walls. He was aware something was behind him but he was not concerned by it. Suddenly he heard two metal objects hit the floor behind him with a sound of metal on concrete. He turned his head slowly to try and see but his head could not twist any further. He began to slowly turn around without any intention from himself, he was on autopilot. As he slowly came round, he saw one of the hammers lying on the floor and he began to feel the onset of fear, he didn't know why he had suddenly become scared, he wasn't being irrational, the hammer surfaced something in his consciousness that he couldn't see but knew was there. He was split between his immediate observations being understood in the present moment and his long-term memory. His long-term memory was separated from him but nevertheless could stir emotion. If he was thinking of his wife in long-term memory he would feel happiness, but he wouldn't know what was causing that happiness and he wouldn't know he was thinking of his wife. Emotions were simply happening with their cause unknown to him.

He slowly began to see the side of the room that was initially blind to him and saw an open door, two paintings with their painted sides facing the wall and the hammers on the floor. The door opening was black

Caliphate

and he could see nothing on the other side of it, and this began to scare him more. He now began to panic and his teeth started to grind to the point where it felt as if he was going to dislocate his jaw if he clenched any harder. His tinnitus began to grow louder. He squeezed harder and harder and his teeth felt like they were going to crumble and split. He couldn't stop, he had no control over it. Then he could hear the scratching behind him of the paintings beginning to turn around. He didn't know why or how but somehow he knew that if he turned around and looked, something would happen, something that he would never recover from. He just stared at the door with his teeth clenched, so tight now he could feel crumbs of enamel on his tongue. He was growing more and more frightened and was beginning to wish for death. Then the paintings next to the doors began scratching against the wall as they slowly began to turn. He began screaming through clenched teeth but he still did not know what was going on. His blood was laced with the most toxic of all fears and this meant something, the day he wasn't scared, he was dead or insane. The painting slowly scratched against the wall with a sharp metal on chalkboard screech. He tried to close his eyes but he couldn't, he just stared at the door, hissing and screaming through his teeth, unable to move. Then out of the blackness, she slowly stepped through the door with her arms stretched out towards him.

Caliphate

His teeth crumbled to dust, his ears felt like shards of glass where being pushed into his eardrums from the tinnitus. The paintings turned. He begged the universe with every drop of his blood to turn the paintings the other way, but it wasn't listening. They slammed against the wall showing him.

The scream.

He opens his eyes and it's dawn. The sunlight is grey as it filters through the dark clouds. The cold wind cries and moans in the silence, gusting over the mud mounds, lifting the loose dust and relocating it like nature was at his funeral mourning his departure, tossing dirt into the grave. The shrubs rustle in their rooted positions, all dancing and rattling in the same direction. Everything cold. He is curled up at the bottom of the mound with the pistol in his hand. He is shaking with cold and fear and places the pistol back in his holster and looks around. He has no idea where he is and it petrifies him. He has no idea how he got here and where his bike is and just sits there with his arms crossed, holding in what warmth he could and looking around, searching. He lets his mind pick up the pieces. His nose is running and his face hurts, but he can partially see out of his left eye now. His left arm feels better, but he doesn't know why it doesn't feel normal and likewise for his leg, although that is still barbed with a drilling

Caliphate

pain. His hands under his armpits, he sits there slumped and shaking, his memory beginning to resonate yesterday's events but this time without the cloud of shock.   Everything seems worse than he initially anticipated. The bike gone, the distance he had to walk, the food and water situation and the people he killed and their faces. When the shock wears off every-thing is seen for what it is and initial prophecies in retrospect seem child-ish. He sits there in the cold morning breeze and goes through the entire feeling of hopelessness all over again. He considers ideas from yesterday and their plausibility and thinks how ridiculous they are. He was going to starve to death and that was that; he couldn't possibly walk 200 kilome-tres. He remembers the road to the south and thinks that is also ridiculous as they would almost certainly see him from there. He sits their, his blurred gaze behind his half open eyelids locked on deep crack in the mud. Sud-denly he becomes aware of how hungry and thirsty he is, his stomach feeling like a deflated balloon desperate for air; the sort of emptiness that a dreadful weakness is sure to follow. This inspires him to think about his pack and rifle, and he panics and spins around, looks up the hill and sees the daysack and the rifle, and the dog sleeping next to them. He lights up with excitement and immediately forgets about the hunger.

'What are you doing here?' he says in a high-pitched voice, the hint of a smile beginning to partially tear his healed lips and face.

Caliphate

The dog's head lifts up and her tail started starts sweeping the floor. She gets up and stretches her hind legs as she leans forward and gingerly trots down the hill to him.

'Come here and see me, come here,' he says, with his eyes welling up.

The dog trots over, nodding and smiling. He grabs her head, rubbing her ears, and presses the good side of his face into her neck, feeling her warmth and kissing her gently with his split lips. He lifts his head and looks at the small body being thrown off balance by her tail. She licks his face, the battered side, and he lets her. She licks it for some time, her rough tongue dragged upwards in long slow laps, like spreading jam on burnt toast with sandpaper. He squeezed his cold hands into fists and held his breath with the pain, but it has to be cleaned or he was going to get infected, ditch medicine. He left her back there and now here she was cleaning his wounds, looking after him. No forgiveness because she felt no malice. She didn't understand why he went but he wasn't going to ridicule her for this because to the dog it didn't matter, she just wanted someone to be with and if that meant chasing him across the desert, then that's what she had to do. A love unparalleled, two completely different species holding on to each other in the cold desert.

Caliphate

It was time to pry his body off the floor and he tries without the bar and manages to climb to his feet, the dog jumping around. He limps gently to gain a feel of the knee situation and finds it manageable but still painful – he would take the bar with him anyway. He gently makes his way up the mound and eases himself down next to his daysack, still shaking, and opens it up. He must have slid down the hill through the night. He feels around inside and finds his NVG's are broken in half. He pulls them out and studies them, lens smashed falling out in small thick shards. He turn them on but nothing, he puts them back in. He takes out a waterproof bag and opens it up and looks at the contents. A pouch of meatballs and pasta, lemon sponge pudding, chicken and herb dumplings, two cheese sachets and two packs of crackers, three grain bars, and four sachets of instant white tea. He pulled out the meatballs and pasta and put away the rest and ripped off the top and looked into the pouch. The tomato sauce looks vulgar cold and he isn't sure whether the meatballs are actually meat. He takes his spoon and stirs the bag, scoops out a single meatball and takes it off the spoon between his front teeth, careful not to split the healing process of his lip. He puts the spoon back in the bag and takes the meatball from his teeth and hands it to the dog in front of him sitting like she was about to be inspected by someone important before a job inter-view. She takes it from his fingers gently and lies down. He scoops out one meatball for himself and some fusilli and carefully spoons them into his mouth. He has to chew with his eyes closed because the taste and coldness required a degree of concentration to stop him retching. It's a peculiar sensation with his new broken teeth. He licks the spoon clean and places it away in his pocket and folds the bag with the rest of the meat-balls and pasta and puts it back in the daysack in its waterproof bag. He would have to be sparing, or was he just prolonging the inevitable. He takes out a bottle of water and takes a sip and rinses out his mouth and swallows, the ghastly cold water sent twitches of cold through him. He puts the bottle away and then sits there thinking for a while, stroking the dog, looking out into the deep, dead land.

'We're going to the road' He took a long breath and let it go in one long sigh   'Maybe try and find a car to steal – are you okay with that?' he says to the dog.

She just looks back, blinking in the wind, licking her nose. A gust carrying sand makes her close her eyes for a second and then she opens them again.

'Let's go then…you little criminal,' he says as he stands slowly up, endlessly shaking from the cold.

He puts on the daysack and slings the rifle. He takes another long look at the land but now with a plan in his eyes and not just a lost

Caliphate

gaze, looking for features on the route his bearing was pointed in. He makes his way down the mound with gentle steps and picks up the bar.

The dog walks alongside him, sometimes running off to shrubs and sniffing them. She gallops around ahead of him chasing mysterious smells only she could find. What could she be possibly smelling in the desert, he thinks. The clouds pass by above, growing more grey by the hour, and the wind comes in cold bursts from the west sometimes knocking him off balance. He waddles with the bar across the flat plains, looking around the lands deserted by everything, so empty and so pointless. Gods imagination stopped here. He has a lot of time to think on the walk. Thinking helps take his mind off the pain and the situation. He wonders for a while how the battery died on the bike so quickly, he put a fresh one on the night of the resupply. Maybe the cold that night killed it. Not a chance, not in one night. Then all the rationale hit at once with the sinking of his gut, he put the almost dead battery back on the radio after he took it off and when Glenn distracted him, he handed him the fully charged one. He just walks in frustration, what's to be done about it? Nothing. He has the radio in the bag, but that only has a distance of maybe two kilometres' transmission distance. He walks between mud mounds and dunes, and looks at the map occasionally to check features against what he could see and look for the easiest routes. He slowly begins to stop doing this as he loses tactical

Caliphate

interest as time goes on as the war between the dryness of his mouth and the temptation to drink all his water raged harder and harder.

Something catches his eye on the side of a mound and he stops. It is shapeless and dark, at some distance, and he can make out no details apart from the fact that it looks like nothing he had passed since he started walking – it looks as if it's moving; not like a bush but methodical movements. The cold wind starts to give him a chill as he stands there staring at it. His hair lifts and rests in the wind and the left side of his face feels like a mask of fire. He takes out the rangefinder and presses them gently to his eyes and steadies them on the movement.

It was the dismembered man from the trench, crawling down the hill with his single arm, grabbing the dirt with his remaining fingertips and pulling his torso down the hill inches at a time. A flush of inertia locks him all over. He takes the rangefinder away and has to check himself, looking around confused, and then he put the rangefinder back to his eyes and steadies them again and realises his eyes aren't deceiving him. The man's mouth wide open as if wailing and eyes looking towards Tom in the distance. His body suddenly feels as if it had just been thrown into a iced over lake, the shock, he squints his eyes shut and opens them again and looks at the figure still crawling. Maybe a kilometre away. He watches him progress maybe a metre in a minute and takes the rangefinder away from

Caliphate

his eyes and the man is right in front of him screaming a blood-curdling scream looking straight at him and reaching with his remaining arm. He jumps and falls to the floor with some cry of horror that he didn't know he allowed to be released, but quickly recovers on to his side and looks again, drawing the pistol in one movement locking it out. The man is gone. He lies there with his heart thumping like a beating drum his arm trembling with the weight of the pistol. His mind questions whether he is awake or dreaming but quickly establishes he is certainly awake and sober. The dog is a hundred metres away looking back at him. If that was real, the dog would have surely investigated it, or at least looked in that direction. Maybe the dog didn't see it. But it saw the vehicles coming down the road from quite a distance back at the trench. He is peppered with anxiety, the fear is blinding, he knows he was hallucinating but that means nothing because it was just too terrifying. The emptiness and loneliness of the desert was teaming with his dehydration and he was now no longer safe in his own mind. Keep the dog close, he thinks, keep her close.

He lowers the pistol and climbs to his feet and picks up the bar. He is scared to look behind him and it involves an element of courage to do so. Nothing there apart from flat cracked desert and mud mounds with trembling shrubs. Something has just happened and there's no one to consult as to whether what he saw was genuine or not. He needed some

Caliphate

sort of verification. He heard a scream and saw something in front of him, he saw this with his eyes as they see now and he had to realise that what he saw was not there but in his mind. If you cannot trust your senses, your mind, then what are you left with? He gets himself together and beats off the chill in a long breath, looks at the dog and starts walking again, keeping one hand on the rifle.

He walked all morning and into the afternoon and didn't stop apart from when he saw the dismembered man and once to drink some water – and to not drink the whole bottle required a feat of discipline he didn't actually possess, the thirst had dried all the way through to his soul, it was all he could think about. He snatched the bottle away from his mouth after one mouthful and put it away, out of his sight. The water felt as though it was stripping wall paper, sticky with paste from the inside of his mouth, swallowing what felt like lumps down to his crumpled stomach. He was dangerously dehydrated and was still terrified of what he saw and wanted to be near some kind of civilisation, no matter how threatening, just see a road light, anything. He had made just over four kilometres by four o'clock and was now seeing pieces of rubbish blown into the desert from the road, a crisp wrapper and an old can, its colours and identifications long faded in the blistering desert sun.

Caliphate

He stops to pick up the can and holds it for a while he walks. He finds comfort in it, something about the can summoning a feeling of human contact. Someone had made this can and someone had drank from it, no matter how long ago – they were born into this world like himself and the can was here to tell him that. He needed to know that there were people out there that he could talk to, drink with, eat with, who would help him. The dismembered man had aroused a shadow of terror in his mind that was ever present but now sharp and it made looking around the desert a terrifying task. He wanted to keep the dog close for comfort but she had her own little agenda of sniffing and scouting, although she always came back to him.

It starts to get dark and even colder. As the darkness grows so does the terror and he feels even more vulnerable. So scared of the dark yet we close our eyes at horror. He thinks that he should stop for the night where he is. He can't see any features that would afford any comfort from the wind. He sits down and calls the dog and she comes over. Exhaustion has set in and he knows the night is going to be cold. He takes off the daysack and gets out his scarf, hat, survival blanket, poncho and the meatballs and pasta, and zips up the pack. The dog is lying in front of him, sniffing his knee. He wraps his head in the scarf until it is completely covered, apart from his eyes, and puts his hat on over that. He takes out his

Caliphate

spoon and gives a meatball to the dog, which she swallowed almost instantaneously, and he has one spoonful for himself. He struggles to not eat the whole bag – he has to remember he is hungry but not starving. He puts the bag away and unfolds the thin foil survival blanket, laying it down next to him on the poncho and placing the rifle on to it to stop it blowing away. The dog walks straight on to it and starts sniffing around, walking in circles. He watches her as she settles down on the corner. Her muzzle is tucked away behind her rear leg and she looks at him through one eye. He puts the daysack at one end of the blanket and the rifle on the edge then slides on to the side the dog is on and adjusts the pack to use as a pillow. He lies down, pulling the poncho and blanket over him and the dog and tucks it under his knees, resting his head on the pack. He lies there with his eyes open, looking across the fading desert. The wind blows against the poncho creating a light rustle, sometimes catching in the open edges making a bubble underneath and then settling with the poncho and blanket returning softly down. He sees nothing in the distance and there is nothing that he could think of that would pacify the anticipation of some spontaneous horror. He checks the pistol is still on his hip. His body is painful but nothing that he couldn't sleep through. The grey sky is now black and the last of the light is making an escape from the night. He closes his eyes and waits for sleep to come. In the middle of the desert flatlands lies a man and a dog taking shelter under a poncho on the cold ground, hungry and broken. Somewhere someone is climbing into their warm bed with their wife and they let the warm duvet sink all over them, the hum of the radiators and the scatter of rain against the bedroom window. The cold ground sucked away warmth and he wakes often, shivering in the darkness and changes his position and drifts off again. The wind bursts in through the gaps in the poncho and circulates around him, and even though he does his best to hold it tight to him, the wind always finds its way in.

He wakes just before midnight, and can hear the first flecks of rain patting on the poncho. He lies there for a while to ascertain whether this was the case or not; he hopes maybe it is the rapping of the poncho in the wind, but he knows it isn't. He closes his eyes once more as if there's a chance he would wake up at home in their next opening.

'Please,' he murmured, his lips barely opening as he said it.

He begins to feel the first few light drops hit his face and he can smell the storm in the air, the humid desert smell like wet dirt, and then hears distant crackles from the thunder, rippling gently and quietly across the desert. He can feel by the way that the wind is hitting the poncho and where the thunder was coming from that the storm is heading his way. He

Caliphate

has to get up and find some sort of shelter off the floor or he would get wet and that would be a game changer. His injuries he could manage and he had the means to curb his hunger for a few more days, but if he got wet, he would probably freeze to death in the night. He feels around with his foot and finds the location of the dog by his feet; she stayed. He takes some deep breaths and tries to get a handle on his shaking and sits up. It is pitch black and he takes out his small torch, puts in his mouth clicking it on and looks around. The beam struggles to penetrate the darkness but he can see the raindrops shoot past the cone of the beam. He looks at the floor and sees the impact craters of the raindrops in the dry mud and then looks to the end of the poncho and sees the dog sleeping curled up. Against the shaking and pain he has to get on his knees and pack away the survival blanket. He gathers some of it up in his hand and looks at the dog and tugs at it gently. She won't move so he pulls a bit harder and she pokes her head up slowly. He pulls it a little more and slides it from under-neath her.

'Sorry,' he says.

He rolls it up and puts it between his legs, grabs and opens the pack and stuffs it inside. He puts the daysack on slowly; every movement created an opening for the wind to breach his clothing and steal his warmth. He picks up the rifle and can feel the cold steel through his glove as he slings it. He kneels, holding the corner of the poncho as it blows in the wind, the dog standing up and smelling the wind and rain. He looks at the floor and clicks off the torch with his teeth and lets it drop, the pattering of the gentle rain on his poncho and his gloves. You have to get up, he imagines her saying. He closes his eyes once more to double-check reality. He gets on to his good leg and pushes himself up, wincing at the aching pain. His body had seized up, the cold turning his movements rusty, and he can feel his joints squeaking and crunching. He gathers the poncho up, pulling it around his neck and over his back and tying it to the straps of his daysack, creating a cape. The wind catches it and flicks it around. He takes out his compass with shaking hands and clicks the torch on and finds his bearing. If there is going to be anything that could help him, it would be near the road. He puts them away and scoops up the bar and checks the pistol is there. He takes a few steps and finds that if it weren't for the cold, his knee would feel a lot better. He bends over and waves his hand around slowly below his waist and he finds the dog next to him, not shaking.

'Let's get going,' he says to her.

The rain isn't heavy and he can't feel it too much on his face but he can hear it crackling, scrunching like screwed-up foil, on the poncho. Every so often there is a distant crash of thunder, slow and rumbling across what felt like the universe and then the fade into silence and quietly returning to the patter of rain. He would lie in bed back home and listen to rain outside on stormy nights, the warm feeling of secure shelter. Out here, it is not something to be reckoned with; rain is as sinister and merciless as the men in the jeep. He can see maybe a metre in front of him, he thinks it's pointless having his eyes open in this darkness and in this terrain as there's nothing to see. But he has to make a special effort to keep them open otherwise he is in danger of falling asleep. When you have nothing but black to look at, there is no point having your eyes open, you need something to look at to keep vision alive, even if it is just a dot, anything but black. But at least black is a colour.

He cranks out the steps, not moving fast enough to be warm but fast enough to stop himself shaking. He checks his bearing every twenty paces, his hobbling was creating a bias in his steps and he was veering off to the left every step and coming off his bearing. There is nothing to look at apart from the distant flash of lightning, too far away to light up anything in his way apart front the matt black sky. The rain continues its drizzle and the wind comes in from the flank, throwing him off balance, making him pause in his stride, tip over to the side slightly and continue. The dog is off somewhere navigating with its nose.

Caliphate

He walks for a long time and checks his watch and sees it is two in the morning. He hadn't been monitoring his progress of distance purely because he was too cold. He would know when he was near the road. He begins to feel the wet in his hat and pulls the poncho over his head. He has to stay as dry as possible, but he knows it's only a matter of time. His knee gives way and he slams into the ground chest first. He didn't try breaking the fall because he had fallen asleep. He rolls on to his side and climbs back up and the pain shoots through his arm and leg once again. The fall startles him and his mind begins to work overtime once again to stay awake. When there is nothing to focus on but darkness, he doesn't know whether his eyes are open or not. He keeps bending over and conducting slow swipes around in the dark with his arms, looking for the dog. Sometimes she is there, sometimes she isn't and he has to call her, he just needs to know he isn't alone.

He's perhaps walked two kilometres in four hours and the rain has started to pick up slightly and the occasional lightning flash shows him what he already knows, the endless mud desert and the black sky. He dreads the flashes; they light up his ignorance of the darkness. Sometimes he sees the dog in the flash, caught in a single frame of whatever she is doing and then gone. Sometimes he sees unexpected shapes, like

Caliphate

figures watching him, adding to his fear. When the flash is over he takes comfort in the darkness and continues walking.

One flash breaches the darkness with a huge white strobe and he sees a dark figure of something in his path and it locks him rigid like an iron suit. Two naked men sewn together back to back with heads twisted around and attached mouth to mouth, clumsily navigating along the desert. The limbs jerking and juddering awkwardly, both heads' eyes white with horror looking to him. Their intestines dragging in the dirt behind them like swelled, tangled blood-worms. He stops and closes his eyes immediately and holds his breath. Don't move, he thinks, don't breathe and wait for the darkness, wait for the darkness, wait for the darkness.

'It's a human spider.' The words of that rider. He clenches his whole body to move the words on and holds his hands close to his chest, searching for something to save him from the thought. The dog with her warm body presses against his leg.

The storm is now close and the lightning becoming more frequent. He hears a slow rumble coming from across the desert and stops, cocking his head in the darkness. Something is coming towards him fast, a giant wall of something spanning the desert. Then it hits him.

Caliphate

He thinks the sky has just dropped everything all at once around him. There is no more patter but a continuous hum of rain belting everything. He pulls the poncho around him and over his head, holding it tight. The flashes of lightning illuminate everything now and it shows him what he could hear, the wall of water haemorrhaging out of the sky and then blackness, the long trundle of thunder sweeping the desert in cracks of ascending pitch like giant boulders being dragged against the earth. The ground no longer sounds like dirt but like a giant shallow puddle as the water sits on top of the baked mud and he can hear the slaps of his feet against it. Long gusts of wind sweep sideways against him continuously carrying a pelting of raindrops against his face. All he can do is turn his face away. He holds out the compass and turns on the torch – he's heading in the right direction – his hand becomes instantly wet and a strong wind catches the poncho and sends it flapping above his head. It is tied to his daysack straps and he gathers it in, squinting eyes against the bombardment. Every second he takes to wrap it around him he gets more wet.

He continues, picking out features on his axis in the lightning and walking in their direction. His feet become wet and he can feel the rubbing and moisture between his toes. A crash of lightning so loud and close makes him fall over into the flooding ground and he once again lets

Caliphate

go of the poncho into the wind and the rain pelts his exposed self with all its force with the ground water running down his sleeve, extinguishing important heat instantly.

'No more!' He shouts into the abyss, the words came without permission or warning, the internal cry of despair.

He climbs back to his feet using the bar, gathers the poncho and carries on. With every crash of lightning, the rain comes in harder and, before long, he is soaked through and shivering.

A flash of lightning shows him the dog maybe a hundred metres away, drinking from a newly formed puddle. The flash is long enough for him to see a small mud hut not too far away and he immediately changes his axis towards that. He thinks it was almost certainly unoccupied but he had to find shelter before he was too exhausted. Every flash brings the hut closer and he can see no vehicles and no signs of occupation. The dog starts running towards it. He becomes colder and colder and rain is finding places he couldn't protect and soaking him. He can feel his thighs becoming sticky with the rain and then his underwear. As he approaches the hut he can see its shape and size. A square building that looks as if it had been pulled out of the mud and moulded like pottery. It was not more than five metres squared. He is looking at it from behind and there appears to be no entrance. As he gets closer, a flash shows him it is made of mud

Caliphate

bricks and has wooden studs protruding from just below the roof. A roof was all he needed. The rain like a blanket saturating everything. He calls the dog and can hear her trotting in the soaking ground as he approaches the building, flicking off the safety catch on the rifle with his thumb. The flashes bring the building closer with each step, until he is at the back wall. He touches the rough mud wall to feel for any heat that may be coming from inside and walks slowly around the corner, and there is a small break from the wind and rain. Using the flashes to guide him and then stopping in the dark, he props the bar against the wall and puts both hands on the weapon. He pokes his head around the corner and waits for a flash. A double strobe of lightning shows him there is a front door and a black plastic bag hanging out of a hole in the wall and a rag on the floor by the door. He creeps to the door and stands to the side of it.

'Salam,' he shouts over the rain.

No response. The rain crashing everywhere, running off his nose and down his lips. A flash shows him the door and he can see no further inside than the doorframe. He waits for the next flash.

'Hello!' He shouts again in the howl of the wind and rain, the rifle pointing at the door.

He sees the dog out of the corner of his eye walk through the door and he goes to say not to but she's already inside. He puts the torch in his mouth and clicks it on, spotlighting the poorly formed doorway and slings the rifle and takes out the pistol, holding it at waist level, entering slowly, shaking now more than before. As he enters, the sound of the rain turns into a loud humming noise on the roof and pouring in the doorway. The room smells strongly of manure, he looks around from the doorway and sees a pile of dirty wool, maybe a metre high, in the middle of the room and the dog next to it sniffing. To the rear is a square kiln with a large metal pot on top, empty, with a metal tube chimney leading to the ceiling from the top of the kiln. There is a small burnt log outside it. He sees nothing else in the room and he doesn't bother to look any more closely as he is beginning to shake badly. He takes off the poncho and drops it to the ground and holsters the pistol. He is drenched and freezing and has to get a fire going. He goes over to the kiln shivering and kneels down in some droppings that littered the whole floor in small piles like green marbles and looks inside the soot-stained opening and sees some remains of tinder inside. He turns around and grabs a handful of the wool and pushes it inside the fire box and unzips his jacket partially.

He takes off his gloves, shaking, and puts them on the floor and opens his jacket and takes out the cigarettes and lighter in the waterproof packet. He struggles to undo the opening of the bag with his rattling, wet hands and eventually takes out the cigarettes and takes one out of the

Caliphate

packet. He pointlessly wipes his mouth with the back of his hand and

places the cigarette between his lips. He takes the lighter and strikes it,

sucking in the hot fumes as he kneels there in the darkness with the cig-

arette's ember glowing. Not a single tactical thought goes through his

head, he is a man on the edge of freezing to death. Behaviour changes

when you are wet and freezing, no matter how trained you are. He strikes

the lighter again and the small flame comes to life and he gently leans into

the fire box and lights the wool and it bursts to life instantly, smouldering

and transforming like a time lapse of the life of a rose-bud. He watches,

holding the cigarette, and grabs another handful of wool and stuffs it in

and then sits there gently blowing inside until the tinder begins to burn. He

takes the remains of the charred log and gently pushes it in and then an-

other handful of wool. It catches light nicely and it starts to light up part of

the room in an flickering orange glow. He turns around and sees the dog

nestled in the wool. He climbs to his feet and puts the cigarettes and

lighter back in his jacket. He takes off his soaked hat and places it on top

of the kiln and then shuffles up to it and sits with his back against it until he

can feel the warmth coming through the baked mud and smokes his cig-

arette, shivering. It takes a while before he can feel any heat and he just

sits and watches the room through the dull orange flames, everything

flickering and quivering. His legs pulled into his chest, listening to the

Caliphate

storm. After a while he goes to the wool and grabs armloads of it and puts it next to the kiln away from the fire box until he has a pile big enough to lie on. He sits on it with his side to the kiln and slides down on to the dirty wool and looks at the door, into the blackness. He slowly stops shaking and his hat on top of the kiln begins to steam a little. The misshaped door and outside the rain crashing down everywhere; he had not been under a roof for months and he felt a little claustrophobic because he couldn't see the sky. No one would be out there in this weather looking for him, but he knows that he has to keep moving and when it gets light he would have to leave this behind.

He wakes a few times, shaking after the fire had gone out and he can feel the fleas under his clothes from the wool. They were running between his hairs and stopping and then running again, like tiny fingernails gently dragging along his skin. He just lies there and lets them until he drifts off again, every now and again they would bite but he is too cold and too exhausted to care. The dog comes over and lies next to him. A huge crash of lightning breaks through the sky like an earthquake and he panics in his exhausted state and opens his eyes, his heart thumping. The lightning lights up the door for maybe a second and he sees rows of people in the distance and in the second flash, they're gone. The projections of his mind

Caliphate

in the desert like a cinema, the door of the room open and the paintings now showing themselves in his waking moments. They were coming through the door and over his senses and his logic and rationale, spilling out everywhere. There was just him and the dog and when you are alone in times like these, he has to treat everything as real.

'Well what else do you suppose we do then? What the fuck do we do, do we just sit around and wait for it all to fall to bits, wait to see how far it can really go? We've done that and now look!' he shouted as he fastened up his pack, he was starting to sweat.

'Do you think I want to go? Do you think I have the mind of a psychopath that craves violence, a mind that wants nothing but to kill? I am a man with a heart, with love'

'But why do *you* have to go, why did *you* volunteer? Are you insane!' she shouted back. She sat on the sofa curled up under a blanket, the wind and rain howled outside, crashing against the window.

'We've done this to death, how many times do we have to do this, how many fucking times' He said under his breath 'I'll tell you what, we'll recruit a load of guys that have no idea what they're doin' and send them'

Caliphate

'Thats not what I'm saying'

'Well you're either saying don't go or send someone else. I know your scared, I'm scared, but in the end, before the wheels completely come off this planet, some of us have to stand up, we just fucking have to! Not for me or for you or for credit or fame or glory, but for humanity. Every war is different but this is not a war, this is the apocalypse. This is thousand year old religious ideas with twenty first century technology, nukes, nerve agent everything at their disposal' He was flicking through the pages of his passport, stamps and visas on most pages, he shook his head 'Everyone, every single family of whoever got the call is thinking the exact same thing, why him, why my dad or boyfriend or whatever'

The dim yellow glow of the streetlight flutters outside the house. He stood up and threw the pack against the wall next to his holdall and boots and went over to her and knelt down on both knees and clasped her small warm feet in his hands. Her tears' paths of descent glistened in the light from the TV on the sides of her face.

'How did this all happen, just…how' She said quietly

He calmed himself 'You want Washington again, Ebola bombers in Europe again then I'll stay, I'll speak to Hereford and withdraw my joining instructions, but remember; If you think we can just talk them into thinking straight then you might as well offer yourself to them' He

Caliphate

paused 'The coalition is absorbed with Syria and Jordan and they almost certainly won't hold, they wont because death looks like you and me, it doesn't wear a uniform. Do you know hard it is to fight like that? To fight a man that looks like he's walking his kids to school carrying bags with milk and bread, smiling at us, but has plastic explosives and nails taped to his and his kids chests with a detonator in his sleeve' He lifted his hands and rubbed his eyes and took a long breath 'Do you understand? Do you understand that now they have surface to air missiles drones cant reach them…'

She shook her head, 'Of course I do, Tom,' she snapped and cut him off. She didn't.

She pulled her feet from his hands and back under the blanket and looked at the fireplace. He looked at her eyes tremble with tears in the light of the fire and he sank down into a cross-legged position.

They sat in silence. She was watching the fire and he watched her eyes study the randomness of the licks of flames. No rhythm to them. The howling of the wind coming through the letterbox. The cat walked out of the rain through the back door cat flap and they heard it slap. He waltzed in, uncaring, and hopped on to a cushion on the sofa and walked on to her lap.

Caliphate

He took a deep breath 'Its a multinational effort. The brief at Hereford said the U.S still has active seal teams that can provide guys for the operation. Even Russia are onboard after their metro strike' he said 'There a good men next to me…good men'

She gently stroked the cat as it closed its eyes and she watched it. She gazed up, looking across the room shaking her head.

She widened her eyes to allow for the tears to escape 'For Christ's sake,' she said quietly as if not to scare the cat. 'They don't have planes or drones or anything. How are you supposed to do anything? What if you get hurt? How on earth can they get to you? I mean, what if they catch you? You don't even know how long you'll be gone for! Why cant we just use the nukes?' she said, looking around the room as if the answers were written on the walls

'No matter how dark this gets, we, the professionals remember their are innocent scattered among the madness'

'They don't know we're coming, you need to understand that. They will die, they will all die before they can get to me.' He took her feet once again in his hands and she let him. 'There is no time for weighing up risks now, we no longer have that luxury, there is no time for safety and consideration and precaution. The days of caution are well and truly be-hind us, we exhausted them. They died with the first million and now the

Caliphate

future is dying with the infected and irradiated. I don't have promises for you, I won't do that, but my heart is solid. I will be all right.'

The cat gently kneaded the blanket and she refused to look at him. Just the flicker of the muted TV and fireplace strobing the dark room.

'I just wish it wasn't you, that's all,' she finally said and nodded to the TV. He turned around and saw the news. Some archive footage of one of the first Ebola bombers and his wife blowing themselves up in a hospital in France. He turned back to her and saw she was looking at him.

She held out her arms and he stood up and leant in and she pulled him towards her. The cat hopped off her lap and she fell sideways on to the sofa with him, and they just lay there, listening to the rain. Relishing their last few hours together for a long time.

He wakes in the grey light of the morning, still wet and cold and curled up next to the kiln with the dog. The rain had subsided slightly and the whole desert from where he was, looked like a sea. He lies on his side and looks out, moving around would let him know how wet he still is and he doesn't want to know right now. His face is streaked with dirt and his hair is lank and half wet. His boots are sodden and his trousers soaked through to his underwear. He can feel the fleas jumping all over him and his hands are white and wrinkled. He sits up slowly and feels wet through to his shirt, his warmth had managed to warm up the wetness and made it less obvious.

Caliphate

He would have to go back outside soon and there was no telling whether or not there was another building he could stop in. He sits cross-legged and feels cramp setting in around his back and legs so he straightens out his body to avoid it. He needs to eat something and he grabs the daysack and drags it over. He eats the last two spoonfuls of meatballs and stuffs the empty packet into the cold, black fire box and returns to the bag and gets out a sachet of cheese and a packet of crackers. He is starting to shake again and the dog wakes up and looks at him. He looks at her and nods to the cracker in his hand with a sparing amount of cheese on and she stands up, stretches and comes over, gently taking it from his offering hand. Then he sits and spreads the salty cheese on all the crackers and eats most of them watching the rain fall outside in periodic crashes as its caught by its accomplice the wind, howling through the chimney like a wolf with infinite lung capacity, never ceasing, never resting its call for him. The dread of going back outside feeding the defeatist in him. I can't do this, the thought drains him of any respect he had for himself and rings out the last of his motivation. The long drenched desert in front of him, an empty colosseum with no audience but still he was the gladiator, the door the entrance into the gauntlet, take your Iron and enter, die in here or die out there. He gives the dog the last cracker and puts the rubbish in the fire box and drinks some of his freezing water, bitter and tasteless like the dirt. He

Caliphate

checks the rifle and gently stands up on to his creaking legs, his joints snapping from the awkward position he had slept in. He picks up his hat, still wet, and puts it on, feeling the pain in the side of his face as he pulls it over. He unzips his jacket and lets it slide down his arms and drops it to the floor. His down jacket is wet but not sodden and he reluctantly un-zipped it and took it off, immediately shaking again. He puts the jacket into a waterproof bag in the daysack, and the scarf. He would be walking again soon and would warm up. He would sweat wearing all this and needed to save it until he really needed it otherwise his body would take the warmth for granted. He pulls on the now heavy jacket and zips it up to the top then puts on the daysack and picks up the rifle, pain in every movement like he aged a hundred overnight. He takes a last look around the room in the dull light. A shepherd's refuge hut, he suspects, surreal. He leans out of the door and looks around, just the rattling of the rain across the desert as far as he could see and the huge plains now covered in water. He was going to get wet and stay that way. He checks the map and his bearing with shaking hands and then puts on his wet gloves, now a size bigger from the rain, and pulls up the poncho over his head. He takes one of the bungees off the corner and wraps it around his waist over the poncho to keep it tight around him. In three kilometres, he would start to

Caliphate

see the road and then he would head west from there. He looks at the dog.

'Are you coming?' he says, shaking under the poncho like an homeless orphan.

She stands looking at the doorway, her fur still damp and matted from last night.

'Am I going to die?' he says to her.

She is just staring at the doorway. He thinks, if she could talk, she would probably say yes.

He steps out into the rain and the rattling begins on the poncho immediately, the water on the ground now a few inches deep, and the dog gingerly steps out into it then runs off and begins her agenda, lapping up water and sniffing. He keeps the rifle under the poncho and makes his way south across the flooded plains, keeping up the pace to try and keep warm, his leg feeling slightly better. The ground has started to absorb the water and his feet are starting to stick. He thinks at this pace and without the bike, he isn't going to make the extraction, there's just no way he could cover the ground in that time while it was like this. If he could make contact with someone he could get a designated area for recovery open, but as there was no contact with Witchcraft One Echo and with Glenn probably a good hundred kilometres west now, the chances are zero. He

Caliphate

trudges for about a kilometre and has to stop and check the map; he doesn't want to stumble across the road, he wants to know exactly where it is. It isn't too far – just short of two kilometres. The rain beads off of his face and on to the map and makes little puddles on the laminate in the creases, he looks at them for a moment while the rain pelts off of him, sweeping in from the sides with the wind and then falling from above again with huge drops. He has seven hundred metres left of map and then he would be without one. Map one is still taped to his knee but he didn't need that for a long time yet. He folds it away and trudges along, the dog by his side. Why didn't she just stay in the hut, he thinks, she could have stayed warm there until the rain passed. But it isn't as easy as that for her, she has to look after him. She walks on, clearing the route of any horror.

He walks on with the sucking and sticking of his feet. He will have to do his laces up tighter at some point as his boots were water-logged and it feels as if his feet are sloshing and sliding around in them as his socks have slipped down. He can hear and feel the air squeeze out of the small breathing holes whenever he puts his foot down. He comes across a small mud mound and sits down on top in the rain and tightens up his laces, wrapping them around the back of the boot and tying them at the front then stands back up and carries on through the bog in the moody, grey light. Shrubs half drowned are sucking up their feed of water

Caliphate

after a long drought. He spends the day hungry and tries to navigate around the thought, but eventually it gets too much and it is making him reckless, so he eats half of one of the grain bars, dry like sawdust, and calls the dog over to give some to her.

After a few hours he stops and sees a bird in a shallow part of the flood. A red-tailed wheatear looking at him. Its red tinted underbelly, its grey and brown head with thin white strips in patterns across its face, back and wings like fine licks of paint. The black beak open, delicate legs springing it around in the water and its black eyes and head darting around, looking at everything. He is hypnotised, watching as it dunks its head and body under the water and quickly comes back up shaking its head with the shake transcending down its wings to its tail, small drops of water flicking and sprinkling around it. It stretches its wings and fans its tail and closes them all up, resuming its settled shape, looking around. The rain beats off his face and the dog is next to him, both watching. He's not seen a bird in a long time. It hops around and pushes its head under water and pulls up something and looks around, twisting its head. It springs up and flutters up into the air, hovers for a second and makes off in the direction he is walking. That bird would be nesting somewhere high.

Caliphate

6

He stands just behind a wet mud mound and looks over the apex to the road. A wide dual carriageway, half tarmac and half dirt, empty and forgotten. From where he is he can see a crater in the tarmac perhaps from a long-ago IED detonation. Probably on a military convoy. He thinks that from where he is standing would be a good overwatch point for whoever was waiting to detonate it as it afforded concealment from the road. The road is long and it stretches in a straight line from the east to the west with no road signs and ditches either side of it. Litter everywhere, tossed from cars and dumped by trucks passing through from towns and cites and he could smell it over the musty, metallic scent of rain and wet mud. Some of the piles have trails of smoke coming from their peaks and it drifts up slowly and fades out like recently shovelled piles of manure. He scans across as far as he can see with the rain trickling off his nose. The dog is off somewhere greeting the thousands of new scents in the rubbish pile, her wet fur dripping and legs muddy. He takes off the daysack under the poncho and holds it to his chest and unzips the side pocket and takes out the handheld AN/PRC-148 radio, battery and antenna and puts the daysack back on. He screws on the battery and the antenna and holds the radio close to his chest and tunes the small knob on the top left of the handset. The screen lights up blue with a series of letters and then the frequency, 467.673. He flips the radio and taped to the back of the handset is the emergency frequency, which he enters by turning another small knob on the top. The rain is pooling on the screen and he has to wipe it with his thumb so he can see. He scans across the road once again and sees a car coming from the east. He kneels down so he can just see over the mound and squeezes the 'press to talk' button on the side of the handset and holds the handset to his mouth.

'Any call sign this is Witchcraft One Delta, Mayday Mayday Mayday,' he says.

Caliphate

He looks at the screen as he releases his finger, it flickers and the transmission bars fill for a second and then go empty. No response. He presses again.

'Anyone please respond, this is Witchcraft One Delta, Mayday Mayday Mayday.'

He waits a few minutes but nothing.

He switches the radio off and slides it into the map pocket on his trousers and buttons it up. He doesn't know who is left or even if there is anyone out there. Glenn could be dead and Witchcraft One Echo was unresponsive to Zero so the chances are he was dead too. Maybe Glenn has made it back, he thinks, but he knows that this is wishful thinking, it is wet and cold and the only reason he survived the night is because of the building he found. If Glenn had managed to call an early extraction for whatever reason then there was a chance a helicopter was out there somewhere and maybe the radio could reach them. Wishful thinking, he reminds himself again. He would try again at last light. The procedure was to turn the radio on at last light and first light, that was when emergency comms were monitored by all those on the ground and those back in Tel Aviv. It would save battery that way. The dog was now standing watching the car approach.

Caliphate

He watches the car come closer and sees it is a box like a yellow taxi. The roof is stacked with suitcases tied down with ratchet straps. He takes out the rangefinder. A man is driving with an elderly woman in the passenger seat and a younger woman next to her. In the back are four children and another young woman. All crammed into the small vehicle. He thinks to flag them down but he can't risk it and it would put their lives in danger – if he was seen with them, they would all be skewered. He had to stay off the road. There would be hasty checkpoints further down and they would be stopped sooner or later – if they were lucky, they had enough money to barter their way through. Maybe the man had a weapon and was going to fight his way through. Brave, he thinks. He watches the car slow down and swerve around the crater then accelerate off down the road. The rain is falling everywhere and the cold wind is coming in from the west. Good luck, he thinks, and turns to the dog.

'You coming or staying?' he says.

Her ears prick up and she finishes smelling whatever ever it was that coaxed her to it; there would be plenty more to smell down the road.

He sees a rusted wreck of a vehicle dragged into the desert off the side of the road. They head off, keeping a fair distance from the tarmac. His feet sink to the heels with every step and it hurts his knee pulling

Caliphate

them out. His boots are caked in mud, looking like astronaut's footwear, and they feel five times heavier than normal. Each step is turning into the task of keeping his boots on and he curls his toes in the boot to stop his foot sliding out, lifting them with a sucking sound, water quickly filling up the newly formed hole. The slow moving is making him cold and frustrated and his hunger is making him weak. His trousers are heavy with mud, and feel as if they're going to fall down, so he tightens his belt. He is a long time reaching the wrecked car and he looks at his watch, 15.12. He thinks he'd best eat while he can see and then walk through the night.

The car is wheels down but half sunk into the ground with the front completely smashed into the driver's seat, like a crushed crisp packet. He looks around inside. Rusted springs from the seats and the guts of the doors. Windows gone and all wiring and electronics looted or corroded. He looks to the road that was maybe a hundred metres away and checks for any approaching vehicles and sits in the boot, lifting his feet off the floor. The cold rusted metal provides little comfort but he is just relieved to have his feet out of the mud and water. The boot door is twisted off and hanging over the side. He takes off the daysack and places it next to him in the rusted boot, unzips it and takes out the bag of chicken and herb dumplings and carefully rips off the top. The smell of rust and putrid wet rubbish stings his nostrils. He takes out the spoon and mashes up the food and eats two big spoonfuls, retching with each one, the rain dripping into the bag and on to the spoon. He calls the dog up into the boot and she jumps up. She is shivering and he has only just noticed it, her little body rattling and drips of water running off her underbelly. He puts down the bag and puts her in his lap. Her little legs juddering and eyes blinking in the raindrops and her tail wagging. He wraps part of the poncho around her and picks up the bag of food and gives her a spoonful with a dumpling and she gently takes it, as always, and then he gives her another. He lets her lick the spoon clean and puts it away, then the rest of the bag of chicken and dumplings. He sits there with the dog and looks around the barren lands: piles of rubbish everywhere and huge black and brown puddles. The Mars-like godforsaken land, silent and siren, more death than life here. The emptiness and uselessness of it all, inhospitable, an arena perfect for nothing. He thinks the rain is a waste as there is nothing for it to nourish. Old habits of the earth carried over from some long ago lush land. The mute earth none the wiser to the events we so live for, and die for. Maybe it's best that way, for our sake.

The road looks inviting with its flat solid surface and he regards it for a while. He would walk the road at night and the desert during the day; either way he was going to get trench-foot if it stayed like this. He looks at

Caliphate

the dog and holds her to him and she stops shaking, sharing what little warmth he has. He starts to get cold and he nudges the dog off his lap into the boot and she jumps up on to her feet. He pushes himself out with his hands and his feet splash into the water, sinking instantly. Looking down the side of the road he just sees rubbish and water and mud mounds, nothing of any use and nowhere to take shelter. Black bin bags flutter in the wind, half full of bottles, nappies and rotten vegetables. Piles of plastic bottles all different colours in different stages of their long process of de-composition before returning to the earth in their various elements. Torn white sacks and sheets, wet and stinking and covered in mud and oil. Old engine parts rusted, a bonnet, a gearbox decaying and piles of cans, wrappers and old boxes. Burst tyres everywhere, of all different shapes and sizes, thousands of blowouts stripped off and thrown along the road. The stench of pollution and rot, everything baked in the sun and then pelted with the rain. Whatever could move rustled in the wind and rain in its black and brown swamps of disease on the dead desert plain. He me-anders around the large piles and avoids the worst of the swamps and the dog walks over the large piles. Feeling the sinking and crushing of bags and bottles underfoot in every step, twisting his ankles and throwing him off balance. Absolute environmental neglect. With it getting dark and him becoming more and more reckless with every minute of it all, he makes his way to the road, trudging over piles and half-full bags, buried and poking out of the black water, his nose stinging from the venomous smell. The tarmac feels wonderful underfoot, hard and confident, and his steps feel solid. He would be careful and look for cover as he went. The white lines of the road are faded and worn from years of tyre tread and there are potholes everywhere. Huge lacerations, scars from metal being dragged through the tarmac, built once and neglected forever. The rain sheeting over everything and the dark sky a blanket of bloated dark clouds bleeding. The dog trotting in front, him limping behind.

He stays on the road until dark and keeps walking. There could be no stopping in the road or on the side – he would contract something from the black water and the smell was too strong. He turns every so often to check the road behind and he begins to see an iota of light through the rain in the distance, he stops and stares, with everything around him black and vile. It is shaking and blurred from the rain lashing into his eyes. As he stares, something changes and it turns into a pair of lights. He quickly steps off the road and back into the swamp lands of rubbish, and clambers his way through in the dark, tripping and sinking into mud and slipping off wet plastic. He falls to his knees in with the cold water stealing his breath and stands back up, wincing at the still present pain in his knee, and turns and keeps moving, grabbing on to whatever he can to help him up. He snaps his head over and moves the poncho out of his vision and sees the lights coming closer in the rain.

'Come 'ere, darlin' – quick!' he yells to the dog out there in the dark and rain.

He can't see her but realises she isn't a target and is probably safe. The headlights bumping and flashing in its collision with potholes and now lighting up part of the road he is parallel to. He gets down and lies behind the nearest pile of rubbish. The stench tests his gag reflex and he grits his teeth to hold in what little food he has in his belly, his back teeth wet with the salivation before vomit. He watches the car approach and sees another pair of headlights behind. He gets lower and closer to the pile, his hands on some slimy bags, full of what felt like potato peelings. He begins to think of hypodermic needles among the rubbish that could prick him and he has to blank this out of his mind to preserve his cover. He pulls up the rifle out of the poncho and holds it on top of the pile and flicks off the safety catch, the rain crashing everywhere and the shaking starting. The cars swerving, avoiding the potholes and the headlights bouncing and shifting in his direction and then the other side. He keeps one eye closed and watches them carefully, and he tries to look for the dog in the head-lights but he can't see her. The vehicle headlights behind spotlight the front car and he can see it is a small people carrier, white with mud

Caliphate

sprayed up the sides and the windows steamed up. He stays low, his heart thumping. They are probably just civilians, he tells himself, but that isn't enough for him to switch the safety catch to safe. The first vehicle comes closer and he becomes colder as it reveals his position is closer to the road than he'd thought. His hairs are standing up and his grip grows tighter on the rifle as the people carrier comes parallel. He holds his breath and puts his head lower to the pile. The headlights light him up briefly and then pass, sweeping across the sea of rubbish and road and leaving him in darkness. He relaxes his breath and holds it again as the second vehicle approaches, the lights again illuminating him, but with the poncho and rubbish flapping in the wind, he imagines he just looks like another bag. The second vehicle was not lit and he could see little of it, he could see enough to know it was civilians, just a typical yellow box car moving west. The headlamps light him up again briefly and wash past, bouncing off the millions of raindrops, like diamonds hanging from invisible strings. The cars continue on their journey down the road and he watches for a little longer before standing up, slinging the rifle under the poncho and applying the safety catch.

'It's all right, come here, you,' he shouts over the rain, his head looking around into the darkness.

Caliphate

The dog was beside him the whole time, shaking in the black puddle surrounding the pile of rubbish. Right there with him.

'We have to keep moving, to stay warm… all right?'

The darkness and the fall of rain everywhere. He leans down and ladles up her chin in the darkness, her little body trembling and his teeth chattering.

'Just stay with me and we'll get away from this place, we'll get to my fireplace at home.'

His heart sinks and the loneliness washes over, absorbing all of his hope and drive. His home might as well not be on Earth, his fireplace quietly crackling as the wood splits and sparks gently. His wife curled up on the sofa under a blanket. His mind rattles;. Don't you dare. You stay here in the rain, dirt and the disease, and you forget about that fire and that blanket, that small part of him still attached to his duty spoke with its dying breaths. You stay out of that place and keep yourself in the nightmare, it's your only chance. There is only now and nothing is going to change that and she is not here. He stands up and looks down the dark empty road.

'Let's go,' he sighs.

Caliphate

He walks for hours along the side of the road and on the tarmac when he can. His feet are stinging, his skin is sliding around like a loose sock. Trundling over the garbage and falling into the black water, arms oaring in front of him, sliding into piles of God-knows-what and the stench like a snakebite to the nose. He tries to keep his mouth closed all the time but walking through the trash is exhausting.

The weakness started not long after he stepped on the tarmac, not a weakness from lack of energy but a weakness that is the precursor to a sickness. It washes over him in a matter of minutes and what little strength he has feels as if it was on its final fumes, every movement clumsy and ill managed. He knows what is coming and an hour later the first stomach cramp tightens inside him on the road and his hunger is replaced by a staggering sensation of shaking and nausea, cramping up like a rope being pulled tight and then loosened. He stops, bent over in the rain, face pressed with pain in the dark waiting for it to pass. His breath shudders and he can feel the vomit at the back of his mouth and he holds it back, swallowing repeatedly until his stomach relaxes and opens again. As soon as he gets stands up straight his bowels begin to feel loose and the surge of diarrhoea squeezed his guts like a ratchet strap straining to tighten. The piles of garbage and their fumes enter his every orifice, contaminating everything. His temperature plummets and his desire to keep moving is

Caliphate

choked by the wanting to stop and do nothing. A cramp knots in his stomach again, bending him in half and he desperately waits for it to pass. But he loses his hold and vomits, a long violent series of retching with little product. His empty stomach has nothing to offer apart from a thick watery phlegm. He kneels as if looking over a steep ledge of a building vomiting in the blackness with the rain beating down in great swaths from the flank, his body convulsing and his back arching with his stomach contracting. The weakness plagues deep into the marrow of his bones and the thought of impending death sails in his mind in the ship of despair. He throws off the poncho and it makes the dog jump, little care about the rain now, he reaches for his belt and struggles to undo it and drops his trousers to his knees and defecates what feels like water. He stays there for a while hoping that whatever organism was rampaging through his system is extracted but he knows this is not the case and that he's going to be rapidly deteriorating over the next few hours. He'd had dysentery and vomiting before, and he knew the only way to combat it was letting whatever it was run its course through him. No comfort at all. He is stripped outside and soon he will be stripped inside too, all remaining nourishment he has conserved will soon be on the floor leaving him with a deep fatigue and enough energy to perhaps crawl off the road. The dog is next to him, sniffing his face, and he gently pushes her head away. Once the surge of sickness is over for the

Caliphate

time being, he gently picks himself up as if he was made of delicate china and lifts his trousers and reattaches the poncho, his shaking now not only a product of the cold but of the parasite inside him. He gets off the road and calls the dog and turns on the torch and heads away, lighting up the piles of waste and navigating between. He needs to find somewhere to lie down out of the rain and away from the black waters surrounding the diseased filth. Each step grows harder and harder with every ounce of energy lost, his boots caked in mud and black sludge, and the stench torturing his senses. With every breath he feels his sickness grow stronger and his life-force grow weaker and, without treatment, there is no hope.

He reaches the outskirts of the dump and continues to follow the direction of the road. Soaked and freezing, his steps are clumsy and his mind is humming with distorted ideas. He sees a box shaped vending machine in the direction he is heading and his heart races, just a silhouette on the near horizon. The Cadbury logo is illuminated on the front in its purple italic writing, barley visible. He thinks the machine will have a cure for him, maybe even a radio to call a search and rescue platform. He hurries his pace but the vending machine grows further and further away and eventually disappears and he can't tell if he is moving forward or not. To him, the vending machine is there and it can't be moving, his mind tells him, but his mind also tells him vending machines have radios and cures.

Caliphate

His whole life forgotten, and he didn't care to remember. He wandered with a mind purged of history, he simply just did not care about anything apart from sitting down, each thought was cold and clinical with no emotion providing the most basic, watered down information; left leg forward, right leg forward, hands are getting frost bite, can't feel my feet or face, hypothermia is setting in, problems just flicked on and off like an old veiwmaster toy, press the switch down and the next image clicks into view and his hope narrows its gaze to see through the small aperture of closing life. Eyelids heavy with exhaustion, desperate and with no energy to hold them open. But the vending machine light remains in the distance. A single light far away, a dot shifting in the rain. He stops and stands, shaking, and takes the radio from his trousers and turns it on. Not a single part of his body is not trembling.

'Anyone… please help… this is Witchcraft… One Delta…' he mumbles with his eyes half closed and the rain dripping off his nose.

No response, as he expected. He thinks he hears something on the radio and before he puts it away he puts it to his ear, listening hard over the pelting of the rain. Something very faint, maybe someone talking, but then it is gone.

'Who's there, please speak to me', he says.

Caliphate

He looks at the dog with the torch. She squints her eyes in the light, looking at him.

'Did you… did…'

He stares at her shaking body and then looks at the floor. The radio left him wandering everywhere, thoughts of primary school he had never thought of now appearing, his teacher reading to the class during an English lesson while he sat at his small wooden chair at his desk, innocent and quiet. People he met long ago once, people in bars, in countries he may never see again. His first car. Nothing he can pin down and vanishing the moment it appears, just a glimpse. A cramp is coming and it is going to be painful, he starts to wince and hold his abdomen. Deep pain, the worst yet, he is sure his body is trying to turn itself inside out. He retches hard and struggles for breath and then falls to the ground. The pressure from the straining forces his eyes to the point of bursting out of his face, the veins on his neck throb and the laceration on his face begins to hurt. He has to take down his trousers again and he fumbles around, the torch dangling around his neck, and drops them. His body discharges every-thing by whatever means. His face is tormented by the pain and his guts are on fire. The dog is watching him, whining. Maybe she thinks these are his last steps and she could be right. He kneels there, trousers down and submerged in the water, shaking and recovering from the violent vomiting, looking at the soaked ground.

He continues for a while in the dark without the light, the weakness now nearly complete. Every so often he stops to purge his body in violent attacks of cramps and diarrhoea, falling to the wet ground, praying for it to be over. He is exhausted, completely drained. He no longer cares about anything apart from death, and he welcomes it. Hopeless and careless, he wanders in the dark with the dog whining and eventually slams into the ground on his side as he fell asleep. He presses himself up out of the water and at long last allows his eyes close.

'I just can't, just let me sit down…'

He undoes the poncho and slides out of his daysack and places it in the waterlogged ground and sits on it. His head is barely able to look up, he sits cross legged, half submerged. He tucks the poncho under his legs and feels for the zip on the daysack, opens it and pulls his wet down jacket out of the waterproof bag and puts it in his lap. He has to put it on but it requires effort and energy he just doesn't have. Every movement is now scrutinised and evaluated in terms of energy. Nothing can be wasted but then what is it being reserved for? He unzips his jacket three quarters of the way down and slowly slides his arms out of it and feels for the arm holes of the down jacket and slides his arms in, pulling the hood over his head and putting his arms through the other jacket and pulling it over his shoulders, his eyes closed throughout. The rain absolutely relentless in its downpour. He feels around for the dog with his flopping arm, his breaths laboured and shallow. She finds him, he feels her warm tongue lap his hand and he feels her shaking. He picks her up under her belly, slides her down the front of the down jacket like an infant kangaroo; she complies without any restraint. Her wet fur is cold against his chest and soon she stops shaking. He sits with eyes closed but not asleep, how could he? The cramps come like clockwork every twenty minutes, buckling him over in pain and retching. Nothing left, empty. He tries eating part of a grain bar but it's turned round before it can get to his stomach. The faint light in the distance flickers in the rain, which has calmed slightly. He sits there curled over with the dog in his jacket and he is shaking violently and he knows that this will be the end. No energy and no strength and his desire to see his wife again dissolved into the beauty and peace of death. It's time to bring this to its inevitable conclusion, he thinks. His mind is relaxed, it knows what is best for him right now. He looks at his watch and wipes off the mud, 02.00. He thinks he won't make it to the morning like this and he wants to drift off into a deep sleep and let it slide over him and take him, but the cramps won't let him, the pain

Caliphate

serves as an antidote to sleep death. But exhaustion takes over the cramps and sends him under.

He was standing in the room, the same as before, looking towards the wall. Where the white walls where, there were now paintings. Not an inch of white wall could be seen, not even on the ceiling, only the backside of the paintings. No strings or nails to hold them in, they just hovered there flush against the wall. Not a sound. He was free to move around but he didn't want to, something about the room was keeping him locked into position. All of his senses were functioning as normal and he saw nothing strange about the situation. He turned, and the movement felt like it took forever. The door to the room as it was before, open and empty, just a black rectangle. The tinnitus began. He was waiting for something to happen. His skin went cold and he began to tighten up. All at once, the paintings started to turn with the slow screeching against the wall like forks dragged against china plates. Every hair on his body stood up as if they were all being plucked from him simultaneously by tweezers. He wanted to hold his breath so whatever was coming wouldn't hear him; he thought that something could hear his thoughts so he desperately tried to blank his mind. The act of complying with his senses made it worse. Try and reason, for Christ's sake, this is not real, it cannot be, it's an illusion. The tinnitus was growing and his teeth began to grind. He set his eyes on the door and kept focus: do not look, he was thinking. Get out now, you have to; some part of him took control. You look at those walls and you die. No use, he couldn't move. The paintings still turning all at once scratching and scraping on their journey to take the life-force from him, to suck out his soul through his eyes.

She emerged at the door. Her small round shoulders likes smooth wooden spheres and slender arms with tiny hands clasped into fists. Her soft breasts pitched out the shirt creating a shelf over her flat stomach. A feeling of heat fell glowed in his torso. She hovered in her summer dress with cartoon sunflowers stamped on the black fabric pinched between her thick thighs that merged into her waist seamlessly. Her calfs tensed and defined in a tip toe strain and her yellow painted nails on her small, nearly non existent toes. He remembers her toes, a flicker of a memory watching them as they slowly clasped and relaxed like a venus fly trap while she was lost in some thought looking through empty eyes, curled up next to him. She came closer slowly, her dress still and her bare feet not touching the floor. His feet were. Her arms extended towards him and her face made a mockery of the impending terror. Her little ears hidden in her hair straight shoulder length hair. Her eyes narrow and sleepy looking but a faint, mildly aggressive shape plucked up in the middle of her

Caliphate

thin eyebrows. His teeth clenching, the enamel on his tongue like pep-pered granite. The taste of chalk. He was starting to cry and wail through his clenched teeth. The paintings halfway round.

He had to engage himself. There is a door and it is open. Think. He remembered the ducks landing in the pond for the briefest second and then his mind flicked back to the paintings.

She nodded slowly as if to show approval; she was hearing his thoughts as they swam through his mind in the sewage of horror and death. The polluted fields of memory reeking from acts of human carnage, the sky dark green and grey. Wade through it, this cannot be all. Out there is the good, you just have to see it. Remember. Lying next to her on green grass in the sun, her leg cocked over his and on her side with her arm over his chest. His teeth started to relax. Stay here. Don't think about stay-ing here, just do it. Do not dilute the memory with questions about the memory, just let it happen.

The paintings slowing down but still turning. He moved his fingers.

'…anyone hear me?' she said through a closed, straight mouth, her voice a grainy low pitch with white noise. The paintings stopped and the room dimmed; he started to hear water.

Caliphate

'I can hear you,' she said in the same voice, the voice was that of a man.

She faded with the room and everything vanished.

'No matter how dark it gets out there, just remember home,' she said 'Whatever you see, don't let it control you,' She brushed his short hair back with her palm as if it was in the way. Her big brown eyes moved around his face as if they were sewing up some memory with a needle and thread. She pulled away her mouth mask and he pulled his down around his neck. He lent in and kissed her warm lips. He was anxious, his stomach floated with that light ball of nervousness of what was in store for him four months from now when the hasty Deep Fire Patrol course was over. He would be released into the growing Caliphate where three days ago a hundred fleeing Christians were filmed. The video reached every corner of the world. Groups of men in black coveralls holding down men and women of all ages and wooden crucifixes hammered down their throats with sledgehammers all the way through to their anus, long heavy swings of the hammer colliding with the top of the cross in a soft thump, sending it in a few inches at a time. They were planted in rows of ten out-side of Kirkuk in some dusty clearing near a smouldering church, a set of goalposts at the end of the clearing. The audience applauded and

Caliphate

cheered with delight as the limp bodies stood in their rows, mouths stretched, jaws dislocated, eyes bulging looking to the sky, insides shredded. Endless moaning though a load speaker at the end of the clearing, crackling with prayers. None of the bodies feet touched the floor. They hovered like limp puppets with only one string that connected to their jaws, the puppet master invisible in the sky.

'Take all the bad stuff and put it in a room and lock the door and never look in it until the next bad thing. It will rot and decay and everything inside it will be useless,'

Another man and woman holding each other by a window. The woman crying into the man's shoulder.

'I'll be right there with you, just remember' She said.

'Passengers for flight EL212 proceed to Gate Three,' the announcement came over the speakers, echoing through the long corridors of the quiet airport.

He is looking at the ground with his chin on his chest and the rain pattering on the poncho. His eyes try to look around but he cant tell if they are open or closed. Nothing to see in the pitch black. He lifts back the poncho and looks towards the light and realises his eyes are open. Dim and far. Unless it was a small window then maybe he was close. A fading cramp in

Caliphate

his stomach. Shaking violently. His feet raw and submerged and he can feel his socks have slid down and gathered at the front of his boot round his toes.

'…any call sign, this is Witchcraft One Echo, I am on foot…' A voice with an American accent comes from his trouser pocket.

He stares at the floor, no longer trusting his senses. How could he, there was no one around to proofread them. He sits there, the dog in his jacket. That's the radio. It slashes though his brain like a sword, that is the radio.

He reaches down with his trembling hands and pulls the radio out of his pocket. He must have left it on accidentally; an accident, maybe not.

'Hello… can… anyone there?' he says into it, his eyes closed.

There is a pause and it is back to the rain and darkness. His strength is gone and his body buckles over in the mud and rain. The day-sack he is sitting on is now submerged and sunk into the bog. Nothing, he knows it.

'Cabin.' The voice comes over the radio again.

No question this time, he knows someone is talking to him. He puts the radio to his mouth. He has to think of the rest of the authentication response.

Caliphate

'Fever,' he says.

'This is Witchcraft One Echo, send your call sign.'

His eyes are now open, his heart thumping. Hope.

'This is Witchcraft One Delta.'

'Tom! Fuck me, man, it's good to hear your voice, tell me your on the bike?'

A hint of a smile rises on his face.

'Wade…fuckin' wade' His face squeezes into sorrow and he lets out a single yelp of a cry '… I'm on foot…' His eyebrows screw together to hold back tears of relief.

'Are you hit? Where are you?' Wade says. The radio clear as day.

He shakes his head slowly and tries to open his eyes but fails.

'I'm finished, mate. I'm sick, I'm, I just can't do it. I've got no map and no bike. Listen, mate… I'm really not going to make it, I need you to tell…'

'You're near the road, right?' Wade interrupts.

He sits up straight and takes some deep breaths; he feels slightly embarrassed.

'Yeah, what about you?' His eyes open slowly and close again. He can sense the dog looking at him.

Caliphate

'Bike's gone, took a couple of rounds to the engine and fuel tank in a mixup back east, sump got a nice hole in it and bled out for a few miles before she kicked the bucket, bless her, radio got zapped too' Tom could hear his laboured breathing, puffs of white noise between sentences 'I buried her miles back and carried what I could' He went away for a moment then came back 'I need to know where you are, what can you see, dude?'

He lifts the poncho again and looks towards the small light. The rain streams off his nose and on to the radio.

'I can see a small light to the west, just next to the road, I think. It's the only one I've seen… look, Wade… my maps are gone.'

'Have you got NVGs?'

'No.'

'Shit…' He could hear he had stopped 'Shit' He says again, there was a pause.

Wade came back 'I have some Metronidazole and it should square you away. I'm going to come to you. I can see a light too. Hold on…'

He goes away for a few seconds and comes back. If their radios are in range, they must be fairly close.

'Which side of the road are you on?'

Caliphate

'I'm on…' He thinks for a second as he gets his bearings. 'The north side, I think… yeah, the north.'

'I'm on the south. Listen carefully, dude. I'm going to come to you, but I need to know which direction I need to go. Do you have a flare?'

'Yeah.'

'That's our only chance, I won't be able to come to you during the daylight as the road is busy. Have you got your rifle?'

He grimaces. His face contorts but his mind finds its sharpness again for a moment, his senses now on emergency reserves. Check the rifle, change the magazine, clean the mud off the working parts, safety catch to fire. The checklist before the fight now scrolling through his mind again like the ticker-tape at the bottom of the television during the news. His shaking completely out of control.

'I'm not a complete fuckwit,' he says, his teeth chattering.

'That building is a checkpoint, dude, and they will probably have a truck. I will get to you… but when they see that flare they are gonna come. Whatever you do, do not write off the vehicle, man.'

There's a pause. He knows this is his only chance, he would not last the next day like this.

'I know… I know,' he says softly, rain pattering everywhere.

Caliphate

'I'm going to start heading north now. It'll take me a while to get across the road because there's been a lotta activity on it lately; I think somethin's goin' down. It's three thirty now. Pop the flare at four, all right, dude, and leave your radio on. Stay with it, man.'

'Flare at four, roger… be careful, mate.'

He smiles slightly then the next stomach cramp begins to knot up and he winces and folds in half.

'All the best dude,' Wade ends.

After a while the cramp subsides and he can concentrate. Each cramp demanded his full attention. He sits in the dark and the rain and thinks. He can barely walk and he is weak beyond any sickness he has encountered before. Out here in the scablands with the rain and the vomit and the cramps, there is nothing and no sacred memory is going to take you away from here; the reality is just too overwhelming. The universe does not care, it's not even alive and it never was, just a cosmic broth boiling and bursting, churning out destruction and emptiness. Who designed that? I am the one who has to act and create purpose, create meaning. Start from scratch, rebuild and retake, for I am the sole survivor of my mind, a champion in the race against nothing.

He wipes the mud from the face of his watch and checks the time, 03.50. He unzips the jacket and gently scoops out the dog and set-

Caliphate

tles her down on all fours on the waterlogged ground and she whines. He zips up the jacket and takes out a pack of crackers and eats as much as he can, and he drinks some freezing water, much to his dislike, feeling it flood his empty stomach. He has to have some food inside him in case he gets caught – run while you still have energy. He drinks a lot of his water until it draws him back into the realm of nausea. He feels his stomach stretch and he has to concentrate for a moment while his body grows accustomed. He unscrews the suppressor off the rifle and stows it in his belt kit and takes off the magazine and checks the weight of it, probably full, then reattaches it. He can feel another stomach cramp coming and he musters everything to hold back the vomit, bending like in some gymnast routine, and eventually it passes and he manages to hold the food and water down. He takes the flare from the daysack and looks around into the darkness. He hears the dog whining then bark once. It makes him jump and he fumbles for the rifle, holding it slumped over, barely able to lift the barrel off the ground.

'What… what is it?' He whispers at the wall of black.

The dog barks again and then comes to him and he can feel her resting against his side and she just stays there whining. He listens carefully around the rain and there is a noise somewhere close. It takes him a while of just staring into the dark with his mouth cocked open to

Caliphate

identify that it is something crying, and after a few moments, it becomes

someone. A gentle cry of sorrow that wouldn't pass for pain. He listens

hard and puts his arm around the dog to stop her whining and she does.

The crying is coming from the ground not too far away, maybe a few me-

tres. The darkness becomes even more threatening with every moment of

listening and he is terrified to the point where he is scared to move even

an inch, eyes wide hunting for light and ears straining hunting for sound

and his mouth open to somehow catch either. The wind carries the sob-

bing closer in loud drifts and he grips the rifle and his head darts around

while it surrounds him then dissolves away. He tries not to blink but it

doesn't matter. He sits on the daysack listening to the crying shift in the

wind like a bedsheet on a washing line, flicking and levitating, tracing the

direction of the invisible wind, then relaxing. The sound always hits him

from the same direction but the constant change in volume makes it diffi-

cult to locate and he measures in a small pause in the wind that it could be

no more than twenty metres away. His mind only gives him a brief mo-

ment to calculate this and then it falls back into fear. He needs to check his

watch but his eyes are fixed on the darkness and on the area of the crying

and he feels he can't break the spell without something jumping at him. He

edges up his arm slowly and brings the watch to his face, he wishes he

could independently move his eyes so he can check the time without giving the darkness the opportunity to strike. In the end, he has to look, and he makes it quick then quickly grabs the rifle again: 03.59. It's time to fire the flare but that's now the last thing he wants to do.

Both the fear and the rationale are on the verge of inference, but he doesn't want to know, despite the flare being the only chance. The wind throws what appears to be another tone of voice crying, from a different direction, maybe to the right of the first and it sounds a lot younger. Both of the voices are almost certainly the cries of women, that much he knows. His head snaps and locks like a radar into both directions when each of them makes contact with his senses. Two people crying out there in the darkness. He has to get that flare up but he desperately does not want to see what is out there. Ignorance is bliss, but there is a time and a place for ignorance and bliss, and this is not it. He slowly takes the long cylindrical flare from his lap and rests the rifle on his knee, eyes never leaving the direction of the crying. He feels around the flare until he identifies the detachable end by feeling for the grooves in the cap. It is on tight and he has barely enough strength to unscrew it, but it slowly turns and comes off in his hand and he places it on the floor, silently. He feels around the cap end of the flare and finds a small circular plastic hoop attached to a small length of string and slides his index finger through it, taking up the slack. He stares into the darkness, as soon as the flare goes,

Caliphate

my hands need to get back on the rifle as quickly as possible, he thinks. He has to take his eyes off the darkness and look to see which way was straight up. Another burst of crying, this time both voices merged, a cacophony of terror.

'Who are you?' he says into the darkness, his eyes stretched wide.

The crying must have heard him and it grows louder, not because of the wind but because it knows he's there and this time there are some unintelligible words among the wailing. He is shot through with horror and points the flare up and angles it into the wind and yanks the pull cord down and closes his eyes. An almighty burst of sparks shoots out of the end of the tube, followed by a high-pitched whoosh as the flare is released, like some small captive sun being released from years of imprisonment. The dog dashes away from him and the unlit flare goes hurtling through the air in an arc and all is silent for a few seconds. He drops the tube and grabs the rifle and pulls it into his shoulder, his whole body shaking and juddering, waiting for the light.

There is the sound of an escalating burn in the sky followed by a dull crack, and the world turns into a throbbing red haze like everything was bathed in blood. He closes his eyes against the brightness then opens them slowly.

Caliphate

'Oh God,' he mumbles. The rain howling all over.

A sea of female heads of all ages, all around him. Some in clusters of three and five, others alone and spaced out, and some back to back. The flare slowly arcs and, in its descent with its small parachute, spirals in the air. He could finally see in front of him, everything painted red. The red light is giving everything a shadow that flickers and moves around its bearer in the same direction, a time lapse of days passing in seconds as the flare spirals. The ground a flat top of shallow red water with half-inflated black footballs scattered around. As the flare turns he can see some of their faces.

Some look directly at him with their red eyes and bloodied faces, others disfigured and battered, teeth smashed out and eye sockets crushed and broken in, leaving the dead eyes looking in different directions. Some wearing black burkas, torn and hanging off floating in the water, others not. The flare turns and all the faces are black again.

'I got it, man, I can see it, I've got a bearing,' the radio says.

He sits there, frozen, waiting for the flare to show him the depravity. Their faces light up once again and their shadows rotate, there is one maybe ten metres away looking at him blinking, her mouth bloodied and shredded and her nose split down the middle; she is crying. Her head moves slowly side to side and she looks at him and around, then back at

Caliphate

him. He sits motionless as if witnessing a God's nightmare. He prays they can't see him and for a moment his shaking stops, his whole body complied to the fear. Her mouth opens and closes, teeth like broken pieces of china, her tongue poking in and out slowly as she moans through her destroyed orifice, her hair matted and tangled around her head like twisted liquorice. Another head a few metres to the left, a young girl's head slumped to the side looking at him, at his eyes. Both her eyebrows split and her teeth exposed through her relatively injury-free lips. All blood washed away by the rain, leaving wounds visible; white and waxy. She looks at him, moaning words fused with cries he can't understand. The flare turns again and the faces are once again veiled by shadows.

'I'm across the road, stay low.' The radio crackles again.

He reaches for it slowly, eyes never leaving the faces and pulls it out of his pocket.

'I'm here… I…' He stops.

A set of headlamps beam into life next to the small light in the distance and he hears a faint ignition of an engine. He grips the cold rifle hard. The building is closer than he thought.

'Here they come, man, get ready to fight. Stay low and don't engage to the south, keep your rounds away from the tyres and engine or we die tonight,' the radio advises.

Caliphate

He stares across the lumps on the ground to the small light that the flare's light couldn't reach and hears metal banging against metal and doors opening and closing. The flare's fizzing grows louder as it comes closer to him and he can see fewer heads. The two closest are still looking at him. On his left, about thirty metres away, is a large pile of rocks, mostly fist sized. The moaning from the women is louder than before, and he thinks that maybe they are calling for his death. He holds the radio to his mouth.

'Wade, listen, Glenn is still out here on his bike, I think. If they get to me, make sure you stay this side of the road and you could proba- bly get him on the net. I have this dog with me… and… you need to look after her. Make sure you look after her, she will find you,' he says looking at the headlights flicking as whoever was occupying it moves in front of the vehicle.

'What's his name?' Wade says, out of breath.

'It's a her.'

'What's her fucking name?'

He pauses but stays staring at the headlights. '…Lucy.'

He can hear the flare's life slowly expiring as the sound grows closer and in each spiral the light's penetrating effect diminishes.

'You called a stray dog Lucy…' Wade pauses. 'Jesus, are you seeing these heads, man?' He sounds out of breath and this gives him a good feeling and now that he can also see the heads he knows he isn't far.

'Yeah, I'm seeing the heads.'

And then the headlights move, they turn away from him and disappear, and, after a few seconds, they emerge over a small slope facing straight towards him and the flare. He can hear the flare burning now as if it's close to his head, the slow crunching burn dying. The light withdraws slowly back to the source until it is complete and the light ends and then there's just a quiet burning. It hits the waterlogged ground with a hiss like a blacksmith plunging his white-hot forged iron in the water.

The headlights bob slowly over the ground. The light reflects off the water like glass, silhouetting some of the heads in its path. He could see one moving, the rest as dead as waxworks. What had they all done that would warrant this? A punishment as wicked as this is can only be the product of a judicial system generated by maniacs who themselves are the ones who should be tried.

He wishes he had never set off the flare but he knows that it was his only chance yet he wants the darkness back as he sees the headlights come towards him. The wind howling in from the west, carrying

Caliphate

screams from the few alive heads and the engine noise of the truck that slowly manoeuvres towards him.

'I've got eyes on the headlights, good luck mate, make fucking believers out of em' he hears Wade say over the radio.

No need to respond. He lies down using the daysack as cover in front of him. The cold water saturates his chest and he immediately favours the risk of being shot to being submerged in freezing water. His breaths gasping and his body juddering as he manoeuvres the rifle on to the pack to try and steady it. The headlights bouncing all over in his direction, he keeps one eye closed every time they glance him. He moves his right arm around in the dark to find the dog.

'Where are you?' he says in a quiet voice, then feels her tail bounce off his hand and he puts it over her hind.

'You're going to have to go and find Wade,' he whispers to her in the blackness. Little whines, her body trembling.

'He's my friend and he's coming to get us, but you have to go and find him now, just in case.' His voice trembles with the cold and sorrow. 'He's a good guy, we're good guys I promise…he'll look after you – He's out there, you just have to find him. Your name is Lucy… okay, Lucy… He'll be calling for you, all right?'

She stays there trembling, as if she heard nothing, and his eye never stops tracking the headlights. They bounce and traverse the open ground, coming closer. From how he is lying, he is level with the heads, he can see some buried deeper than others; the ones in deep holes who survived the stoning have drowned. Some of those who survive in shallow holes look around but he can't see their faces, and he is grateful for that, but still, the wailing in the dark, the songs of agony and pleas and worship in different tones and pitches are sounds to dissolve the courage of any soul.

Close now, he can hear the sloshing of the tyres in the water and mud, in the sea of misogynistic mayhem. His grip on the rifle tightens, as if something is about to take it from him. His eye is open and steady. A cramp is on its way but he has to keep the barrel pointing towards the truck and he can let no amount of pain or emaciation stop that; while alive, there is always fight left somewhere inside. He waits for it to arrive, he knows the body holds special reserves unknown to the mind, a supply of fire, stoked by the horizon of death and calmed by life. Enough for a short fight. There is nothing that can give indication of the fire's place, any in-quest will douse it, it lies at the bedrock of being, a matter controlled by time, only triggered by the unconquerable moment of cessation. The prim-itive, final-gasp attempt at survival.

Caliphate

He flicks off the safety catch with his thumb in one click, his stomach knotted and his entire body shaking. The rain trickles off of his nose in a steady stream on to the stock of the rifle and his open eye blinks away the entering rain. Concentrate. Lucy with him, always with him. Forget the cold and hunger and forbid the pain, it's voluntary. He aims the small red cross-hairs above the left headlight and holds it there, tracking the bumps, waiting for a steady opportunity. Blink and breathe. The cramp in its final stages and the pain is there and he allows it no attention, like tensing a muscle, he can't do this for long. The truck slowing, maybe eighty metres away just off his direction, approaching a flat area. He takes up the first pressure of the trigger and holds half a breath, the truck steadies and he fires. The blast from the rifle barrel is deafening and the flash revealing, like a gas burner being suddenly lit then extinguished. A single round placed above the left headlight and the empty case hissing as it hits the water. The truck stops suddenly and some voices shout and then the truck makes a sharp turn and the headlights are straight on him. He shuffles the rifle into his shoulder and fires three more rounds at the driver's side and the truck stalls and the horn begins to screech and then a single burst comes from the bed of the truck and cracks over his head. He squeezes himself into the ground and reshuffles the stock into his shoulder and fires again, at the last muzzle flash on the bed, the flashes his only guidance to know what is where. Two constant muzzle flashes, this time one from the bed and another from the passenger side of the bonnet. The thumps and snaps seem everywhere. The men in the jeep fire generously at him, and he squeezes lower until he has to put his chin on the ground. His face winces, his teeth gritting. The freezing water runs down the front of his jacket with rounds striking to his left sending water and mud over his back.

'Wade, Wade!' he screams.

The firing slows and he hears shouting and he waits for a pause and then shuffles his elbows up and fires again at the bed. He is careless in his return fire, looking over the sights, anything to stop the barrage coming again. Another flash from the bed. Three men. Change your magazine snaps into his mind, but the thought of taking his finger off the trigger terrifies him. All three flashes now open up from around the truck. Some heads close by are screaming. An ungodly racket of cracking and snapping above his head, a hail of rounds seemingly coming from all directions, the thumping from the vehicle like hundreds of people banging on a wooden wall. The dog barking. There is no way he can look up under such a rate of fire. He wants to dig down, but there is nothing he can do. The fire is constant; while one is reloading, the others pick up the slack in the rate of fire. A round thumps into the pack he is leaning on and rico-

chets into the ground. He changes his magazine with his face half submerged in the water, the freezing water running down his sleeve. He finds
the magazine housing with his shaking hand and slides the fresh magazine home and shuffles into some makeshift fire position. You need to run,
the thought strikes his brain like lightning. No chance, they'll cut you in
half. He fires again in quick succession, desperately trying to avoid the
engine, and two of the men seem to take cover, but the one on the passenger side maintains but less accurately. Then the firing stops from the
truck but he can still hear cracks in front of him. A single shot from the bed
of the truck and then two cracks and a thump shot over the truck.

'Wade!' he shouts.

He gets on to his knee and adjusts his position and fires at what
appears to be the bed. He can hear rounds hitting the blind side of the
truck. Wade is approaching from the south-east so with himself firing from
the north-east they have a good base of fire on the group.

'The tyres, man!' he hears over the radio.

All firing stops. Nothing but the monotonous slow wail from the
surviving heads, and the rain. He keeps the rifle trained on the truck and
doesn't move an inch. His body no longer shakes but this won't last long.
He kneels there, the raindrops landing on his hot barrel with little hisses as
if he's holding a bunch of small snakes. The truck's headlights as still as

Caliphate

stars, silhouetting the rain and a single dead head. He stays still and can hear a faint sloshing and sucking of the mud as someone walks to his left quite far away. His eyes never leave the headlights. He takes one hand off the rifle and feels around for the dog. He can't find her. He puts his hand back on the rifle and takes off the other hand and feels around the other side. No sign of her. His heart sinks slightly then he refocuses his mind on the truck. She's fine, she's scared, he thinks. The sound of sticky walking getting closer to the vehicle.

'Check fire,' he hears over the radio.

He takes out the radio with one hand.

'I'm good, go firm and I'll move to the truck' he says.

'Roger, move.'

He stows the radio and stands up with the daysack in his hand and slings one arm through the soaked strap while holding the weapon on the vehicle, then the other. He shrugs up the pack and starts to walk towards the vehicle.

He walks briskly, each foot sinking and sucking deep in the mud making it difficult to keep the weapon steady on the vehicle. After four steps, his feet have gained in weight tenfold. The poncho hanging off his back flapping in the wind like a cape. His weakness begins finding its way back into his limbs and his stomach starts to curdle, his breathing comes

Caliphate

heavy and sluggish and the shaking starts to creep back in. He checks

over to his left every few paces to look for Wade but he can't see him. A

door opens on the truck.

'Go firm,' he hears from his pocket and he drops to his knee

and two rounds snap, with two violent short hisses following, into the side

of the vehicle. He turns to the direction the rounds came from and now

has an idea of where Wade is.

'Move,' Wade says over the radio.

He puts his hand on his knee and pushes himself up. He is

back to shaking again and keeping the rifle up is difficult and exhausting.

He takes his steps slowly, each one requiring more than one attempt to

remove his foot from the sucking mud. He slings the rifle and draws the

pistol and trains it on the vehicle – lighter and easier to aim. The rain

sheeting in from the west is teaming up with the cold wind. He can't take

his eyes off the headlights and as he gets closer he can start to make out

the rough outline of the truck, tracing the dull straight lines silhouetted by

the headlights reflecting off the water. The engine is ticking and cracking

slowly and the wind cooing through some open window or door. He takes

the torch in his mouth, clicks it on and holds it in his teeth so he can see in

front of him and approaches the truck slowly. He walks over to the bed

and scans along the side with the torch. The driver's door window smashed. One man slumped in the driver's seat against the door. He slowly walks along the side of the vehicle, holding on to the edge and peers behind the cab into the bed. A man on his back with one arm thrown behind his head and empty cases all around him and a M16 tangled in its sling. A thick pool of dark red blood gathering around the man's waist, drowning some empty cases, and his face dead in its last plain expression. There is an exit wound behind his neck and his trousers had half fallen down on one side. He moves to the rear, keeping the pistol in front of him, and comes around the back end and round the other side, and sees another man face down in the water next to the rear tyre, blood mixing with the muddy water like red cream in coffee. He steps around and sees the last body on its back in the water with one leg still in the cab. A expression of disgust on his face half submerged in the water, his long hair floating on the surface slowly stirring in the ripples. He shoots the man in the face and shoots the remainders in the head. Standard procedure.

'We're good,' he says into the radio and throws it on the cab seat.

'Roger, I'm en route.'

He looks at the little light in the distance coming from the building. He can hear Wade's steps tramping in the distance not too far away. He climbs in the passenger side of the truck with the last of his strength

Caliphate

and kicks out the stiff leg and it splashes into the water next to its owner. He pulls his feet out of the mud and puts them in the footwell and slumps against the seat and turns on the interior light. He sits there looking though the shattered windscreen, resting his head back against the headrest, looking through half-open eyes, his shaking out of control and his clothes soaked through. His breathing laboured and his long hair matted over his face. He should be watching the building but the adrenalin is gone and he is left with nothing but fumes, and the pistol feels like some heavy kettle bell in his hand. He focuses through the windscreen and sees the silhouette of Wade coming towards him. He can barely keep his eyes open and his blinks are long and slow. The feeling of shelter dissolves the last vestige of motivation. Nothing to give and nothing to take, the fever coursing his veins turns his life-force to ash inside him. He wants to put the pistol in its holster but he can't lift it from his lap. He sees two small green blobs floating around the front of the vehicle and come around to the side. He doesn't know what they are but as they get closer he can see it's Wade's NVG. Wade steps around the door and snaps them up, takes a quick look at the body next to the door and looks back at him sitting in the cab.

He was tall, maybe 6'2, well built, and he looked Mediterranean. Broad square shoulders with hands that made his rifle look like a toy. He wore a long black beard that covered most of his face and was

Caliphate

down to his collarbones, and his helmet barely contained his long black curly hair. His eyes were buried in their dark sockets but the blueness pierced through, looking at him. His lips hidden in the beard but the lines in his cheeks showed he was smiling underneath. A man purpose built for these conditions. His lower half caked in mud from his journey in the saturated wasteland, he was shaking slightly from the cold. His jacket, a half trench coat snug with his warm layers underneath and his belt kit over the top. Everything soaking wet.

'Mate, Zero is pissed off with you' he whimpers as he drops his pistol into his lap and slowly holds out his hand to Wade.

Wade takes his hand gently and puts his other hand around the side of his head and leans in and hugs him; he can feel his warm breath against his cheek. Wade pushes back and looks Tom over.

'Jesus' Wade says quietly, staring at the side of his face. The constant rain had washed away the blood and dirt and he could see his wounds. 'Stay put.'

'Is the dog there?' he says in a long blink.

Wade steps out of the vehicle door. 'Dog!' he shouts over the bonnet.

'Lucy,' Tom says, rolling his head slowly.

Wade looks back at him and then back over the bonnet.

Caliphate

'Lucy!' he shouts.

He hears the pattering of something running in the water and the dog comes around the back of the truck, does a cursory sniff of the face of one of the bodies and then stands looking at Wade.

'You're Lucy, I take it – get in.' He looks at her then looks at Tom in the cab.

The dog just stands, switching her wide eyes between them, wagging her tail, trembling, and he leans down, scoops her up under the belly and gently puts her in the truck cab.

'Dan Dresden?' Tom says

'Iv'e been holding two runways for three weeks, found him a while back'

'How'd he go?'

Wade looked to the building and just shook his head 'If I ever get hold of one of these motherfuckers Tom' He raised his hands to his chest, open and half clenched like Iron gauntlets

'If ever' He clamped his hands closed.

Wade slides his arms out of his daysack and puts it on the bonnet and takes out a medical kit in a bag the size of a small shoebox. He comes back to the door, puts the bag on the seat and pulls open the Velcro.

Caliphate

Three small compartments hold various emergency treatments; tourniquets, Israeli first field dressings, two morphine coffins with injectors, some
hypodermic needles and syringes, and three small vials of fluid. Wade
takes one of the vials and places it to the side and picks up a syringe,
removing the plastic packaging and dropping it in the cab, then takes out
one of the hypodermic needles. Tom sits, eyes half closed, watching him
with his head resting against the headrest and the dog sits shaking, also
watching, her ears up. Wade steps back and takes a glance over to the
building in the distance and has a scan around while screwing the needle
on the syringe, then steps back into the door. He looks at Tom and picks
up the vial.

'I heard the drop at your red point, the day before I lost the bike.
What the fuck have you been doin'?'

'Don't ask.' He takes a long blink. Wade pauses and peels the
small metal cover from the vial and pushes the tip of the needle into rubber and into the fluid.

'I dropped and got seen by a follow-up, my position was terrible,
I should've…' He takes a deep shuddering breath. 'We had a replen but I
got your bag and my radio died. I take it you didn't need any batteries?' A
creeping smile begins but falls before it can be completed. Wade looks
back, shaking his head and holds up the vial, drawing back the syringe

plunger with his thumb. 'They chased, I came off. Complete write it off, burnt to a crisp.'

'Them?' he says, not taking his eyes off the syringe.

He closes his eyes. 'They hit a mine chasing me.'

Wade looks at him with a quick glance. 'Mysterious…I will give him that.' He puts down the vial. 'Just hold up that torch,' he says.

He slowly picks up the light dangling from his neck and holds it up. Wade checks the syringe in the light, holding it close to his eyes, flicking the side of the vessel and shifting the pockets of bubbles to the top. Pressing the plunger with his shivering hands, squeezing the air to the tip of the needle.

'We need to hurry, I think that building is worth checking out, fuel, food and all that. Roll up your sleeve.'

He can't roll up his sleeve because of how many layers he is wearing so Wade helps, but can only get it halfway up his forearm and then assesses any potential points for injection. He slaps his forearm with his cold hands, trying to summon anything large enough to inject, but nothing surfaces.'All this rain and you didn't even take a drink'

He doesn't have enough water to even remotely rehydrate; no amount of water either of them is carrying could hydrate Tom enough to a healthy standard.

Caliphate

Tom's head against the seat, he smiles a weak smile looking through the windscreen. Wade picks up his hand, turns it over and removes his glove, exposing his white, waxy, shaking hand. His wrinkled skin from constant saturation. Wade rubs it between his, bringing it to life and studies the top of it. A large vein just above the wrist joint.

He looks at Tom. 'Still,' he says. Tom's hand shaking. Wade holds it tight and navigates the tip of the needle at an angle on to the vein, carefully resting the tip on the point he wanted to puncture and then pushes it softy into the skin. The rain drumming on the roof like thousands of small ball-bearings in a washing machine. He holds it there for a second or so then slowly readjusts his hand and squeezes the plunger down, and slowly the fluid courses into Tom's vein on its journey to seek and destroy the parasite. He draws out the needle and pulls a small piece of foam from a tear in the seat and presses it over the hole, getting Tom to hold it there with his other hand.

'Can you do this?' Wade says.

'I don't know', he says, staring through the smashed screen, thinking it looked like a map. It looks flat, but he knows that if he looked through a microscope at it, it would be a vast terrain of valleys and mountains. The wind whistling through every crack and opening in the vehicle and the dog trembling in the footwell, good as gold. He takes a deep

Caliphate

breath and shuffles his weight up and slowly takes off his daysack and places it next to the dog, his face showing the constant battle raging inside him against death. Wade watches him. He takes a hold of his rifle and takes off the magazine, puts a fresh one on and blows hard out of his mouth, the vestige of aggression taking form again inside him. For now the injection has a placebo effect.

'Yes you do,' Wade says, who then turns and goes to the bed and releases the hinges of the tail-gate and eases it down with a slow, rusty creaking. He reaches in and takes the body by the arm under its owner's head and drags it out, empty cases under the body scratching against the metal bed and leaving a slimy trail of arterial blood on the way. He gets it halfway over and grabs it by the belt and pulls it the last few inches and lets it slam into the floor like a sack of potatoes, splashing red and brown water over his legs. He closes the tail-gate and goes around to the driver's side, three bullet holes scattered around the door, opens it, steps to one side, and lets the limp body slide off the seat and fall to the floor. Tom and the dog watching him. He looks disgusted at the blood caked around the back of the headrest with its thick trails running down the seat and pooling around the female seat belt connector. He looks at Tom.

'You wanna drive?' Wade says.

Caliphate

'You treat yourself,' Tom says with a small smile as he reaches over and slowly pulls the passenger door, closing it as gently as he can, some glass rattling from the windscreen on to the dash. Wade turns and looks around at the heads. The screaming now just moaning.

'The new dark age… this is the new dark age, man,' Wade says as he gets in and gently closes the door.

'We never left it,' Tom mumbles.

Wade draws his pistol and punches part of the windscreen out with the barrel until he has a hole big enough to see the headlight coverage. He slips the gears into neutral and grips the keys and looks at Tom.

'If this don't start, it's because of your shooting.'

Tom looks at him then looks through the screen and has a long blink.

'If it don't start, I'm going to die.'

'Before you do, you're going to fix this truck for me.'

He twists the key and the engine fires to life with a short shake. Wade looks at Tom and slaps the steering wheel.

'Not today, not today, brother.' He looks at the dog watching everything. 'See, he may've smashed up his bike, but at least he can shoot.'

Caliphate

The new dark ages, he thinks. He imagined the Earth alone in the cosmos, the small sphere in the dark void of space, turning slowly. Insanity. There is no God watching. Its crust crawls with the desperate few learning and the desperate many squirming with their lust for ignorance. There are those few who read the pages not of the book, but of the light and the infinite, with its tales of promise and plight. He thinks of those spending their limited days and nights watching it for signs, staring into the sky and studying its messages of construction and destruction. But he knows the messages are all written in each of us, in the atoms that we fight.

They drive slowly towards the building, carefully navigating around the heads on the surface, the water creating drifts submerging some which reappeared after the wave travelled far enough, dead eyes lighting up like cats-eyes caught in headlights with a glassy effect, mouths open, yawning in their final moments. They can't hear the few moans over the engine and are grateful for that. There was no help for those buried; the situation epitomised the moral fragility of when situations are just too formidable, and individual survival has to take precedence. It was not in their nature to leave them there but they both knew it was their sheer desperation for rescue that drove them away.

Wade turns on the heating in the cab, instantly giving them a sensation craved during those long weeks in the cold, relentless condi-

Caliphate

tions of the winter desert. The feeling is as slow as a trickle, but it's something.

Tom opens the window and steadies his rifle on the edge and
keeps it trained on the door.

'If it goes noisy in there…' Wade says.

'They're not expecting us, but we are expecting them,' Tom
says.

Wade would clear the building while Tom stayed in the truck, he
would do more harm than good in his condition. They pass the last of the
heads, and the headlights light up a flat clearing next to the small building
where they assume they usually park the truck. The building is on a slightly elevated piece of ground and is relatively clear of flooding. The lights
now light up the whole building. The building's size suggests that there
couldn't be any more than two rooms inside. A semi-square building with
mud walls and a roof of corrugated iron. Some makeshift, poorly con-
structed box near the road not designed with permanent residence in
mind. The notorious light they had been seeing was strangely enough not
a vending machine but a window, a hole smashed out of the wall with
some transparent sheet nailed to the outside of it, loosely flapping in the
wind. There was a satellite dish on the roof and the cables ran through the
window. Behind the building was an old Portaloo filthy with mud, with a

Caliphate

pipe running from the bottom and hanging over a small slope off the elevated ground at the rear, where a shallow hole was excavated to capture the exiting waste. The notorious black flag with white Arabic writing, tied to an old stick, was flapping in the wind violently. They were now back into the edge of the landfill that littered the sides of the road and the smell began to creep up on their noses again. Wade stops the vehicle short, silhouetting the building with the headlights and waits for a few moments to observe any movement; the lights beaming up the start of the gradual slope illuminating the side of the building against the blackness, the rain coming across the beam in waves, loudly hammering on the iron roof of the building. They sit in silence and wait for someone to emerge.

'Check out through the window and toilet first,' Tom says.

'Yeah…' Wade says, staring intensely at the building, nodding his head. 'Yeah… hopefully they're all back there in the mud.'

Tom turns his head to Wade. 'When the shooting starts, I'll be right behind you. I can still fight.'

Wade keeps staring at the building. 'I know.' Then he turns to him. 'Just don't get caught, okay… as long as one of us can still shoot, we're good. Keep the engine on. Are you ready?'

He sits there slopped against the seat, head back against the headrest, stomach empty and shrunken. The barrel of his weapon hanging out of the window, his hand half on the grip. 'I'm more ready now than I will be in ten minutes.'

Wade checks his weapon and unscrews his suppressor and puts it away. If there was shooting on his part, Tom needs to hear it.

The vehicle edges up the slope, Tom with his weapon trained on the front door. As they get closer they can see it's a metal front door, the only entrance on the front of the building and they can hear the faint noise of a generator whirring away, perhaps behind the building. Next to the door is a large cooking oil container, the size of a suitcase, and two shovels. A track led from the front of the building to the road but in the darkness they can't see it from here, but each side of the track is littered with trash. Tom looks over his sights at the door and Wade pulls the truck up the crest of the slope and on to the flat ground with a slight wheel-spin, and brings it to a stop. The blue door rattling in the wind slightly with a dead bolt holding it to the rough mud walls.

Wade opens the driver's door and climbs out, leaving it open and creating a wind tunnel, then makes his way around the back of the vehicle. The dog silent and sleeping in the footwell between the seats on the muddy floor mats. Tom checks to the right of the building and sees Wade creep past with his weapon in the shoulder, then he disappears out of view for a minute or so. He can hear the scratching of the iron roof as the sheets rub against each other in the wind, creaking and twisting. A plastic sheet underneath the iron rustles in the wind. Wade creeps back around the corner and approaches the front door, glances at Tom and shakes his head. He reaches the door and stands with his back to the wall on the hinge side and reaches down for the dead bolt and looks at Tom.

Tom's hands make a fresh grip on the rifle, his shaking half subsided even though he is still very cold and soaked. He squints his eyes to clear them, adjusts his position so it is more central to the door and pulls in the stock tight. Wade watches him the whole time, then slowly nods his head once, and Tom replies with a nod in return. His heart racing once again and his nerves on edge then Wade brings up his weapon with his right hand and nods once, then twice and on the third nod he slides back the bolt and pushes in the door all in one swift movement. The door gets sucked by the draught of wind and slams inwards into the building and smashes into the wall with a rattling crash. Wade steps back immediately away from the door and Tom peers in from his elevated position in the truck cab. A single light bulb hung from the centre of the ceiling reveals everything inside. At the back of the room, half asleep under a few blankets on an old metal bed, a man is leaning up on one arm with his hands over his ears, staring straight back at Tom.

'Don't move, don't you fucking move,' Tom shouts over the wind and rain through the door. 'One man, rear of the room.' The shout demands a lot of energy from his meagre reserves.

Wade peels around the wall and steps in, clearing both the sides he couldn't see from the doorway.

'Clear!' Wade shouts, his voice muffled by the wind and rain.

Tom takes some deep breaths and opens the door; he can see Wade has the man at gunpoint. He climbs out of the cab, using the door for stability and limps to the doorway and cradles it, holding himself up, and catches his breath; it was only three steps from the truck to the door. He limps into the room and sits down on the bed closest to the door and points his rifle at the man, both of them shaking. The room smells of some kind of cooking, the smell of some curry and fresh bread. The man is wearing black trousers and an orange long-sleeved t-shirt with his socks still on. His skin is light brown and his hair black and he has a patchy beard dotted around his neck. His dark eyes are wide with horror and his yellow-stained teeth are exposed as his mouth slackens open with surprise.

Wade turns and sees Tom has the man in his sights and slings his weapon and drags the man from the bed to the floor. He begins to utter a prayer as Wade handles him on to his front with his face to the floor and kneels on the centre of his back and grabs a fistful of his long hair.

'Who else is coming?' Wade says into the man's ear in a calm tone then cracks the man's head into the hard floor with a dull thud. 'Who else is coming?' Again slamming his head into the floor. Wade's eyes like lasers, bulging with rage looking into the man's soul. He repeats this a further eight times, the same sentence, and by the last the man is utterly shocked and looks like he has concussion, his face turned white and his right eyebrow beginning to bleed. The man had not a single chance to get a word out between each slam as Wade wouldn't let him.

'I know what you are.' Crack.

'I know what you want.' Crack again, the man now trying to structure some kind of response.

'Who else is coming?' This strike releases a strange yell from the man.

'What year is it?' This strike makes the man retch and his hands flail around.

'Do you know who we are?' Crack. Every strike looked as if it was removing fragments of the man's memories. Tom could see the creases in the corners of Wade's eyes as he seethed under his beard.

Tom turns on the bed and points his rifle to the door. He does a quick scan of the room. It's just a room and the single window that they

Caliphate

have seen. There are five metal beds around the edge of the room, all half made and recently used.

'Are you okay? We're here to help.' Crack. Now a high-pitched cry. The man struggled aggressively and Wade tightened up his grip so hard the man could not move.

There's a leak from one corner of the room and a bucket underneath collecting the drops. In the right corner, on the door end, are two crates of water, a sack of rice, a plastic bag containing flatbread, tomatoes, onions and a tray of eggs, half empty, all on top of a dirty fridge with black finger-streaks around the handle. Next to the fridge, an old Motorola VHF radio, its antenna cable running through the ceiling. In the corner near the door, a small box television on two stacked crates and a cable also running to the ceiling, and next to that a basket containing one AK-47. In a rear corner is an electric stove, recently used. On top is a large cooking pot with a ladle handle poking out and a lid covered in foil balanced on top. There are dirty rugs tucked under each bed with various clothes hanging from make-shift hangers, nails banged into the walls. A dirty Manchester United t-shirt hangs from one; he does a double-take of that. The soft noise of the generator out back.

Caliphate

'We have been sent for you by your God.' Crack. This one sounds more muffled and soft. There's a steady stream of blood coming from the middle of the man's forehead.

Wade leans into his ear further still, almost touching.

'Who… where…'

The man tries to squeeze out something that has absolutely no importance to Wade.

'Go on, princess! Go on, I'm listening now.'

The man tries to speak but Wade jabs him in the throat hard and the man screams and goes to vomit but Wade covers the man's mouth and the man blows hard through his nostrils.

'I've seen what you have done and now here we are.' Wade looks up and smiles through his beard at Tom and then looks back at the man.

'Your little friends building nukes in your bedrooms stateside, huh! Man, all my dreams have come true tonight. I'm a lucky guy, a lucky fucking guy! We caught you in bed! Ha! In bed!' He looks at Tom and lets out a single laugh and then he's back to the man, winching this head higher. 'In fucking bed, what are you doing in bed! Are you tired? Do you wanna go back to sleep?' He lets out a hysterical fake laugh. 'Do you know what we've just done to your friends while you was dreaming of

Caliphate

virgins? Did you hear Snow White? No, you didn't. Well, sweetheart, we fucking switched them all off from the fucking mains, tight groupings too, and then I burst through the door and here's you! Sleeping away in bed!' Wade's face now straight and stern with focus. 'Now I've got you all to myself!' He pulls up the man's head more and he is gasping for air, dribbling.

Tom thinks Wade must look entirely demonic to the man on the ground, and he is probably right; Wade had uncaged the demon that was tormented inside him.

'There's no going back now, cunt. You are about to go on a journey to a very very dark place with me, you listening in there? Huh? The day you stepped on to your path of jihad I was released from a dungeon.' Wade's blue eyes suck the life from the man, his teeth clenched like he was refraining himself from biting off the man's lips. 'I am the last fucking animal you would've ever wanted coming for you through the mist. I am the spectre, the shepherd of the barbarians. You have not seen someone like me before, boy, there is only one, your suffering will be legendary, even to your kind.'

He throws him over on to his back and kneels on his arms and holds his head in both hands; he looks like he is going to rip his ears off.

'I came a long way for this. I'm not even tired, can you see me?

Caliphate

This mud! It means nothing to me, I'm not even hungry, I'll walk through the rain for another hundred years for you, hunting, chasing, fucking relentless, constant, non-stop, foaming at the mouth, the prophet of trauma, the champion of the cannibals.' He pushes his face closer to the man, until their noses are touching.

'I'm gonna fucking eat you, eat your fucking brains – whatcha think about that?'

The man had wet himself, his face as though he had just woken up in hell after a life in heaven; Wade was the last thing anyone guilty of infanticide would want to wake up to. One final crack of the back of his head and Wade rolls him on to his front and grabs his arms and centres them on his back, holding them there with his knee. The man's face is turned to the side with one eye looking at Tom. Blinking erratically, his other eye is now looking a different direction to the first. His left eye socket has been badly fractured and is bleeding and the eye has dropped slightly. He is babbling some kind of English and his face is twitching with pain. Wade retrieves three heavy-duty zip ties from his pack and ties the man's hands behind his back and his feet, then ties his hands and feet together leaving him a stressful shape on the cold floor.

'Inshallah,' Tom says, looking at the man, Tom's face unsurprised by Wade's monstrous outburst.

Caliphate

Wade stands up. 'He dies at first light', he says as he walks to the door, his voice and expression changed dramatically back to calm and reasonable. He goes out to the truck, switches off the engine and closes the doors.

'Why would you do something like that?' Tom says calmly, nodding to the burial ground of women. 'See that man' Nodding to wade 'Do you think I would stop him? Do you think he knows when enough is enough. He doesn't...not for you. He will do what he wants until you give up your life, because thats what he wants' He leans forward as far as his pain would let him 'Your life over in his hands, in his mouth...all over the floor' Tom shifted his weight, glaring at the man who was just straining, veins bulging in his neck.

'I would never stop him...even if I could'

Wade comes back in with the dog under his arm. Her ears are pricked up and she is growling through a closed mouth at the man on the floor. Wade tears a blanket off one of the beds and places the dog on it and she sniffs it and walks in circles on it.

'I am... I... I', the man whimpers, struggling to breathe.

Wade closes the door against the wind and locks the dead bolt and just the hissing of the wind comes through the ill-fitted frame of mud.

Caliphate

A cramp is coming, the first since before the fight. Tom shuffles back on the bed and rests against the wall. The room is warm from the stove and he can feel the warmth on his face but he is still in his soaked clothes shaking. Wade is rummaging around the room, putting on the radio and turning it up. If a distress call had been sent during the shooting, they would want to know if someone was coming. Wade walked over to the stove, stepping over the man, and lifted the lid.

'They made us some supper!'

Tom stares at the man on the floor, desperately trying to maintain a face that doesn't show his stomach cramping. He looks at his watch, 06.23.

'We can't stay long, mate,' he says.

Wade walks over to the fridge and comes back to the stove with three plastic bowls and two spoons and ladles the steaming food into one of the bowls and takes it over to the dog who is now curled up in the blanket snug. He places it next to her and her eyes open instantly and she crawls to the bowl and begins lapping up the steaming, thick soup. He goes back to the stove and brings Tom a bowl and places it next to the bed and takes off his pack. He takes out the med kit and the vial and a needle and syringe. Tom watches him. Wade, a man with two hearts. A barbarian prowling the dark side of the earth with a heart carved from nothing short of benevolence. He was the kind of thing sent when the conversation is over, when our words become useless and cannot penetrate them. He was forever in his debt and Wade was none the wiser. Tom always felt safe with him on his flank, but he knew Wade, he knew he was nursing some deep trauma that he kept hidden, in the darkest part of himself. He'd always thought there is no greater virtue than a human who holds no ledger for the compassion they give to others.

Wade kneels next to the bed and prepares the syringe, holding it against the light, the clear liquid still and bubble free.

'You're going to have to rest or you will die, man. You look like you've lost a fight with a cheese grater.' He pauses. 'Do you remember talking to me on the radio?'

Tom is slumped against the wall, his body now involuntarily shutting down in the new warm climate. His lips still as split as the day of the crash and his face feels ruined, sandpapered on one side where the skin must be raw. His veins collapsing from dehydration. Part of him thinks that his body held on just to find somewhere warm to die. He was terrified to check his feet.

'I spoke to you, yeah, I remember' Tom says, sleepily.

Caliphate

'No. You was talking on the radio but you wasn't talking to me. I didn't know it was you but it was your voice and that's all I knew, man… You was just, I dunno man, talking about death, I think.'

Tom fixes him with a strong glare while Wade rolls up his sleeve to look for a vein. His nearly translucent forearm is showing no sign of circulation and Wade shakes his head, so slightly he can barely tell. Wade slaps his arm and tries to arouse some sort of circulation, takes his hand and does the same, and manages to find the same vein as before.

'What do you mean, death? The first time I spoke to you was when you woke me.'

Wade gently places the needle above the vein and pushes it gently in and draws the plunger back slightly, and no blood enters the syringe. The vein was too weak or small and he went straight through it. He takes Tom's other hand and massages it until it gains some colour; any colour apart from death-white. He summons a vein and quickly takes the needle and gently pushes it in. He draws back the plunger slightly and a cloud of blood swamps into the needle like a red cloud squeezing through the hole, and gives him the whole injection. Wade looks up at him.

'What do you mean, death?' Tom says, quite sternly and con-fused.

Wade takes out the needle and starts to dismantle it.

Caliphate

'I don't know, I mean, walking alone in the dark was enough without you rabbiting on about weird shit. You told me you had… I don't know.'

He holds the puncture hole for a few seconds, waiting for the platelets to create their genius dam, then stands up and gets some flat-bread from the fridge and comes back over and picks up Tom's bowl, still steaming, and hands it to him.

'Before you sleep, you need to eat. You eat the whole bowl and the bread and then you sleep. Don't worry, I'll take care of jihad boy over here and prep the vehicle, but you have to sleep, dude.'

Tom could have kissed him for that. Wade collects his own bowl and bread, and sits on a bed opposite, next to the man on the floor. He is now unconscious in a small pool of his own blood. They gave him no time to grasp their entry and no time to think of who they were, confused, in pain and terrified – exactly how they wanted him. And how he deserved to be.

Tom does his best to sit up but after a short battle between his strength and motivation, he is slumped against the wall. Wade comes over and rips Tom's flatbread into mouth-sized pieces and goes back over to sit down. Tom takes one piece of bread and dips it into the bowl of hot, thick mush with torn chicken, allows the bread to absorb some of whatever it

Caliphate

was and pushes it into the good side of his mouth, opening it as far as his split lips will let him. He tastes, as if for the first time his taste buds are awoken by the most delicious food the world has to offer. He can taste every mineral and vitamin, his body desperate for something of flavour and nourishment, and he sits there chewing slowly and difficultly. He sees Wade, also eating, watching. The heat gives a strange sensation to his chipped teeth.

'You sounded like someone reading from a text book, like, a robot, something without personality, you know?' Wade says looking into his bowl, slowly eating. 'You were describing something – I tried talking back but you just kept talking.'

Tom simply sits and listens, gingerly feeding bread and soup into his mouth.

'Whatever it was, it must've been terrifying,' Wade says as he looks up at him.

Something stirs in Tom, like a spark in a pitch-black room.

'I can see, but I have no eyes, I can hear but I have no ears, I can breathe but there is no air. There is no colour to see, no white no black and nothing between; imagine no colours. I am solid and still. I can hear silence, the sound of nothing like a rock, but I have no ears to hear it. I can see the infinite stood still, I can see and have no time to see. Nothing

Caliphate

going nowhere, the vacuum of vacuum, forever.' He pauses. 'You said that and I remember clear as day.'

Tom stares at him, chewing slowly, the rain crashing down on the roof, the door rattling in the wind. Parts of his thoughts come back to him, like jigsaw pieces scattered across the earth slowly being found and put back together by old archaeologists. He had no idea he had been dreaming until now. The thoughts assemble slowly: the hammers, the men and the paintings; his wife. He remembers the room and the door. A narration of the nothingness. But the paintings he could not see, only the backs, and he would never see them in the waking world. The sensation of memory resonance, like when someone wakes from many years in a coma, picks through pictures of their childhood, and things begin to make sense.

'I remember' Tom says.

Wade looks at him and eats slowly. 'You remember talking to me?'

'No, I know what the words mean. I saw…'

'I've got no idea what you're saying, what were you talking about? do you think maybe it was just sleep talking' Wade says, stirring the bowl with his spoon.

The man on the floor hummed a flat tone and then stopped. They both looked.

'I know what it's like to be dead.' Tom says

Caliphate

'What, Like those… those people who survive death… near-death experience kinda thing,' Wade says.

'No, not near dead…dead.'

Wade looks at the man on the floor and then at Tom.

'Sounds like dehydration, you need rest, bro. Eat,' Wade says smiling under his beard.

Tom sits, musing at the man on the floor for a moment.

'The paintings were the end of everything, the terminus of consciousness and existence of everything for me. I had consciously experienced it, I know that's impossible and I know its probably bullshit but I did feel something and that counts' Tom says and then takes a bite of bread soft with sauce and swallows nearly instantly.

'There is no afterlife, Wade and there is no God, this is all there is. Theres no plan for everything, for us, for the lot of it and thats why shit like this is happening, because we all have our own different plans, different ideas about the future. You don't have to believe me, it doesn't matter if you do, but I know you know. Everybody does.'

Wade is spooning heaped deliveries of the food into his mouth, looking over his fist as he listens.

'Why would those who claim to be so sure in the afterlife spend their whole lives desperately avoiding death, wearing warm clothes during the cold, eating food, going to the doctors, calling an ambulance, crying at the deathbed of their friends, all the time worried about the end. Why not just go outside naked into the cold and accept death with a smile? We do know and we have all along. But it only dawns on us in our final moments. I heard you last night. You brought me back, I had given up.'

Wade stops eating, looks at him and ponders what he has said.

'Paintings' He did a small nod during the mouthful 'Then why was you calling for your misses'

She came crashing into his mind with the force of a hydrogen bomb. He missed her to the point it set fire to his eyes and throat. He felt like every organ in his body was crying and squeezing against each other. He sits there nodding slowly; his eyes hypnotised by the bread in his hand, with the first tear rolling down his ravaged face. His shaking stops.

'I don't know why we are being pulled off the ground but something is happening, something this world hasn't seen before' Wade says.

They both finish their meals, eat the rest of the food in the pot, then drink a lot of water. The injections had subsided Tom's fever and allowed him the process of digestion. As the warm food fills his stomach, he can feel his strength kindling. Wade gets up and checks outside the front door and sees the first evidence of daylight lighting up the deep grey sky; the rain picking up again, thrashing all around.

Caliphate

'Here comes the daylight. I'm gonna take him outside…' The words from Wade slur and echo in Tom's mind as he sinks into the bed and drifts into a deep sleep, still holding his spoon.

7

He sleeps for a long time, at least it feels like a long time. He opens his eyes slowly and panics. He has no idea where he is or what has happened in the last few days. He just stays still and looks around the room, the drumming of the rain still on the roof, his stomach desperate for food. He focuses. A woman is lying on a bed across the room under a blanket, looking straight back at him. Her face bloody and her eyes open. She just stares straight back unflinching, still and silent under the blanket. He is stunned, he doesn't want to move an inch in case she thinks he is dead, in which case he wants her to remain thinking that. She is soaking wet and her hair is muddy and matted and all over the pillow in twisted knots. She has a spilt down the front of her nose and her eyebrows that had stopped bleeding.

'Who are you?' he says after resisting the urge to stay silent. His voice is croaky and ill toned. He has seen her before not too long ago, he is sure of it.

She just stares back, head silent on the wet bloody pillow. His situation comes back in fragments: the stove, the door, the TV. How long has he been asleep? Why is he asleep? Wade.

He sits up slowly and realises the dog is sleeping by his feet and he is careful not to wake her, his eyes never leaving the girl. He thinks she is a girl because he can see through the blood and cuts her small lips and smooth skin. Her brown iris with perfectly white sclera tracking his every movement.

'What happened to you? Where's Wade?' he says. He assumes Wade knows who she is otherwise she would've been dead before she could open the front door.

Nothing, mute as space. She looks as though she is looking at a monster that can't see her through a crack in the wall. He swings his legs off the bed and sits up. He is semi dry, and he has no boots on. He is barefoot and his feet look white and heavily wrinkled. His toenails are black and he has fresh zinc oxide tape around his ankles. He looks over to the stove and sees his socks hanging off a nail above it and his boots propped up against it. His belt kit and daysack are next to the bed and his rifle is laid on top. He reaches down and grabs the pistol, and slowly draws it out and holds it on her. Who is she? Is she one of them? The confusion scurrying for answers.

'Who are you? Where's Wade?' he finally says.

He stands up and walks to the stove, his knee hurting a lot, feeling like some kind of sand in the joint crunching with every step. He takes his socks off the nail, dry as bone, and grabs his boots, not dry but not waterlogged. His keeps his vision on the girl as much as he can. He sits on the bed next to the cooker and puts the pistol down.

'I'm going to put my boots on,' he says to her. The same stare.

He slides his feet into the warm socks – it feels wonderful – then slides his feet into the boots; they feel as though they had shrunk. They go in with a squeeze and it hurts his ankles and heels pushing them in. Once he's done them up, he rolls up his trouser-leg and checks his left knee. The map is gone and a SAM Splint has been moulded around his knee, allowing it enough bend to walk but keeping it relatively rigid. It is held on by more zinc tape. He starts to panic. Where is Wade and why has he left him? He stands up and picks up his belt kit, puts it on and picks up the rifle.

Caliphate

'I'm going outside, okay, outside,' he says, pointing to the door.

He makes his way over to the door, the girl tracking him, unlocks the bolt and slowly opens the door, peering out of the crack. Dull daylight, the grey clouds still looming overhead and the rain cascading down all around. He can see everywhere. The small track leading to the road and the stinking trash everywhere with plots of steam scattered around, the piles of trash breathing their toxic breath. The road no more than three hundred metres away. At the end of the road is a large old billboard sign with a faded cigarette manufacturer advertisement. He could just make out 'Gauloises' written across the plastic canvas. Attached to the bottom of the sign are four ropes. He looks through the rain at the bodies for a few moments and feels the rage boil inside him, the rage for the whole of humanity contained inside him. An old man and woman hang in their individual nooses, slowly swinging in the bitter wind, arms taut and rigid, feet tied together and clothes flapping. Four children next to them, hanging, one noose around two of their small necks. They gently swing in pairs, back to back from the billboard like sacks of rice. Their small faces expressionless and empty. A yellow box car with suitcases on the roof parked next to the sign with some spray-paint on the windscreen. A warning to people on the road. Too close to the road to cut them down.

Caliphate

He turns and looks at the girl in the bed and goes over to her and kneels down. His throat tight and his eyes trembling. He smoothes her hair back and she stares at him. The sight of the hanging immediately draws him to her, it is clear she needs them and he knows this immediately as the feeling of compassion pours over him.

'I'm so sorry,' he says 'You have to run from here, far away, okay? I have to go and find Wade, I'll be back shortly.'

A single tear falls from her eye and travels down her broken nose and stops; she doesn't blink once.

He goes back to the door and only just realises the truck is gone and he grows suddenly more alert. He walks out and around the building and looks to the east and sees the truck static in flooded ground among the now half-submerged heads.

Wade is standing there with his rifle and the man with his orange shirt is digging around one of the heads. Tom watches in the rain. The man drops the shovel and kneels down and starts to pull the woman out of the ground and falls on to his back, the woman landing in his lap motionless. Tom can hear nothing from this distance – it looks like a silent movie. Wade goes over and scoops up the woman and carries her through the bogging ground. Wade looks over at him, his face stern and grey, and gently slides her body into the bed of the truck, and goes over to

Caliphate

the man and grabs him by the hair, lifting him to his feet and signals with his head to get into the truck. Tom stands in the rain watching everything. They both get into the truck, Wade in the passenger seat. He hears the truck start and then it begins to turn towards the building and make its way over. The water waving from the tyres, washing across the open ground. It pulls up the slope with a short wheel-spin, flicking mud and rubbish behind it, and pulls on to the flat ground next to him. Wade throws open the door and looks at Tom.

'Deal with this motherfucker right now,' Wade says, as he moves to the bed of the truck.

Tom turns his head straight to the man slumped in the driver's seat. His face pulverised.

'Get out of the fucking truck,' he says as he draws out his pistol.

The man switches off the truck, sobbing, opens the door and steps out, slams the door shut and comes around the front, limping, his hands above his head.

Tom stares at him as he goes into the building and follows him in. He goes back to the place where he was zip tied up and kneels down with his hands on his head, looking at Tom through his broken face. The girl in the bed pulls the blanket over her head. Tom glances at her then back at the man.

Caliphate

Wade kicks open the door and lies the woman's body on the floor in the middle of the room, throws his rifle on to the bed, drops to his knees, then tilts her head back and leans down and puts his ear to her mouth. He is drenched, beads of water running off his curly hair and beard on to the woman's face. His boots are caked in mud and his hands are shaking. He stays there for a few seconds and then begins mouth to mouth. Blowing hard into her lungs, watching her chest rise and then re-turning his ear. Nothing. He moves to her chest and begins CPR, his face staring at the woman dead on the floor. He does this for a while. Tom watches the man staring at Wade.

'She's dead, mate,' Tom says.

Wade continues. Robotic.

'She's dead'

Tom watches as Wade stands straight up and reaches into his pocket and pulls out a phone and tosses it at him, as he storms past and nods to the man on the floor. He switches on the phone and looks for the video folder. He finds it; he will wish he hadn't.

He scrolls using the touchscreen, to the first video and clicks and waits for it to load. His heart stops. Children screaming and gargling and men chanting – the sound makes him immediately turn the phone off. He puts the phone in his pocket and stands up, grabbing the man and

Caliphate

yanking him to his feet. Wade's grey face expressionless as he loads a pot filled with water and eggs on the stove.

'Allahu Akhbar, Allahu Akhbar…' The man says hurriedly and frantically as he is dragged up.

Tom head-butts him straight in the nose and the man falls to his knees but is dragged straight back up before his knees can touch the floor. He grabs the man's hair and grabs his rifle, and tows the man outside. Wade, the woman and the dog watch him as he kicks open the door. He throws him to the front of the jeep and the man slams into the wet mud with a slap. Tom walks over to the driver's door and opens it, leans in and opens the bonnet using the catch under the steering wheel. The man jumps up and begins to run to the road and Tom draws up his rifle and steadies it on the man's legs and fires two rounds; loud thumps dulled by the pouring rain. The first one misses, striking the mud in-between his legs. The second cracks through his thigh and the man crumples to the floor silently as if he ran into a step that tripped him. Tom walks over, glancing across to the hanging bodies and then back to the man blowing into the dirt, mumbling. He picks him up by the armpits and dragged him over to the truck, his leg beginning to hurt with the odd walking of carrying someone. He throws him to the floor again and glances inside the building and sees Wade and the woman staring at him. He reaches under the bonnet and feels for the release catch, tugging it so the bonnet clunks open. He lifts the man by his hair on to the ram bar and holds him there. He is panting, his lips fluttering with every breath. His leg bleeding with blood pooling on the wet ground trickling from the bottom of his trouser-leg. His arms desperately grabbing Tom's arms who snatches them away and throws them off. Tom throws up the bonnet and holds it up with his bad arm and the pain shoots through his elbow. He tows the man up by the scruff of his shirt and places his head on the bonnet frame, where the bonnet meets the chassis and holds his head there. He stares into the man's uneven eyes, his face bloody and torn, with missing front teeth.

'God is not great.' he hisses at him, and slams the bonnet down on the man's head with a mighty crash. The man lets out a high-pitched squeal and his arms flay in the air, slapping Tom, who raises the bonnet again and brings it down harder, with all his strength. A prominent crack of the man's skull shattering. He raises the bonnet and the man's head is dented and his ear is hanging off by a thread. His eyes roll back in his head and his mouth judders. He brings the bonnet down again, this time there's just the sound of metal.

Some part of Tom is satisfied with this method of dispatch; a necessary statement, he briefly thinks; a statement he only wishes the man's companions could have witnessed. The man's lifeless body slides

Caliphate

off the car into the mud. His body lying there in the blood around his leg and head, both legs tucked behind him like some yoga position. His head hideously deformed.

He drags the man's limp body to the wall and sits him up against it and stares at him in the rain. Just the sound of the muffled generator around the back, and rain on the iron sheeting.

He turns and takes a quick glance at the road – nothing. Just the piles of trash and the gently swinging bodies hanging from the billboard sign; rain and wind howling over the ruined land. Chilling.

He shoots the man in the top of the head and goes back inside and closes the door.

He does not seek approval from Wade; he knows Wade cared nothing for the man and his cruel demise. And he did not do it for the girl on the bed as some medieval justice. We are all products of our environment, but some products just can't be deprogrammed. This time the execution had to be just so, because the three of them needed to know that the man spent his last few moments alive in unimaginable pain. They would settle for no other deal.

We have our monsters and they have theirs. Months among the ruins of humanity and death turn the riders into savages. Relentless and merciless, neither notices it in the other. It becomes a standard. Emotionless to

Caliphate

it. But they remember who is innocent and who is guilty. In a world where the gamblers of God roam, giving the world no choice but death, a certain kind of person needs to be deployed in reaction. Dark for dark. Fire with fire, indiscriminate fire versus just fire. There is no other way; they will destroy all before they listen.

They all sat in silence for a long time. Wade boiling eggs and the woman still and motionless.

'How long have I been out?' Tom says, as he ruffles the dog's head. She laps his hand and gently bites it with a little growl.

'Since about seven this morning,' Wade says. Tom looks at his watch; it's approaching four in the afternoon. There is a silence for a minute.

'Thank you, mate… I owe you everything,' Tom says.

'Don't sweat it, man, the truck's ready to go. How you feeling? We've got just under half a can of gas and I've loaded the food. We should move some time tonight though – we *are* pushing our luck.'

'Wade……thank you'

Wade takes a breath, his big chest rises and slowly sinks in. His eyes flicked to different parts of the room every half a second, comfortable with no permanent sight, lost.

Caliphate

'I don't wanna die out here, man' Wade says quietly across to him

They both can't look at each other for a moment.

'Do you want to get some shut-eye? I'm feeling pretty good…. what about the TV?' Tom eases back in.

'I've tried it, but there's just one channel. It's a news channel but I couldn't understand it. The guy whose head you just smashed like a melon was rambling about God revealing himself.'

Tom stands up and walks past the girl, who is now asleep, and switches on the TV. It flicks to life and is heavily distorted, but he can make out it was a news channel. He leans around the back and wiggles the antenna cable in its port and the screen flicks and jumps, but no improvement. He stands back and checks it out.

'I'm gonna go and check the antenna outside.'

'Roger,' Wade says.

He goes outside and walks around the back of the building, the cold wind forcing its way down his jacket. He stands on the generator and peers over on to the roof and reaches for the dish. He pulls it towards him and turns it slowly. He's there for about a minute when Wade shouts through the window.

'That's good, leave it there. You better come and see this.'

Caliphate

He goes back inside and closes the door. Wade is stood with his arms crossed, looking intensely at the screen.

'SETI? Any idea what that means? It's the only English on there,' Wade says.

The screen is fuzzy with slight static. No sound but a workable picture. A shot of a field – somewhere in the U.S perhaps, filled with huge satellites pointing to the sky – is on a loop, with Arabic writing across the bottom; the letters SETI and the numbers 438 written among the Arabic. Tom looks for a moment, trying to decipher the message. Then it dawns on him with the coldness of the wind outside, his hairs on end.

'Search for Extra-Terrestrial Intelligence,' Tom says, in a low tone.

Wade looks at him. His eyes look as though he is piecing something together in his mind.

'I thought them programmes got shut down after the Washington nuke,' he says.

'I guess not,' Tom says.

Then the radio crackles and fuzzes then stops. They both turn to look at it and then it crackles again and they can hear someone speaking. It's very quiet, maybe due to the distance, but then the volume increases and they can hear it clearly. Someone speaking in Arabic, shout-

Caliphate

ing. They stand, listening for a moment. Ears straining and hunting for familiar words. Neither understands the language.

'They're coming,' says the woman in the bed. Her bloody face and eyes shifting between them.

8

Wade spins his head to her. 'How far?'

'I don't know.'

'Let's go – now,' Tom says, looking at Wade.

They both grab their kit and throw it on. Tom is still hungry and begins shovelling bread into his mouth while getting his kit.

'I knew we should have moved earlier, I knew it,' Wade says as he checks the magazine on his weapon. Tom goes to the door and un-locks it and opens it slightly and peers out over the bed of the truck. Blood streaks in the water across the bed and empty cases littered all around. Wade has strapped the crates of water into the back with the can of fuel.

The sun is setting on the horizon and the day looks more grey than before. The cold rain still thrashing down everywhere. He turns and sees Wade stuffing the boiled eggs into a plastic bag by the stove. The girl looks back at Tom.

'Please… don't leave me,' she says in a small voice. Her face filthy and bloody but her eyes shining through with a thousand pleads.

He contemplates her, trying not to let his emotion numb his survival. He has no idea who she is and what she has done before now, but the thought doesn't complain. Though strangers as they are, what is clear is her current situation and if he ignores that, he is no human. He looks back towards the road, headlights coming from the east a few miles away, maybe two.

'Here they come, mate, here they fucking come. Keys! Gimme the keys,' Tom shouts.

He swings open the door and opens the passenger side of the truck, looks around and sees Wade throw the keys at him. He catches them and leans over the seat and stuffs them into the ignition and turns on the engine. He pushes himself back out and sticks his head through the door and looks at the dog with her ears pricked up, looking at him with wide eyes.

Caliphate

'Lucy, come on. In the truck,' he nods over his shoulder and points at the door.

She springs up instantly and runs across the room and hops into the truck. He looks back at the woman. Food and water the driving factor for leaving her. You know what they will do to her when they get here, are you prepared to do that to her? To be in control of her destiny and to choose to throw her back into the pit where the dogs lie hungry and waiting. Is there a being in you so careless, so hideously selfish? The thought punishes him for such neglect and he cowers as it does.

Tom hurries over to the woman.

'Can you walk?' he says coldly as he checks his weapons.

'Yes, I think so.' Her eyes are wrapped in anxiety as she awaits their decision.

Wade throws one of the beds upside down and grabs a pair of old military boots and the AK-47 in the basket and trots past Tom, who is helping the woman up, and throws them in the truck. Tom gets the woman up and outside, her legs still slightly unworkable from being buried, but she can just about walk. She sees the vehicles in the distance and starts to cry. She is still wrapped in the blanket shaking, with her black burka, cov-ered in mud, underneath. She is thin and fragile and Tom can feel that as he helps her up. Wade is next to the man's body against the wall, taking the pin out of a grenade and holding the fly-off lever down. He throws the man's body face down into the dirt and rolls the body over slightly and places the grenade between the body and the dirt so that it holds on the fly-off lever.

Tom climbs in the vehicle with the woman and dog.

'Come on! Come on!' he says as he slams the door.

Wade gently lowers the man's body down on to the grenade and slowly moves his hands away and stands up looking over to the approaching vehicles, which were maybe a mile away. Still a good distance thanks to the potholes – they could only see their headlights through the rain.

Wade climbs in the driver's seat and slams the door. He reverses the vehicle around so it is facing towards the road and speeds off down the track towards the junction, kicking up dirt over the dead man on the floor.

'Keep the lights off' Wade says looking through the hole in the windscreen, the wind whistling through.

'How can you be so sure they don't know?' Tom says as he winds down his window and pulls up his rifle.

'I'm not, but we did kill everyone.'

Caliphate

Tom looks at the woman and she looks back, her face full of terror at the thought of being buried again. He turns and looks through the back window and looks up the road as Wade pulls out of the junction and heads west along the ruined road. The vehicles in the distance are closing but he can't see them that well because of the rain, and he hopes vice versa. Tom picks up the AK-47 and checks the magazine and a round is chambered, and places the M4 on the dash. The dog is between him and the woman, looking everywhere, and he puts his hand on her head. His vision is glued to the back window watching every movement of the vehicles slowly coming down the road. The rain crashing everywhere, seeping through the cracks of the shattered windscreen.

'How we looking?' Wade says, watching everything in front. Squinting against thin rain blasting in through the hole.

'You'll know when it's looking bad,' he says holding on to the passenger side of the dash, twisted in the chair looking back. The vehicles approach the junction, he can see four, all vehicles with roofs. A right indicator, pulsing orange, through the rain. The first vehicle turns up the track to the building, then the second. He swallows hard and his nerves start twitching. The third approaches and turns right down the track, by now the first vehicle is at the building and he can just about see them dismounting. He flicks his eyes back to the last vehicle. 'Come on,' he whispers to him-

Caliphate

self. The fourth vehicle drives past the junction, and is heading towards them.

'Here we go,' Tom says as he swings around with the AK to the passenger window. He looks at the woman.

'You are going to have to fight, there is no other way,' he says, his face scabbed and filthy and long wet hair matted swept back. His hazel eyes look like the last thing alive in his battered body. He pulls out the slack of the seat-belt until it stops, hooks his right arm through it, doubles the slack over his shoulder and manoeuvres his top half through the open window, pulling the AK into his shoulder. The seat-belt tight, holding him rigid to the car, keeping him steady. He hangs out of the window with the elements like a wind tunnel against his back. His hair flying everywhere, his hood flapping against the back of his head. His legs are stiff against the seat and his body follows the vehicles shudders and bounces as it rumbles across the rough road. He takes off the safety catch and trains the rifle sights on the windscreen of the car in the distance. It is still far away and he couldn't see it too well, could just make out the headlights through the rain. And then there is an explosion from the building.

A small thump echoes across the area and he locks his gaze straight to the building which is now just a slight smudge in the wall of rain. A plume of black smoke, no bigger than a small car. They know now, it is a matter of minutes before they come hurtling down the road in pursuit. He swallows hard and clenches his teeth, the smooth wooden grip of the weapon in his hand and the inescapable miasma of the landfill. Out of the corner of his eye he can see the woman watching him with a face stretched with terror. He can hear nothing from this distance but he can just about make out some figures scatter from the area.

'Was that what I think it was?' Wade shouts.

'Yep', Tom shouts through the wind and rain, eyes still on the building. Are you prepared to watch her die in front of you? Hear Wade's ghastly bellows as he has his throat sawn open and his head twisted off? His body tightens and he grabs the magazine once more to make sure it is on tight.

He looks back at the car and sees it has stopped and is turning in the road. It does a U-turn, wheels kicking up mud as it pulls away from the muddy edge of the road. He lowers the rifle and watches it take off back towards the junction. He pulls himself back in through the window and pulls the seat-belt off his arm and holds the AK in his lap.

'Don't get comfy,' he says.

The road is saturated and rubbish parallels it for miles. Wisps of steam emitted from scattered piles of waste create a vile fog and black bags blow

Caliphate

through the air in the wind, sometimes sticking to the windows and doors before the gale winds move them along. The holes in the road are signified now as puddles, making it difficult to determine their depth. Wade navigates the truck around the worst of them, meandering around the road.

They pass a car at the side of the road on its roof with the rear window smashed and a few suitcases sprawled behind it in the trash partially sunk in a black pool. The fresh swerving tracks in the roadside mud show it doesn't look like it has been there long. A few miles further, a man and a woman crucified on some makeshift crosses made from scaffolding on the side of the road, next to each other. The contraptions tilting at the weight in the wet ground, the grey light silhouetting them. Sacrifices to the land of decay. Absolute misery. Signs around their necks with some painted slogan badly written on the black wooden board. Bound naked, wire running around their arms and legs and necks tight to slash the skin. Their bloodied heads cocked to the side like some depressed statue. They hang there against the backdrop of endless trash and rain in the nearly dark sky, water pouring off their extremities and hair. They all stare as they pass them. As they did, the crucified man on his cross sinks slightly and the whole structure which he is bound to falls backwards slowly as its shoring gives way, and it gently eases on to a pile of trash. The man doesn't move

Caliphate

an inch, he's just still with his head cocked. It is as if their collective stares and empathy had somehow forced the cross down. If only.

'Christians,' the woman said, gently and quietly. Too common a sight for surprise.

They come to a junction on the freeway with a small road cutting off to the left and a road sign that is badly mangled and unreadable. Wade pulls over and Tom studies the map.

'We should get off here and hang off the motorway for a while. If there's gonna be activity, it's gonna be on the freeway.' He looks up to Wade for approval.

'What about gas?'

Tom ponders this for a moment. 'The road handrails this freeway and we can join it again just before Ar Rutba, maybe thirty miles down, it's not too far out of our way.'

Wade looks a bit uneasy with the decision. He wants to punch straight down the freeway to the border but Tom answers this as if he can read his mind.

'They're coming, mate. They're gonna see we've been at that checkpoint and come hammering down the road in them twin turbo V8's. I just think we should take them off the scent for a few miles.'

Caliphate

Neither of them looks at the woman and they speak as if she isn't there, but she is looking at Wade.

Wade nods a few times as if slowly building the confidence to approve and then pulls off down the slip road.

It is now dark and Wade slows down as the rain in the head-lights makes vision difficult. It is colder and the heating on full blast couldn't quite cut it.

'What's your name?' Tom says to the woman as she sits with the dog on her lap. He is peeling some boiled eggs.

'Luna,' she says. Tom recognises a hint of German in her ac-cent; maybe she was an immigrant during the Capitulations.

'Luna…' Wade says, quietly to himself.

'I'm sorry about your family, Luna. We need to know we can trust you, okay? We're not going to hurt you, it's important you know that. Do you know that?' Tom says, handing a peeled egg to Wade across her lap. He takes it without taking his eyes off the road and pushes it into his mouth.

'Yes.'

'But we need to know we can we trust you. Can we?' Tom says.

'Yes,' she says, looking at him.

Caliphate

'How do we know?' Wade says. She turns to Wade and then back to Tom, her eyes beginning to glisten with tears.

'Yes, yes… please, you can trust me.'

Tom's face, emotionless as stone, looks back at her. He peels another egg.

'I'll bury you. Do you understand what I'm saying, Luna? We'll stop the car and I will shoot you. Okay, I don't want to, but we need to know we can trust you.' He wants truth from her, and he has to cut through to her fear of the mystery of who they are to summon it – they don't know her and her allegiances, and callousness is what he uses to separate him from his altruist side for a moment.

She is crying silently, with the blanket pulled around her head and shoulders. Tears roll down her bruised cheeks. She is shaking.

'How can we trust you, Luna?' He puts down the egg and draws out his pistol and holds it by his side.

'Please please please! I… am good! I am a good person!' Her head darts from Wade to Tom. 'I don't want to do anything. You must believe me. The people in space! They have talked to us. We know now! Please. My family and I saw the news. You have spoken to the people in space, we believe you!' She spoke with a light voice in broken english.

Caliphate

Wade looks at Tom and back to the road. Tom's eyes are still on Luna with the pistol in his hand.

'There are others, hundreds! Thousands of us. We're leaving! You understand? We are going to the west. My family and I, we were leaving but they stopped us and killed my brothers and sisters and parents! You saw them! They don't believe any more. I don't believe!'

She is sobbing uncontrollably, tears streaming down her face, her hands under her chin as if guarding herself from something. Her eyes give the evidence Tom desires and he holsters the pistol. He figures he had put the point across as brutally and quickly as possible. He didn't want to do this after what she had been through and it was clear in his eyes as they gingerly moved back to the road, but it was important she knew the policy, for all their sake.

'The people in space?' Wade says, half smiling, his hands and lap wet from the rain coming through the hole in the windscreen. He glances at Tom, then the woman, then back to the road. He navigates around a huge hole filled with water in the road and then back on to the flats.

She looks at them both. Confused as if she isn't clear in what she says. 'Yes yes! The people in space!' she says, shaking. Still crying. 'You know?' She stares at Tom.

Caliphate

'No, we don't know. What are you talking about?' Wade says.

'Luna, carefully now, remember what I said. What are you talking about?' Tom says, staring at her more intensely now.

Her head fixes on Tom, her pupils chasing his every eye
movement, giving him no room to look away.

'You don't know?' she says, her face wide with shock.

'Jesus,' Wade says under his breath.

Tom's back goes cold. He changes his gaze to Wade. Wade
looks at him and their eyes meet with a look that neither has seen in the
other before.

'You don't know,' she says flatly, her mouth slightly open with
shock.

Tom is in a daze looking out of the passenger window. She has
delivered a blow they were both unprepared for. There is a long silence
between them all. One does not simply understand such information.
There is a period of instant consciousness-raising that takes place and the
information has to filter through everything you have ever learnt. Part of
him doesn't believe her. He thinks about the TV and SETI. Something is
happening and he is certain about that and there is enough evidence to
suggest so. The operation has been halted before the end date and that

had swung him slightly. Why would they pull us off the ground, there is still

a threat, he thinks. Maybe not everyone believes. To some it will be God,

to some it will be unity and to others it will be a conspiracy. They had been

in the desert a long time and to them the world is as it was when they left,

shut down and dug in, waiting for someone to make the first move. Why

hadn't Zero told them? Because they didn't want them distracted, he an-

swers himself again. His mind an ocean of thought and he still doesn't

quite believe her but he fantasises about the prospect. Religion refuted

and in pandemonium, societies in mental turmoil and books burning in

their tens of thousands. Old primitive quarrels stopped in their tracks and

turned instantly to dust. Demagogues silent and local differences mean-

ingless. The final freedom of humanity. The world paused in unison look-

ing to the sky all sharing the same thought like a flock of hummingbirds,

hovering together and each bird's colour meaningless. No words needed,

but a single thought like a laser running through all of humanity's con-

sciousness; others.

It is pitch black outside and they stop on the side of the road in front of an

old sign. The headlamps light the sign, bent up at the edges with scattered

bullet holes punched through, some hastily spray-painted writing across it

and the name of the approaching town in white printed letters, Ar Rutba,

Caliphate

11m, on the faded blue background. The last town before the Syrian border.

Tom sits studying Wade's map in his lap with his torch in his mouth. The engine rumbling and the rain clapping away over the metal roof.

'What are our options?' Wade says.

'We can flank the town to the north.' He brings his head closer to the map. 'The highway runs parallel a few miles down the road and we can get back on there – we may have to do a little cross-country,' Tom says, tracing the roads with his dirty finger.

'Can't we go through the town?' Luna says.

'No, no way, man. We don't know what condition it's in,' Wade says. He goes to say something else then stops and just stares at the sign.

'My father said it was okay,' Luna says gently.

'Well, your father may be wrong, and I'm not taking chances right now. Chance means luck and we haven't had much of that,' Wade says.

'We have been lucky.' She says.

'Well that depends on your definition of luck. Just because we're not dead, doesn't mean we've been lucky.'

Caliphate

'Another five miles and we'll peel off on to a small track, keep an eye out for it, that'll take us around the town and we'll have to cross-country from there a few miles down that road and make a surprise entrance on to the freeway,' Tom says, still looking at the map. 'We stay away from the town.'

'That highway, I dunno, man. If this exodus is as she says it is, that road's gonna be packed with refugees, and they'll be swarming.'

'We have to. We get stuck off the road and we're walking again. We use the highway for as long as we can, if we can, then push into the desert and try and make comms,' Tom says, folding the map into a manageable size. 'We use the night… we're not that far. How we looking for fuel?'

'About half a tank,' Wade says, squinting his eyes at the dash.

'We're not that far,' he says, looking out of the window, musing. He turns to them. 'If what you're saying is true, Luna, I just… I dunno, I just need to see it.'

Wade pulls slowly back on to the road and the sign disappears into the night. The lights illuminate the saturated road and the trash. They eat the rest of the eggs with some of the flatbread and after a while Wade begins to fall asleep at the wheel so they stop the truck in the middle of the road and swap. Tom could now see how much concentration is demanded

Caliphate

to drive a vehicle with a smashed windscreen with a small aperture at night. It was a wonder Wade had managed to drive for this long. No sooner has Wade got into the passenger seat, he's asleep with the dog in his lap with his head and enormous bob of black curls head propped against the door. Luna is awake, peering out of the passenger window into the darkness.

'How old are you?' Tom says.

'Seventeen,' she says, still looking through the window.

Tom grips the steering wheel hard. The rage once again courses through his veins like molten metal. He goes to say something then stops himself.

'Madness,' he mutters under his breath. He lets the rage settle for a moment.

'Who are you? Why are you here?' She says, peering through her hair at him.

'That man back at the building is why we are here. You should put them boots on,' he says. 'You never know when we might need to run.'

'Are there lots of you, like, out there?'

That cold desert air combing the ruined wastelands, endless rain far into the distance, for hundreds of miles, beyond sight where no

Caliphate

man should lurk. He casts himself into the blackness, into the marooned, silently watching desert and wonders about the rest.

'Just me and him,' he says as he checks the mirrors.

She looks around the floor and finds the boots. They are too big but she has no shoes. She rips a hole in the seat and pulls out some handfuls of foam and pushes them into the boot, packing out the toe end.

'Where were you going?' He says.

'Anywhere. We, I have family in Germany and we were going to try and get to there. We had all our money and were going to buy our way out or something… somehow. There wasn't really a plan, just drive as far as we could to escape. No one had any plans. West, everyone said, go west.'

Tom peers through the windscreen, a dusting of raindrops coming through on to his hands.

'You know you won't get there, don't you?'

'Things have changed now…'

He stares through the hole in the window screen and into the thin road that cuts through the swamps of waste. The hazy light in the rain. The future.

There is silence for a while. He can't imagine how much trauma she has witnessed in the last few days. Buried to her neck and pelted with

Caliphate

stones until the edge of death. She is innocent and exposed. Every time she speaks, every piece of information he gathers about her, only makes it harder.

'How did you survive?' he says.

'They said the rain would drown me and then they just walked off,' she says as if it was obvious. She is looking at the boots. How much damage has been done to her, he thinks. How much can a seventeen-year-old girl take before she becomes a husk, a wandering wreck searching for death?

'Your friend?' she says as she looks at Wade sleeping. Then her eyes trickle back to the dog in his lap. 'I thought he was an angel.'

Tom smiles. 'An angel!' Gently he laughs though his nose and cocks his head, nodding in some form of mocking agreement as he thinks of Wade and the man back at the building.

But the smile fades and his face drops back to its flat state as he remembers hearing Wade on the radio for the first time, hearing his voice as he ventured on to the cusp of death.

'An angel.' He gently nodded.

Tom slows the vehicle and navigates around a discarded wheel from some truck that is lying flat in the road. Tyre shredded to ribbons.

Caliphate

'It was my father's choice to leave Munich, to take me out of university,' she finally says. 'Other families thought it would be safer here, you know, with the bombings and everything.'

The rain thrashes all over and comes through the aperture in the windscreen. They have to talk louder than normal because of the constant drum of the assaulting downpour. She strokes the dog and he watches the road.

'This is no place for a woman,' she says.

He glances at her. Her lips trembling and eyes glazed, she brings her hand to her mouth to hide some of the approaching anguish. But in the end she pulls down her hand and Tom can see her face. Her eyes shift around in their sockets swollen with tears and her throat swallows frantically, defending her expression against the surge of melancholy.

'For anything,' she adds gently.

He reaches over and gently takes her small hand by the fingers gently and holds them. She looks at him. Her face needs stitches on each eyebrow and on the corner of her forehead. He feels how cold her hands are. He feels.

'I'm sorry we couldn't help your family,' he says.

She just stares at the dog, and he puts her hand down.

Caliphate

'I heard you,' she says, rubbing the tears from her eyes. 'I heard you on the radio that night and then the light went up and I saw you.'

He glances at her then returns his gaze to the hole in the screen.

'You were sat down and you were sick. I could hear you crying and stuff while you sat there. I didn't know what you were but I could hear you.'

He thinks back and remembers the faces of the women when the flare went up. The chaos of it. Hideously senseless, defining evil. The moment that flare cracked in the sky he saw the absolute desperation of man, how utterly terrified we can be of death and what we will do when we think God is watching.

'I wasn't doing too well, I'm still not,' he says.

'I heard what you said on the radio. Is it true?'

He swallows and runs his fingers through his hair, brushing it out of his eyes. He takes a few seconds to prepare his answer. He didn't really know how to explain it to himself.

'It's true to me.' He wipes his mouth. 'I know that I will die and be met with nothingness. It's just a case of realising it, admitting it.' He squints to study some detail of the road, 'Right there in that spot, I died

Caliphate

and saw what comes next and it was terrifying.' He looks at her. 'But in that moment I felt something… everything about life became precious.'

She is looking at him with her hands under her armpits. Her hair still mostly wet.

'I see' she says.

He looks at her again. 'Too precious to pretend there's more.'

The headlights shine on the road and it's slow going. Wade is fast asleep and his body is limp so as the truck hits the bumps, his head rolls around. After a while she speaks again but a change in her tone reflects a shift in motivation, a determination to do something has been aroused. She ties up the bootlaces, pulling them tight and doubling them around the back of the boot.

'That man you killed, he was the one who buried me and killed my family.'

He doesn't look at her. 'I know.'

Caliphate

9

They begin to see the lights of the outskirts of the town. Small white blobs in the rain twinkling like stars. They are already closer than he liked. He slows down further still and approaches slowly until they find the track – he would have missed it if the girl hadn't spotted some tyre tracks leading off on to it. He turns and takes it and there is a small slope down the road bank then the road begins. Trash everywhere blowing in the gale. The smell is suffocating, forcing them to breathe through their mouths to avoid it. The track is a lot worse than the road and Tom carefully fords the deep gorges and holes filled with the black water. They can still see the lights from the town on their left, moodily floating in the darkness like a band of lost ghosts. Tom wants to turn the headlights off but it would end with them stuck in one of the hundreds of quagmires of rot. They begin to hear something in the night over the engine, some kind of dull blurring noise, an unrecognisable hum. They start to see some kind of wall in the distance, maybe the ramp to some other road that hadn't been mapped. There isn't enough moonlight to silhouette it but something from what seems to be behind it is highlighting it. After a while they begin to realise what it is, a man-made mound stretching along the horizon. He tries to think what purpose it serves but he could think of none, maybe a perimeter of the town. They stop in front of it and the headlights light up the gradual slope and they slowly drive up and crest, come over the top and can see the highway in the distance. He stops the truck at the top of the slope and looks in disbelief.

'Wake him up,'

She nudges him with her elbow a few times and he startles awake and looks at them stunned.

'What's going on, where are we?' Wade says, head shifting everywhere. It takes him a few seconds to understand what the dog was in his lap.

Tom gets out of the vehicle slowly, unflinching against the rain. Eyes locked on the freeway. Spellbound. All thoughts drop out leaving him

Caliphate

floating in inertia, the mud squashed underfoot and the cold wind fuming in from the flank with its icy promise. The rain casts at him in bursts as if it is trying to awaken him. His hand grips the cold metal of the top of the door and his lips separate, allowing the news to flow through every opening and then finally a shift in thought takes place like the dropping of a pebble in a still lake. Luna was right.

Thousands of vehicle headlights and brake lights in a line as far as they could see light up the night like a giant runway. Some moving and some static. Tracer bullets fly off in every direction towards the west of the line, disappearing into the night. They can hear the distant crackle of gunfire everywhere. The fighters of the Caliphate desperate to cage the apostates of the new zeitgeist. The exodus fighting their way through the hastily formed checkpoints to stop the movement. Headlights moving around the vehicles that have the dead slumped over the steering wheel. Vehicles of every kind driving around each other on and off the road, some turning back heading east on the flooded sides of the road and some stuck. Those without four-wheel drive were sticking to the tarmac and some of those with it leave the road towards the north-west across the desert, like distant fleeing lanterns. They can hear the endless dull racket of car horns and the larger engines chugging and thumping like dull bass instruments penetrating deep into the thick black night, a million-strong orchestra without a conductor. The exit from inhumanity.

'Take a look at the end of a civilisation,' he says into the truck. They can't see through the smashed screen and they get out and stands in awe as if the sun was minutes from colliding with the Earth.

'Damn,' Wade says as he puts the dog into the seat, his voice croaky from sleep.

Luna gets out the driver's side and looks.

'Do you see now?'

He pauses for a moment. Scanning along to endless vehicles screeching in the distance.

'Yes I do,' he says, a slight smile growing under his beard. 'Yes I do.'

He can feel a sort of excitement growing inside him about how home would be in response to the contact, but as the situation creeps back into his mind, he thinks about how unlikely it is that anyone will come and get them. He gets back in the truck because of the rain and sits for a moment to allow the scene to etch itself into his memory. He takes out the map and starts to study the highway. There is no way around it so they would have to cross it. Driving across the desert in the rain would be trouble but they had no choice, and because of the fuel, they had to go as the crow flies. It is maybe a kilometre to the highway from their position and they could find a break in the traffic and punch through to the other side and back into the northern desert. Luna and Wade get back in and close the door.

'Straight through?' Wade says.

'Yeah, I think that's our best bet,' Tom says then looks at Luna. 'Do you want to get out when we get to the road? I can't say you'd be safer but I just think you'd have a better chance of getting out of here with them.'

She is silent for a while and stares at the dash. He says nothing further.

Wade draws his pistol and opens the window, then he removes his small Velcro US flag on his right shoulder and Tom removes his UK flag patch and they put them in their pockets. Wade puts the dog on to Luna's lap and Luna holds her. Tom punches the hole in the windscreen around the edges with the pistol barrel to give him more field of view and then pulls off. The truck tyres slip in the mud and trash then find their grip and pull away, down a short slope of the road into the landfill and trundle along. He avoids the pools of black water and piles of metal and navigates between the biggest of the piles. The stench is breath-taking and they all cover their mouths and noses. As they get closer to the road the noises grow out of a disharmony and they could understand what noise was coming from where. Truck horns and car horns, the roar of people shouting, women, men and babies screaming. Up and down the seemingly endless line is chaos. Gridlocked traffic, bumper to bumper. People on foot walking by the sides of the road holding children's hands and carrying them on their shoulders. Abandoned cars with their engines still running, trembling mountains of belongings on the roofs held on with thick ratchet straps. A man, dead on the side of the road wearing all black. His body peppered with gunshots. A small car not too far away half sunk in the mud with a woman and young boy pushing the rear and a man in the driver's seat desperately accelerating, scattering mud all over those pushing. Tom and Wade watch everything, endlessly scanning up and down the freeway. They had not seen such a site in a long time, maybe ever. How had they not seen these people? Tom thinks, how did we not see them! Alone in the desert for such a long time and now seemingly every human in the land suddenly planted on one road. He felt the isolation of the desert finally lift, finally.

The landfill begins to thin out and then the wet mud starts. Tom can't stop the truck without the vehicle sinking so he has to keep it in second gear and keep going through, straight to the road. The truck's wheels spin off the last of the trash and the wheels sink straight away, slip and then gain grip with the truck kicking mud up everywhere.

'Over to the right, right there, see it, next to the tanker,' Wade says, his head out of the window pointing to a spot on the road with a potential breakpoint.

A tanker had jack-knifed sideways in the road blocking most of the lanes apart from the outer ones, and cars were slowly feeding around the sides individually, trying to avoid the mud slopes on the edges.

'Yeah, roger,' Tom says as he pulls the wheel around, head ducked, peering through the hole. The truck slides from side to side and as they get closer they can see the road raised slightly.

They could now see people and cars, thousands of them. People crammed into any available space. Small jeeps with the beds filled with people standing up and sitting down. All with hoods up and heads down with their precious few belongings in their arms. A bus crammed so full the windows had been kicked out with people half sitting in the frames and people sitting on top on the cargo of suitcases and bags on the roof in the howling rain. All kinds of cars full of families and belongings. A small taxi stuffed with people and a plasma TV on the roof with a smashed screen, their faces carved with a determined fear, the children covering their ears, eyes wide. People on motorcycles weaving in and out of the traffic, wobbling with bags bungeed to the back. There are clothes on the side of road and as they get closer they can see they are all burkas. Every woman they see is wearing jeans or trousers and jumpers and coats, their hair in ponytails or loose blowing in the wind. This stirs him, he had seen no women not covered from head to toe for a long time, apart from the roadside slaughter back at the red point. Humanity's primitive practices lying empty, like shed chrysalises. We finally look at ourselves for who we are outside the cocoon, he thinks. Our wings struggle and eventually un-fold, the colours and patterns embroidered on the delicate fabric wave and stretch and quiver as they find movement, surprised at the freedom, we find flight. But we always knew.

The tanker is now maybe a hundred metres away and they slow down slightly. The noise from the road rattles the windows of the truck. They reach the slope that leads to the side of the road and stop the truck with the tyres out of the water. Wade holsters his pistol and grabs his rifle and opens the door. The dog goes to jump out and Luna holds her still, her little ears standing up scanning the barrage, head twitching everywhere, absorbing the unfathomable scents and noises, her little body shaking while Luna comforts her. Tom can see Wade come around the front of the truck and make his way up the slope to the slow-moving cars peeling around the tanker, his awkward steps in the ground. He reaches the top and steps in front of an old BMW and holds out his hand with his other hand on the rifle. In the windscreen he can see a middle-aged man driving and another younger man in the passenger seat with a small girl on his lap. They both stares at him as if he had two heads and Tom remembers what they are doing here and the nature of the rallies.

'Wait, please,' Wade says as he holds up his hand in a stop gesture and they stop instantly with a short skid.

'Stay low,' Tom says to Luna, watching stoically as her civilisation desperately flees.

Wade turns and looks down the hill to the truck and signals for Tom to drive up with a quick thumbs-up. The back wheels of the truck skid and it slowly snakes up the hill. The front wheels hit the tarmac, jolting the truck forward and then the back wheels skid up. Traffic horns everywhere, heavy gunfire cackling to the west, men and women shouting all around. Wade turns to open the door and a round snaps past the top of the truck and another thumps into the side of the bed.

'Shit, get in! Get in,' Tom shouts as he ducks down lower.

Wade spins around, raising the rifle and looking everywhere for someone firing, and then he notices most people are carrying weapons. A woman is on the roof of a transit van holding a pump action shotgun; a

Caliphate

teenage boy is in a passenger seat with an old Lee-Enfield bolt action rifle. Many have AK-47s and M16s but they don't seem interested in pointing them at him. He considers the two rounds a warning to move and lowers his weapon and climbs in the truck and slams the door. Tom pulls into the central reservation, where the tanker is on its side. There is a huge thick gash in the belly of the trailer, where it had collided with a concrete bollard in the middle of the central reservation. The central reservation is a slight dip and now it is a pond of thick black oil, half submerging the tyres of the truck. They drive through it to the other side of the carriageway where the cab is a smashed wreck on its side with a burst front tyre, the rubber in torn rags around the rim, in the middle of two lanes, leaving an open lane closest to the opposite edge. A small people carrier drives slowly around the cab and Tom looks into the back window. The vehicle is laden with all generations of a small family, an old woman staring out of the window, maybe a grandmother. Her face white and still as a statue, her eyes look- ing straight into Tom's. The car moves slowly past and her face changes not a millimetre, just her eyes following with her face pressed up against the window, her mouth closed. He stares back. Too inculcated, some people are too far gone from before, too committed, they believed so hard. Space dementia on Earth. Maybe we are not ready, but when would we

Caliphate

be? He wonders what messages had been received that had done such damage, what motivated such chaos.

They edge forward as the woman's people carrier passes and out of the oil pit. The tyres sticky and slippery with the earth's blood, trailing the slime behind them. They push into the open lane and a car skids to a halt as they emerge round the smashed cab and the driver in the car starts punching the horn. A man slams into the driver's side door shouting some plea to take him with them. His arms waving and banging on the door. He's wearing filthy robes that look as though they may have belonged to an imam. Now he has been shunned and excommunicated by the masses with their new knowledge. He attempts to climb in the bed and Wade leans out with the pistol over the roof through the window and holds it on the man. The man looks up and sees him and slowly climbs off the side of the truck and steps away with his arms out to the side, his feet bare. Wade stares at him. The man is soaked in the rain and shaking.

'Liar,' Wade says to him. He stares a moment longer and pulls the pistol down and slowly climbs back in through the window. Luna in the footwell with the dog, crying.

Tom pulls over the edge and on to the slope heading down into the flat desert. The racket from the road makes it hard to hear if the engine is on or not. The truck slides down the slope and hits the flat ground and they pull off. Along the edges of the road they can see headlights stuck at the bottom of the slope trying to join them and others heading out in their direction. Sporadic headlights are slowly bobbing around in the open desert heading north, stretching across the landscape like randomly placed flickering candles, wobbling on the horizon, leaving the exodus of the road to avoid the battle out of the Caliphate.

They pass alongside vehicles that are stuck deep in the mud in the hammering rain. Their headlights illuminate those buried to the wheel arches, the occupants sitting inside looking through steamed-up windows at them as they drive past. Children and women asleep in the back seats and usually a man in the front keeping watch with his weapon in his lap. They can't help them; trying to tow them out would only bury them too. They give the stuck vehicles a wide berth to stop them being jacked or ambushed. Figures begin to appear in the headlights and they pass people, sometimes groups of people banded together, slogging through the desert with heavy packs on their backs and suitcases caked in mud in their arms, walking the tracks of successful vehicles. Travellers looking for a new world. Their shattered beliefs leaving them disorientated, wandering in the desert, but their fresh minds now capable of anything. More investment in this life and not the next. All goals changed and refreshed with a new vision of reality. Their road is going to be hard but not long.

They eat some of the tomatoes and onions wrapped in the last of the bread, the grit from the unwashed vegetables crunching in their teeth. They stop the truck and Tom empties the half can of fuel into the truck's tank and throws the can back in the bed, replenishing the fuel tank to just under half. By Wade's guess, they won't have enough fuel to make it to the extraction point and will at some point have to abandon the vehicle and make the distance on foot, unless there's an abandoned vehicle they can syphon out of. Tom takes out the mobile phone and switches it on and waits for some signal to come through. Nothing does and the battery has one bar left. They should be sparing but there's no way to know they have signal unless they turn it on, so they agree to turn it on every ten kilometres and check. The rain begins to lessen and the early-morning twilight begins to emerge on the eastern horizon behind them, the grey clouds and light showing the tracks from vehicles everywhere but no one in sight. Tom switches on his radio and tries to reach someone for nearly thirty minutes but there is the same dead traffic coming through.

The terrain starts to become less flat, with high mounds and dunes emerging again. Luna is asleep in the seat with the dog and Wade is looking tiredly out the passenger window.

Caliphate

To Wade it's too late, Tom thinks – he lost everything in the first strike, on Washington. He was in Alaska, intercepting uranium smugglers when it hit. He kissed his wife and children and went to work one day and eight days later at 07.29 in the morning, while his wife was getting the children into their school uniform, they were instantly turned to ash. No warnings and no funeral, his family danced with the other hundreds of thousands in the wind as they blew through the uninhabitable streets of burnt rubble for as long as the Earth exists.

'Check it out, man,' Wade says, nodding to the one of the larger mounds.

On the top, a group of about twenty people are standing around a fire with some vehicles around them. As they get closer they could see that they are all women and they are all looking at them. Luna is now awake, looking back.

'Please, can we stop?' she says.

'No chance, we stay away from them. We don't know what their agenda is,' Tom says.

'Please, please! Look. They are free. I can talk to them, I have to,' she says like a child wanting some gift.

Caliphate

'I know, but they have rifles and I don't want another fight.'

'These are my people. They are like me, they won't shoot, please.'

'Just do it, man,' Wade says.

Tom shakes his head and turns the vehicle to them.

'It's your grave, mate,' Tom says as he reaches for the rifle and pulls it into his lap. They get closer and the women begin to reach for their weapons and take cover behind their vehicles.

'We'd better swap places,' Wade says, and then he and Luna change seats.

'Here we go, great idea, Wade,' Tom says, fuming.

Luna leans out of the window and starts shouting something in Arabic and the women lower their weapons and return to the fire.

'See, see!' Luna says.

They approach the trucks slowly and stop at the bottom of the dune. Luna opens the door and steps out in the mud and clambers up the mound and the dog jumps out too and follows her. Tom goes to say something and gets as far as inhaling and decides not to. Wade gets out with his rifle and Tom sits there, shaking his head. He punches the seat between his legs and opens the door and steps out and looks over the bonnet. He steps round the truck and holds the weapon in one hand, careful

Caliphate

not to look too threatening. There are three hard-top jeeps caked in mud, parked around, with various bags strapped to the roofs. One of the vehicles has bullet holes in the trunk door. Luna walks up the mound in her boots that are too big and half the group looks at her, the other half looks at Wade and Tom at the bottom of the hill now standing next to each other.

'Are you going up?'

'Of course I am, there's a fire up there,' Wade says.

'Wade, we don't have time for this, mate,' Tom says, but Wade is already halfway up the mound slinging his weapon over his back.

'For fuck sake,' Tom mutters t himself.

Tom watches Luna greet the group and there is nodding and waves from most of the women and they maintain their positions standing around the fire with their hands in their pockets. She is talking to one of the women standing apart from the group. The woman wears a military trench coat and some jeans that look too big for her tucked into military black boots with an old AK-47 slung over her shoulder in a sling made out of string. Her long black hair rustles in the wind around her face and her eyes are brilliant green. Tom's heart flutters when he sees her eyes as he remembers the woman from the roadside massacre. She is no older than thirty, he thinks, and she has elegant features, high cheekbones and thin lips, and when she speaks he can see her teeth are in good condition.

Caliphate

She has a map poking out of her pocket and pouches clipped on to the belt on her waist, presumably containing ammunition and trauma control. Tom thinks she looks remarkably professional for a freedom fighter. The right side of her face is dusted with carbon and gun oil from firing. Luna starts to wipe her eyes with the blanket around her and the green-eyed woman puts her arms around her and holds her close, muttering something in her ear. She kisses her on the top of her head and the woman take Luna's head in both her palms and looks at her eyes nodding and talking, shaking her head and then brings her head back to her chest. Tom knows what the green-eyed woman has heard and shares her sympathy. This is mourning and he doesn't belong here, he thinks. Here are these people finding somewhere to start again, fleeing from what terrible lives they had been chained to for so long, and he feels some remorse that he could have done more that day of the execution and for a moment he is catapulted back there. How could you just watch, he thinks as his head gently shakes. Wade reaches the top and looks around the group and holds his hands out to the fire. The group just stare at him, his curly hair bobbing in the wind and rain, and his clothes unfamiliar. Tom looks around and heads up the mound and he can feel the twinge of pain in his knee; he had not walked up a hill for a while. He doesn't want to look at the women's eyes but he can't help it. Some are wearing men's clothing that is

Caliphate

too big for their small frames. They are all different ages and he guesses that maybe the youngest is now Luna and the oldest looks to be a thirty-something woman sitting on a crate. The fire is large and there is a large cooking pot held on a metal tripod above the flames. He can smell something sweet coming from the steam. The women take turns looking him over and he watches them, all standing there staring at the fire with their hands in their pockets, heads nuzzled into the collars of their jackets. Tom looks around the relatively silent crowd and gives a few nods as he zips up his jacket further; he had taken the truck heat for granted. Some nod back. One smiles, her woollen hat pulled over her ears and nearly her eyes. He attempts a smile back but its intention barely makes it to his lips. Luna turns around to them, her eyes red from crying.

'I stay here now, is that okay?' she says, pulling her hair from her mouth as the wind tosses it everywhere, one hand holding the blanket around her.

They both look at her. Wade nods gently, and Tom sees him swallow a lump in his throat. He had caught fire inside. Wade had accidentally cared for her future. Tom thinks this was a mistake and he could see that back in the building when he woke up. Tom is more detached than Wade – he keeps everything in its rightful place in his mind and never

Caliphate

lets feelings cross-contaminate with those which don't belong together. But this is wrong and he knows it. Life is not something as clinical as that.

Luna walks up to Wade and throws her arms around his neck and stands on her tiptoes and presses against his filthy jacket. He is a lot taller than her and her head comes to about his mid chest. He puts one arm around her and holds the rifle in the other hand. He just looks over to the fire and his eyes never leave it but something leaves his eyes. The others watch her and the green-eyed woman looks at Tom.

'I won't forget you,' Luna says with her head in his chest.

She pushes away slowly and runs her hands down his free arm and holds his hand in both of hers. She has tears streaking down her face, creating little channels in the dirt and dried blood from the corners of her eyes to her lips.

'I know,' Wade says.

She looks at him for a moment longer then holds out her hand to Tom and he looks around at the group all waiting for his response. He takes her hand and shakes it gently, her thin fingers and her shaking stopping his heart.

'It is always now,' she says, her eyes shifting around his face. He can feel her looking at the gash on his head.

'And that's all there ever was,' he says.

Caliphate

He looks around the surrounding desert. A vehicle way off in the distance stuck and silent, some tracks dotted around that will probably be there for a long time after the rain has passed.

'You should take the rifle in the truck. You know what these women are doing, don't you?' And then he lets go of her hand.

'Yes, I do.' And she steps away and walks down the slope to the truck. Tom walks past Wade who hasn't moved and approaches the green-eyed woman and stands in front of her.

She shrugs the rifle sling more on to her shoulder and her eyes study his face as if she is looking at a bad painting. She is.

'Single aimed shots, never automatic,' he says.

She glances at her rifle quickly and then back to him and responds with a quick nod. He takes a deep breath and turns and walks down the slope to the truck and passes Luna on the way back up.

'Good luck,' he says.

'You too' she responds.

He gets into the driver's side of the truck and leans over and looks through the open passenger door and looks for the dog and sees her by the fire.

'Come on, Lucy,' he shouts through the door.

Caliphate

The dog just stands there and then sits down next to Luna who is looking at her. Her ears pricked up and her nose twitching, looking back with her little eyes in her wet fur. Wade comes down the slope, watching his footing, and gets in the truck, then also looks at the dog.

'She not coming?' Wade says.

Lucy watches them from the top of the slope and then lies down next to the fire and closes her eyes. Luna crouches down and rubs her belly and she rolls on her side. Luna stands up and looks back at them and gives a little wave under the blanket.

Tom feels his heart capsize at the coldness of her betrayal and no amount of hard swallowing can hide that. He has to look away at the desolate desert to reinsert himself back into it but he has to look back at the dog. He takes it personally and he realises that he has to; he'd invested some spark of love in something transient that he'd thought was eternal. He knew it all along, but he was desperate for something that brought his mind, if only for a second, away from the desert and death. Something that could look back and nod and say 'I'm still here, right next to you. You're not alone.' A temporary replaced manifestation of something dearly missed. But she was just a dog and that was that; though not at the time. One last choking gulp, an attempt to masquerade his inner self from Wade.

Caliphate

'Not any more,' Tom says as he looks away.

They drive off in the early sunrise, leaving the group behind, and head north-west again. The rain has greatly reduced, a light drizzle now, but the clouds remain grey and bloated. The mud now more sticky and the tread on the tyres slips a lot and it's slow going. They pass fewer people, some stuck in the mud, digging their wheels out with hands and anything else that can shift it. On hands and knees pulling armfuls of sludge from in front of the wheels and tossing it to the side. Their breath steaming in the morning cold and their hands blue. The people digging never look at them once.

'Fuel light's on,' Tom says.

'Surprised it got us this far.'

Tom tosses Wade the phone and he turns it on and checks the signal and sits there shaking his head. He turns on Tom's radio and listens for any traffic. Just the crackle of white noise and he turns it off. The desert grows more features as they go, lines of mud dunes with thick cracks and water running off them. A huge square hole; maybe some excavation site some time ago. They see an old man pushing a motorbike through the mud, his head down and his hands on the throttle and mud kicking up all over his legs. The back of the bike loaded to capacity with plastic bags and a rolled-up blanket in a bin liner. The man looks at them for a few seconds and Tom looks back. The man's face a mask of mud, his eyes white as snow peering out. The bike's engine so caked in mud he wondered how it worked. They couldn't help him.

They come across some tracks in the mud coming around a dune and stop the truck. Three dead bodies are sprawled out in the dirt. One older man, a younger man and an elderly woman wearing some loose jeans and a parka jacket. Both men are naked. The blood is curdled in the mud around them. There are some suitcases emptied and tossed around and left lying in the soaked ground. Clothes scattered around as if they'd tossed all of their belongings around them in some strange cult sacrifice. The younger man and elderly woman had both been shot in the head. The elderly man had maybe eight holes in his chest and one in the lower part of his face. Tom stops the truck and looks at them over the bonnet and Wade leans out of the window and takes a quick look then pushes himself back in. Tom scans their bodies. The woman face down with her arms around the young man half underneath her and the elderly man face up with his arms out to the side. He looks at the tracks of their vehicle leading off into the distance.

He's tired, of everything. These people wanted no part of this – they just wanted to escape, he thinks. But you don't just get up and leave; they won't let you. And that is why they have to be destroyed. Violence

Caliphate

won't stop them, but it will slow them down because the fact has to be realised that they are moving. It's not a case of revenge for what has happened or preparation against what could happen, it is what *is* happening. How does this all happen, how did it get so far? No such questions can have any value in such depth of desert he thinks. Too late, his eyes flicker, we are just too late. Such observations were made hundreds, maybe thousands of years ago, when we really didn't understand; when we really can look back and say 'we didn't know any better'. He wants to look at Wade but he knows him well enough. Look and laugh, the human abortion, are you proud? He closes his eyes – every tool the cosmos could divinely conceive and all the time of your choosing to achieve it in, divine hoax. Bastard, he thinks.

Tom pulls the truck away and handrails the tracks, following them around and along the steep dune. The tracks move off their intended bearing slightly and he can see that Wade is unhappy with this deviation, given the fuel situation.

'We need the diesel, mate,' Tom says, glancing at him.

'It's not about the gas, is it?' Wade says, looking through the passenger window at the mud ground as it passes by slowly.

'Not entirely, no.'

Caliphate

They follow the tracks for maybe twenty minutes before they come to two sets of soaked black coveralls lying in the tracks and footprints stamped in the mud all around where the truck had stopped temporarily. The ends of the sleeves and trouser-legs flick in the wind. They push on and come to a stop at the end of a series of dunes that mark the boundaries to a long flat plane of spotted shrubbery and mounds. A vehicle is in the distance, maybe 300 metres away, static beside a large row of mounds. Tom takes out his rangefinder and presses it to his eyes. It's a silver Toyota Land Cruiser with a plastic sheet wrapping blowing off the roof in the wind like a dysfunctional ghost tied to a wall. There appears to be no one in the vehicle and he assumes they had ran out of fuel and continued on foot. He puts the rangefinder on the seat and creeps the truck forward another 150 metres, Wade picks up his rifle, takes off the magazine and checks it, and slides it back on, holding it in his lap. Tom stops again; he could now see the number plate and its Arabic writing. He picks up the rangefinder and looks again. The Land Cruiser is unoccupied and there are footprints from the driver's door leading to the front and disappearing. He can't see the passenger side.

'You still want to check it out?' Wade says.

Tom holds the rangefinder in both hands, resting his forearms on the steering wheel, looking through the hole. His eyes shift down to the top of the steering wheel and he just rests them there in a trance. The thought of walking again trumps everything.

'Tom?' Wade says.

The windscreen bursts with an almighty crack and something hits Wade in the chest. Tom flies back in his seat and scrambles for the door handle and stalls the truck, keeping his head low.

'Front! Front!' Tom yelps.

The door swings open with the assistance of the wind and he falls out into the mud and quickly pulls himself out of the sucking ground, grabbing on to the doorframe and pulling himself to his knees. Another crack thumps into the door and another the bonnet and then there is a series of cracks over the roof. He pulls himself half into the footwell and grabs his rifle and shoots his gaze up to Wade. He is leaning on his left forearm in his seat with his mouth gasping for air. He can hear him wheezing.

'Wade, fucking climb over now!'

Another three rounds snap into the seat where Tom has been sat and send foam bursting over the dash. Tom pushes himself out and peers over the inside doorframe, over the bonnet towards the Land Cruiser and sees two heads exposed over the mound. He pulls up the rifle and balances it in the join of the door and the frame and flicks off the safety catch, immediately firing four shots in quick succession. The heads take cover. He spins his head towards Wade and sees him still on his forearm. His face changes to a white colour and his eyes are wide as he sucks in air with foamy blood leaking from the corners of his mouth. His right hand reaches around to his belt kit and draws out one of his magazines and throws it towards Tom on to the driver's seat.

'Stay down, please, just stay low.'

Tom's eyes go straight back to his sights and he sees one of the men emerge over the mound and bring up a weapon. He steadies the red cross-hairs on the man's centre and sucks in his breath and fires one well-placed round over the bonnet into his chest. He follows it up by firing again rapidly, some rounds clipping the edge of the mound and maybe one more hits the man. He sees his body slump over the crest of the mound then he's dragged over behind.

He looks back at Wade and sees him reach out for the dash and grab on to a windscreen wiper and pull himself up. He gets a few inches up and another round snaps into his hand, ricocheting into the roof. A dusting of blood sprays over Wade's face and he lets out a deep whine as he tumbles into the footwell.

'Get the clutch, get the clutch!' Tom shouts.

Caliphate

Wade is on his stomach in the footwell, curved around the gear stick. He pulls his arm from underneath him and pushes in the clutch. There is a steady pool of blood forming.

Tom fires again, the mud from the mound kicking up in small splashes. He leans in with his right arm and switches on the truck. Wade lets up the clutch and the truck creeps forward under the idling revs. Tom walks with the truck using it for cover, keeping his rifle pointing over the bonnet. He fires three more rounds and his rifle stops. He ejects the empty magazine and reaches into the driver's seat, patting around for one of the mags Wade threw him. He finds one and stuffs it on to the rifle and re-leases the working parts forward. The man comes around the side of the mound and fires a burst but misses the truck. Tom returns three rounds and the rifle stops. Empty again.

'Stay with it, Wade, hang on!'

He keeps his eyes on the mound, waiting for the next emer-gence, walking alongside the truck. They are about forty metres from the Land Cruiser now. He finds Wade's last magazine on the seat and reloads the rifle and controls his breathing. The truck moves slowly closer, he keeps his eyes on the place he thinks the man would emerge from again on top of the mound. Breathing slowly. The next rounds come from in front of the Land Cruiser, snapping into the engine block and radiator. He jolts

Caliphate

the rifle's direction to the man hanging over the bonnet of the truck and fires and he sees the sparks as his round hit the man's rifle and he falls back. The man falls in a manner that allows Tom to see his arm, and he shoots it twice, missing the first time.

He steps away from the vehicle and walks at a brisk pace to the man, his rifle steadied on him. His feet sucking in the mud. Twenty metres now. He can see the top half of the man's body and he stops and fires another two rounds at his gut. The rifle stops and he discards it and draws out his pistol. His heart is thumping and his legs are shaking. He gets to the Land Cruiser and sees the man on the floor looking at him, his face screwed up in pain. He shoots him in the face twice instantly and steps over him. He checks the slide of the pistol with a flash of a look, it is fully forward. He moves around the side of the mound keeping the pistol in front of him and edges slowly round. He hears the truck bump into the Land Cruiser and stall again. He emerges around the side and sees the second man sat with his back against the mound with a huge laceration in his face that allows Tom to see his teeth. The man slowly reaches for the rifle next to him and Tom shoots him three times in the neck and side of the head. The man slumps instantly into his own lap position and then slides down the slope. He moves back to the Land Cruiser and looks in the passenger window and sees nothing but interior. He tries to run to

Wade and falls in the mud and quickly picks himself up and goes to the passenger door.

Wade is sitting up against the gear-stick with his arm hooked over the seat, his hand missing its ring finger down to the knuckle and lying in a still pool of blood that ran between the seats. His radio next to the blood. In his lap is his pack opened and his hand inside it. Tom clambers over the seat and steps one foot into the footwell and grabs Wade by the armpits and hoists his heavy body into the centre seat. His body is limp and lifeless. He kneels next to him and unzips Wade's outer jacket and then his other jacket. He takes hold of the neck of his thermal top that is soaked in blood and rips it down the middle in two sharp yanks and pulls it apart. He studies his bloodied chest frantically. A large tattoo of a frog with angry red eyes on his left pectoral and a hole the size of a jellybean below his left collarbone. He reaches his hand around his left armpit and finds no sign of an exit wound.

'Don't let it take you mate, Don't let it,' Tom says in a voice collapsing from sorrow.

He reaches around his right armpit and further round and pulls his hand away. It is covered in thick warm blood. The bullet had travelled through both lungs after it ricocheted off his ribs. He checks his pulse with his bloody hand and after a moment falls into the seat and sits next to him looking through the frame of the windscreen at the plastic sheet flapping in the wind; the silence around the flapping terrifying. Wade's electric eyes fixed on his final sight before he allowed himself into the darkness. His chin resting on his chest looks as if he is staring into his lap. His curly hair flutters in the breeze. He puts his arm around Wade's shoulders and pulls him into his lap and just sits there holding him.

And it was all lost in a moment. Everything he meant to say to him, everything he ever wanted to ask him slowly dissolves away, leaving a void of confusion. Memories are all that remain now, and Wade, the keeper and caretaker of his place in Tom's mind and heart, has walked away and left, leaving only his history collecting dust. Look when you wish, but remember: each memory is delicate and will perish more and more with every summoning. Why does it hurt so bad? We know why.

He stays there a long time. He weeps and stops and weeps again, and then he just falls asleep. Machines with human hearts

Caliphate

10

The white room was no longer white. Paintings filled every space of the room all around him and beneath his feet. Some large and some small but all neatly fitted together with no spaces between. All he could see was the brown canvasses of the backs of them; they looked like hessian.

This time he knew where he was. He moved his arm and felt his face and then looked at his hand and turned it. His hand felt cold and plastic-like. He moved his head around and looked himself over. He was wearing what he had fallen asleep in and he was just as filthy. He could see mud-caked boots. He stood there a while and tried to compose himself but could think of nothing other than where he was, a room filled from top to bottom with paintings. If he tried to think outside this, it was as if he hit his head on some ceiling and fell and returned to the room, as if he was trying to think beyond the existing universe. He moved his foot out to take a step and he could do it and it felt no different as if he took a step on the pavement – the same feeling of contact with material and gravity – and then he took another step and stood still. He turned his head and looked at the open door and then returned it to the far wall in front of him. He went to walk forward but something was aroused in him that began to scare him. A haze of anxiety dropped over him like turning out the light while looking in the mirror and hesitating to turn it on again. He stepped backwards and turned around to the door and walked slowly towards it. He approached the walls opposite the door and reached out to one of the paintings. A small one the size of a shoebox. He pinched the corner of the painting and it felt very cold, like reaching into a freezer. He pulled the corner away and slowly turned it around and held it in both hands. It was an oil painting of his first cat his family had when he was small, it was in the jaws of a large dog and appeared to be being tossed around. The cat's eyes were nearly protruding out of its skull and its front legs were helplessly crossed over underneath it. In the background he could see a silhouette of his father who was running towards the dog and everything else remained blurred. It caused him to remember that moment and it felt like the first memory he had, and he had never thought of it until now, but the thought was there all along. It just happened so long ago, it got lost in all the clutter of his life. That was the first cat he had and it was killed by a neighbour's dog when he was two years old. Remembering it felt like an injection of some ghastly concoction into his veins coursing its way through to his brain. He put the painting back and it turned itself around. He picked up the one next to it that was about the size of a coffee table top. He turned it around and a feeling of anguish stabbed his brain like a red-hot poker and he dropped it face up. A perfect painting of the hacked-up man in the tank trench crawling towards him. So well painted it looked 3D as if the man was reaching out to him. He stepped back and the picture moved back to the wall into its original place without a sound and turned around exposing the canvas. He became stiff again and moving was difficult as if he was slowly being sealed in drying concrete. His jaw became tight and his teeth clenched slightly and the tinnitus began. And then the paintings started to move. This time he knew what was going to happen and he could feel his heart slow down and his vision began to blur. Then he saw her come slowly through the door. Her steps gentle and elegant. One hand outstretched reaching for him and her fingers looked soft and warm; perfect, he thought. He tried to pry his arm up from his side and it was like bending an iron bar. The paintings a quarter way round.

Caliphate

The hideous silence of it all. His teeth crunching against each other. He widened his eyes as far as they would go and with all his strength bent his iron arm slightly. She had a soft warm smile that told a thousand stories, each of which he couldn't remember. Her hair across one side of her face and her flowery dress flowed with her movements. She came closer and he could feel her warmth, like a growing fire. She took his hand and the paintings slowed down their turn. His body relaxed slightly and his jaw loosened and his arm lost the iron feel. She extended her other arm and reached for his other hand. He took a single step and pried his other arm away from his side and took it, his body relaxed further and he now had more control. She remained smiling and nodded to him as approval. He took a few steps holding her hands and she walked backwards to the doorway pulling him to it. His teeth now completely loosened off and his heart started to function normally again and the details of his vision came back. She stepped back through the door into the darkness and pulled him halfway through. His body became warm as she disappeared with his hands and forearms as if she walked through a black wall. Then he felt a sharp tug and he was absorbed completely into the blackness, followed by an enormous slam all around him.

The room, the last broadcast of the mind before death, the chamber of the worst of the paintings and the revealing of them all simultaneously was the end. He had transcended the horizon of death and it was terrifying, but he knew now. And he was now out of it. Stay away from the room if you can. But the endless horror of the desert sent him back there time and time again and eventually he forgot what else there was in the world. But she did as she said, she guarded the door.

He opens his eyes to the rumble of thunder echoing around the desert. His lifts his head and looks around. Wade is still in his lap, his body cold, and the Land Cruiser is still in front of him with the bumper of the truck resting against it. The clouds are grey and the rain is gently showering all around. He checks Wade's pulse again and still finds nothing; he knew what he was expecting. He looks at his watch, 13.46. He takes a moment to absorb the situation. He is incredibly thirsty and the thought of drinking a lot of water cuts though his every decision he was aligning in their order. He gently lowers Wade's body on to the seat and slides himself out from underneath it, then gently lowers his cold head on to the seat with his hand and steps out into the mud. He reaches over into the bed and rips open the plastic packaging of one of the crates of water and takes a bottle, twists the lid from its seal and sucks the bottle dry. The water is freezing and it turns his stomach into a sack of ice. He tosses the bottle and re-peats. He drinks half rapidly and has to stop to retch. Nausea blurts through his gut for a few seconds, passes and he drinks again. He leans on the side of the truck and looks around. The loneliness again. Everything around him dead and empty. He takes some deep breaths to keep the sorrow at bay and walks over to the Land Cruiser. He opens the door, reaches in and turns the key. The batteries are fine but the fuel light is on. That's why they stopped. He turns the key and the engine turns over, but doesn't start. He tries a few more times and concludes it's empty. He looks around the inside of the car for anything of use. Some passports in the glove box, one woman's and two men's. The boot is full of possessions, a large vase, some elegant china sets, suitcases crammed full of old photos in their frames and fashionable cloths and suits. Nothing of any use. He pushes out of the driver's door and releases the knot of the thick plastic sheet rapping in the wind, balls it up under his arm and walks back to the truck. The thunder creeping closer with accompanying black clouds. He looks at Wade's body on the seat and sees his hand that was inside the pack was grasping his flare. He stands for a moment and thinks about this. He grabs Wade's radio that is on the seat and finds it is switched on and he can hear white noise very faintly coming from it. He picks it up and turns up the volume.

'Any call sign, this is Witchcraft One Delta, Mayday Mayday Mayday.'

Caliphate

He holds it there looking into the screen. The signal bar still. He looks around, the tracks leading back the way they came. Then there is a crackle of white noise.

He looks at the signal bar and sees it flutter with signal, two bars then three, back to one bar and then nothing. Something had heard him. His body goes hot, a flush running from his heart all around him, right through to the fingertips.

'Anyone this is Witchcraft One Delta, please help.'

He pauses in anticipation, staring at the signal bar, dead and silent for a few seconds then two bars shoot to life and he hears some faint voice, so distant in the interference he reserves part of his judgement to him just hearing things. He can't understand any of it, just the crackle singing in different tones. But someone was hearing him. He turns it up to full volume and throws the radio in his pocket along with the flare. He lays out the plastic sheet, using some empty magazines to hold down the corners from the wind, and slides out Wade's heavy body, holding him under the armpits, and lowers him on to it. There is thick crimson blood all over the seat. He goes to the bed and takes two bungees that Wade had used to tie down the crates. He takes Wade's full pistol magazines and the map out of his pockets; all his rifle magazines were empty. He wraps Wade's body in the plastic sheet and ties it tight around his feet, using one of the bungees until he could tighten it no more, and joins the hooks. He does the same around Wade's waist, pulling them tight until his body was mummified in the tarp. He grabs his own pack and takes anything from Wade's pack that he needs; a packet of crackers, maps, a radio battery, NVG, his wallet in its waterproof bag and the thousand dollars. He opens his own pack and sees his remaining rations had burst in their packaging, takes them out and studies them, and sees a bullet had torn through them. He eats what he can of them and salvages the remaining cheese and crackers. He packs away all the items and some water from the crates into his daysack then eats an onion and some tomatoes with some of the crackers and leaves the rest then opens the map.

He studies his chosen route to the border then gets a grid from his rangefinder and plots it. He's not far from the Syrian border, maybe twenty kilometres. He takes a bearing and puts everything away and shoulders the daysack. He goes over to the men he killed and plunders them and comes away with a fairly well-kept AK-47 with one and a half magazines. Their bodies can stay exactly where he initiated their decomposition. He pops the bonnet of the truck and inspects the engine. The radiator had been shot through and had emptied while he was asleep and the engine block has a few entry holes. He checks underneath and sees a large pool of oil sitting on the ground curdling in the watery mud. He tries the engine but it doesn't even turn over. Foot it is.

He takes the corners of the poncho and ties them around his waist and sets off walking west on his bearing, dragging his friend behind him.

Walking is hard work. His knee begins to hurt again as soon as he sets off, with the weight and having to pull his feet out of the sucking mud. He slips over constantly, landing on his hands and knees, and after a while he is soaked again. There are no tracks anywhere but he sticks to his bearing regardless of how remote it gets. He walks for hours and is constantly out of breath, his legs trembling from the stress but he can't stop with the Syrian border so close. He stares at the ground most of the time, his mind elsewhere, anywhere but here. Sometimes stray emotions surface and he sheds tears which fall to the mud; the rest of the tears are the sky as if the clouds are crying with him.

The dark sky is towed from the east over to the west. He checks occasionally and sees the mist of the downpour in the far east spewing out of the approaching darkness and the flashes of lightning ignited the clouds in a strobe. Another storm rolls towards him, maybe a few hours away; if he is caught in this one, he will die. He leaves the radio on and checks it occasionally, asking for anyone; sometimes he receives

Caliphate

four bars of signal but it is the same response of white noise every time. But the signal means one thing; someone is trying to talk to him.

After about ten kilometres he stops, gasping for air. He has to rest, the mud and his exhaustion catching up with his will and he just stands there looking around, panting. He can hear through the rain a faint rattling of something in the wind, and he holds his breath between pants to try and get a direction of it, but the teasers are ushered by the wind back the way they came. He takes out the rangefinder and scans around, trying to keep it steady by holding his breath. To the south-west he can see a large ridge running across the horizon from north to south then disappearing off as it curves around to the north. It looks like a wall of mud. He runs the rangefinder across it slowly and can see some barbed wire on the top. He scans further still to the north-west and sees a breach in the wall and studies it. A large chain link gate open, maybe the size of an arctic lorry trailer, swinging in the wind crashing into its other half.

This is the border and he's been here before. If he were a betting man he would say there would be patrols around here by now, but he isn't a betting man, so he will just grant that there are. He checks Wade's body and sees that it is still tight. He puts the rangefinder away and takes out the radio.

'Any call sign this is Witchcraft One Delta, is anyone…'

Caliphate

Before he can finish he looks to his north and sees a small black mushroom-shaped cloud rising from the ground. He instantly knows what it is; he has seen many before. There is no noise from it for a moment and then a very slight rumble and thump comes his way, so brief and quiet he would not have heard it if he wasn't looking or mistaken it for approaching thunder. The adrenalin is released instantly, coursing through his every vein.

'Witchcraft One Charlie this is Witchcraft One Delta!' he says purposefully into the radio.

That's Glenn. He is sure of it; there's no doubt in his mind. But how could it be? He's way past the extraction date, he thinks. What if they delayed because of the weather? How would they know we aren't all dead? Because Glenn couldn't make it in the weather on his bike and he still has the radio to reschedule. Maybe, probably, definitely. What matters is that was an engagement from a deep fire patrol and his certainty crafts that into truth.

He makes a bearing to the now perishing cloud from the rocket and sets off. It is no more than three miles. It couldn't be. He speeds up his pace and slows down after maybe a hundred metres because of fatigue. He isn't getting there any time soon and the ground is hard work, soon to be harder when the next storm blots out the sun. The thought of being rescued is now what is on his mind, no matter what else he thinks about – his state, Wade, the mud, the border – the thought always merges into what is going on in that area. He looks at the sky and sees the black and grey blanket rolling closer. The thunder now torments him. He comes parallel with the chain link fence and stops. One gate is locked in place with a hole cut through the corner. The other half is bent up at the bottom corner, swinging in the wind from some vehicle ramming. There is another mud wall that runs parallel, following it all the way north and south. Two huge walls of mud scrape out of the ground and forge into a tall barrier maybe ten metres high. Between is a labyrinth of old rusted razor wire that not even the most professional contortionist could worm through with all the time in the world. There is a large portable cabin between the walls behind the gate that was probably the border control point. It is peppered with shrapnel and was initially white but now has a huge black blast stain on the front and the empty window-frames have a thick dusting of soot and smoke stains climbing above them from a fire. There is graffiti on the side and empty water bottles and rubbish scattered, blowing around everywhere. He looks at it, catching his breath. They were dropped on the other side of the border and came through this control point. The familiar sight is comforting, like seeing the signs for your home-town after a long tiring journey. He catches his breath and continues, the border wall a few hundred metres to his left. Wade's body becomes heavier and heavier, not because of the weight but because of his diminishing strength. He stops every twenty or so metres to catch his breath and uses this time to check for any movement where he saw the mushroom cloud. Nothing, he is too far away and there are mounds in the way. He turns around slowly, scanning the landscape and sees them. He wishes he was a gambling man.

'No…'

He can see the glint of two windscreens coming along the wall from the south. Then three. He knows exactly who they are. He falls to his knees and turns and looks to where he is going. He takes out the rangefinder and glasses the vehicles. Of course they're not refugees, his mind snaps at its optimistic side. He looks around hurriedly and collides with the desolation as if he has just woken up here.

This is the end of the road. This is going to be his failed final stand. There is nowhere to run and nowhere to hide and anything worth running to is too far to get to before he is seen. He looks back to the oncoming trucks. Seven now, staggered behind each other. Headlights on and bouncing up and down coming straight at him. He looks to the approaching storm to the east; its darkness swamping everything underneath, coming closer. The rain is beginning to pick up again, the wind has grown colder. His hope and passion to live hit a wall. A car crash of emotion shattering everything. There is nothing he could do and so he looks at Wade. His body muddy and his face white and wet. What's the point of it all? Endless warfare making tramps of good, strong men. He is not a murderer but an emergency killer of murderers. Way out in the untouched lands where only hordes of death roam, there are no courts, no police and no order. War is an emergency, a return to a form of morality which we have worked so hard to come from and in this emergency there is a difference between emergency killers of murderers and murderers of emergency killers. Wade's eyes long entered the glazed, murky glass looking stare with a yellow tinge that comes after death, locked in glaucoma.

You came as far you could, the thought settles over him like a warm blanket. He feels his hand hover to his pistol. It's the right thing to do. His hands clasp the grip, the freezing metal. Each thought of each movement rehearsing over and over: remove pistol from holster, check the chamber, open your mouth and rest the cold, carbon-stained steel on your tongue and find your most cherished thought, let it take the mind away. Relax and let the finger pull back the trigger. You won't feel a thing, do it quick. His eyes shift up to the vehicles and the blanket is lifted; every thought is cold again.

Fight. Fight until there is nothing left. Until the end. It is only the end when you can truly know all is lost, and you wont even know. He closes his eyes and can hear their engines in the distance, so quiet, everything so hideously quiet like a graveyard. The gate rattles again with a gentle crash and he looks at it swing back open.

He jabs the pistol back into the holster, where it belongs, swings around the AK-47 off his back into both hands and checks the chamber.

'Okay,' he says, he looks to the dark clouds. 'Okay.'

So go into the void violently, kicking, screaming, biting. Make it as hard as possible. He takes out the radio.

'Anyone, this is Witchcraft One Delta, if there is anyone who can hear me I need immediate support at Entry Rendezvous Bravo.'

He waits for a response as he looks at the vehicles that would otherwise be here by now if it wasn't for the bogging ground. He lays the radio on Wade's chest and takes off his daysack and places it next to him. He gets behind his body for cover and rests the rifle on his chest and looks over the sights in the growing rain. The cold wet mud now shaking him again. He sees a small figure slowly emerge out of the sunroof of the first vehicle, a black mound of a figure lacking any human form and he steadies his sights on the first car's windscreen driver's side and resists his shaking. He shuffles his elbows down into the dirt until his platform is stable with the foregrip of the rifle resting on Wade's abdomen. He takes a few breaths then holds, perfectly aligning the front and rear sight. All he can hear is the rain and his cowering heart thumping in the wet mud, each beat marking the seconds of the clock face with its old batteries behind. He squeezes the trigger and the blast is deafening and it has more recoil than he anticipated. The lead vehicle slides to a halt, like a sidewinder snake, profiling its side. The man out of the sunroof drops down. The other vehicles stop in a more controlled fashion. He fires a few shots again at the side of the door and waits. All the vehicles have stopped in a pack. Nothing moves and no doors opens and he could just see the fumes from the exhausts. He is about to fire again when he hears a distant sound behind him as if a balloon had been popped. He rolls on to his side and looks behind and sees the throbbing red flare arcing in descent in the distance.

In his thirty years on the planet, he had never felt so much comfort from a mere object. Suddenly he feels invincible; everything he has ever loved returns into consciousness with the freshness of birth. The beautiful colours of life painted instantly over the greyness and bleakness of melancholy.

'Yes! Yes!' he mutters.

He rolls back over and grabs the flare from his pocket and unscrews the end while looking to the pack of trucks. They stay still. He tosses the end cap of the flare, rolls on to his back and holds it up, pulling the release cord and sending it whooshing straight up into space, and stares at it until the phosphorous strikes to life like a giant match. He watches it as if a God had finally revealed itself to its so-desperate creation. We waited so long and did everything as you asked but you watched all along like a masochist as we manufactured every tool to bring about our own death, you should have come before we split the atom. He looks at the other flare in the distance twisting around held on by its little parachute. And then he hears the thumping, that familiar sound. The sound of safety, the feeling of responsibility shifting. He looks back at the trucks and sees men climbing from the doors slowly, walking to the front of the pack where the lead vehicle is sideways. Black figures wearing the mismatched uniforms of the cult of endless death. None are armed but that does not have any value to him right now.

The thumping of the helicopter blades grows slightly louder and he turns again and see two of them slowly emerge out over the horizon of the long wall of mud. He looks at his flare and sees it slowly descending, he is desperate for them to see it, his life depends on it. They must have seen it, must have, he thinks. The helicopters approach where the other flare is falling and the lead one slows to a hover and the other swoops around it and begins circling the immediate area. The first lifts its nose and begins climbing down to the surface slowly and then disappears behind the mounds, and he can then only see the other helicopter circling around. He glances at the group of men and back to the flare hissing in the rain like a surrounded snake. What if they don't see the flare, he thinks, but responds immediately; they absolutely have seen it. The flare is now starting to crackle, its final sounds that give warning of its approaching demise. He nearly breaks his neck looking in all three directions so quickly. As the seconds pass the feeling of grief begins to creep back through his thoughts as the roof of hope starts to leak. The circling helicopter now on its second loop. The flare straining in its final burn. The group static and watching him. He sees the first helicopter slowly rise from the surface.

'Here! I'm…' He stopped himself. Pointless.

He watches as it rises and then stops, hovering like a genie. The moment that will decide whether he lives or dies. His eyes lock on the circling aircraft as it swoops around like a kestrel in the opposite direction, it circles slowly around to the north and then it banks to the west. His heart races. The hovering helicopter snatches its nose towards his direction and dips as it begins thumping towards him.

He rises to his knees, the feeling of isolation washing from his being. He reaches into his pocket and takes out his Velcro Union Jack flag and slaps it on to the Velcro patch of his arm. He feels surrounded by the warmth of everything that matters to him. Old plans now resurface and

Caliphate

chambered desires are freed as the prospect of life chops through the air like the true saviour. For the first time in as long as he can remember, he feels his drained, emaciated body succumb to the fight. Death and life lay down their swords and turn into their respective directions to light and dark to postpone the battle for which they had fought for so long. He raises his filthy hands into the air and places them on his wet matted hair. No words to speak. Just the trembling of his body as it resynchronises. The first Black Hawk pointing straight to him and the second banking around and now in pursuit. It follows the wall towards him and as it grows closer he can see the pilots' heads looking around at the myriad of controls. The awesome chopping and whirring of the rotor fends off the frightening silence of the empty desert. The door gunner leaning out, looking straight towards Tom and Wade. Tom gazes in awe and marvels at the ingenuity of the aircraft. The first Black Hawk pulls up its nose as it slows and he is looking almost directly up at it. It flicks its tail to the side and the door gunner sights the mini gun on the group and peers over the sights. The second Black Hawk whooshes past towards the group and circles them with its action side pointing towards them. Tom cocks his head, closes his eyes as the down-draught nearly knocks him off his knees and the helicopter slowly drops in front of him. The deafening screaming of the engine.

Caliphate

He looks up to the side door and sees four men climb down into the dirt and move towards him, one man with his rifle pointing towards him and the other three aimed at the group. They come slowly closer. They are all wearing multi cam trousers and shirts that look brand new in comparison to his. Their small helmets have NVGs folded up and their body armour is littered with uniformed pouches containing medical treatment and magazines. Their rifles look bright and well cleaned. The faces behind their goggles look alien to him. He hadn't seen someone so clean in many weeks and he could almost smell their freshness. The man with his rifle pointing towards Tom stops a few metres in front of him and takes out an A6 plastic card from a stowage panel on his chest and holds it in one hand.

Tom kneels there and bathes in the warm breeze of the helicopter and squints. His hair is tossed in the wind and whips his neck and face. He is shaking violently, not from the cold.

'Your name?' the man in front shouts over the engine. He was almost certainly from the US.

Tom blinks erratically; he can't take his eyes off him. He has to swallow multiple times in order to summon some language.

'Thomas… Thomas Marshall,' he says as loudly as he can, his voice tight and laced with the precursor of tears.

Caliphate

'Troop?'

'C... C Troop, C Troop.' He takes a few seconds to remember, he had not thought of these things for some time.

'Parent unit?' The man screams again, his rifle pointing straight at Tom's face. The two men on Tom's flank never looked at him once.

'...22 ...Special Air Service.' His voice growing worse.

'Your spouses name?'

And this is the question that boils over the emotion. His mouth waters and his eyes burst with tears. He takes one hand from his head to cover his mouth and looks at the door of the helicopter. The man lowers his rifle and kneels down in front of him and leans into his ear and puts his hand on his shoulder.

'What's your wife called?' the man says.

He looks into the man's eyes, but he might as well not be there. His love had been reborn while he knelt there in the mud. He is shaking and his lungs juddering from the suppression of hysterical crying and he tries to squeeze out her name, but it is the hardest thing he has ever had to say.

'Her... her name is... is Lucy.'

Caliphate

He couldn't say anything more for all the money in the world. The tears left his eyes to be vaporised by the helicopter fumes; he was human, after all.

The man slings his rifle instantly and puts away the card and throws Tom's arm around his neck.

'You're going home, Tom, you're going home to Lucy, okay, buddy? Can you walk? Try and stand up if you can.'

He tries to get to his knees but he's a wreck and then tries again and manages.

'That's it, Tom, all the way up. We just have to get you over there. Vince! Vince! get his other arm.'

'Okay…' Tom says, like a confused child, as he holds on to the man for dear life. 'Okay.'

Another man comes to his side and takes his other arm and he makes it to his feet.

'That's it, everything's going to be all right, you're in safe hands now, get you some hot food and a beer, how does that sound huh,'

Tom just looks at the helicopter doors as they come closer.

'Have you got Wade?'

'Yeah we've got him, I'm sorry.'

Caliphate

He stops and looks around and sees the other two men dragging Wade's body behind them.

Two men in pristine condition, well fed and strong carry the most broken man they have ever seen. He looks like an ancient relic found deep in some rotten dungeon of despair. As they approach the door of the Black Hawk, the door gunner looks at Tom as if he is witnessing some ghastly crime, shaking his head slowly and reaching out as if to help him on. The men either side of him help him on and he steps up on to the metal floor. He takes his eyes off the door gunner and looks around in amazement. On the floor are two men just like the ones who helped him, wearing surgical gloves and tending to a man between them. Glenn is lying on a stretcher with most of his trousers and shirt cut away and the two men are operating on his legs, half of Glenns right foot is missing. His eyes travel to Glenn's face and he sees him looking back at him over the oxygen mask. Glenn opens his hand inside its oil- and blood-stained glove and gives a gentle thumbs-up. He rode from the red point to here with half a foot. He wanted to touch Glenn but was guided to a seat, he wanted to know this was real. It is all too overwhelming and he falls back as his face loses all its colour and the men step into the door and help him into the seat at the back. He is crying, looking at Glenn, all noise muted by the

Caliphate

bellow of the engine. Wade's body wrapped in the plastic tarp is slid into the doorway and the final two men get in.

The helicopter slowly begins to ascend and one of the men takes off his goggles and sits next to him and takes Tom's hand in both of his and holds it tight and leans in and looks into Toms bloodshot eyes as they struggle to take in everything. Tom puts his other hand over his mouth and holds on to his face as if it was falling apart. He had been re-lieved of his role as the sole tender to his survival and now he is surround-ed by people performing the task for him, and the relief is all too quick. He could see one of the pilots has turned around and is looking at him and gives him a nod. Another man comes over, pulls on some plastic gloves and begins to examine the ravaged side of his face, gently pressing around the laceration. He looks over the door gunner's shoulder as the helicopter banks over the group of men on the ground, who all have their hands above their heads looking at the helicopters. He watches as they disappear out of view to be left in the desert and then the punishing grounds vanish as the helicopter straightens its course, their surrender too late. Just the low, grey and black sky stretched far across the world chas-ing them but always in front. One of the men throws a survival blanket over him and pulls it over his shoulders and he can smell the soap the

Caliphate

man had used whenever he last washed; he even picks up the aroma of coffee and toothpaste from one of them as they speak to him.

He looks around at the crew of the helicopter and feels the heat from the engine warm him. The arena of slaughter below now felt light-years from him as it is swept away into the past and he sits there wrapped in the blanket and just lets it slip away. All the dead and open graves, the stench of rot and the wandering depraved, the wanton violence and perpetual pain, the day the medieval world went away.

He looks out of the side door once during the journey and sees the desert gone and civilisation emerging from the fringes of the dirt. The lush green trees bathing in the sun, swaying gently in the cool, salty ocean breeze and the birds clinging to their branches in the shade like fruit. The long stretching blue rivers meandering through the land like maps of nerves and veins. The rows of houses side by side like little cakes stacked neatly against the flat tarmac roads with their ant occupants cooking and talking. Roads, he thinks. Interconnecting us from one end of the Earth to the other, snaking and twisting up the mountains and under the oceans, through the different cultures and cities in their journey back to where they started. We built them, he thinks, no road should lead to despair or misery and, if they do, they should be destroyed and rebuilt.

Caliphate

The last thing he read in the book the day he watched Wade's family turn to dust on the news: 'We must always takes sides. Neutrality helps the oppressor, never the victim. Silence encourages the tormentor, never the tormented'.

Caliphate

11

He tries to open his eyes but his eyelids seem glued together. He pulls up his hand and rubs his right eye with the knuckle of his index finger and feels the eyelids separate but closes his eye instantly against the sharp light and waits for it to adjust. He opens it again and can see a window-frame with golden sunlight beaming through and across an empty hospital bed a few feet away beside the one he is lying on. The sheets are neatly folded as if it has never been used and there are some machines on wheels with screens that are not turned on and wires coming from them. There are birds conversing outside in a tree and he can hear the rustling of the leaves. Their little chirps and songs so perfect and harmonic that he lies there for a second and lets them serenade him. He shifts his gaze to look down to the end of the bed and sees his feet under the warm duvet. His arm is cannulated in the crook of the elbow and he manages to open his other eye but that needs to adjust too and he lies there squinting one eye. He can feel his stomach completely empty and he is hungry instantly and his thirst for water is overwhelming. The smell of some antiseptic cleaning agent highjacks the sweet smell of clean air, and it is this that has caused him to realise he doesn't need to look for his weapons. There is no danger, no rain and cold. Careful, he thinks, you could wake up in the tank trench any time.

With both eyes now open he leans up on his arm and looks to his right to the corner of the room. On the chair under the woollen blanket is Lucy, her head buried in a pillow. He leans there on his arm and watches her sleep and smiles. Am I dead.

'Lucy,' he whispers.

Her eyes creak open and her pupils instantly dilate and before they are fully open she shoots out of the chair and wraps her arms around him, crying into the side of his neck. He falls back and she falls with him. He can feel the most precious beads of salt water running cold down his neck. He wraps his arms around her and sinks his face into her hair. The smell of her in that instant will haunt his memory for his remaining years. Her hair is as light as the finest silk ever crafted and her lips as warm as he remembered. His arms engulf her small back and her hands grip his hair as if humanity would vanish the second she let go.

He takes her soft hands in his. Skin so supple and delicately formed. He traces her arms with his eyes to her small round shoulders. Shoulders to her neck and neck to her face. We have come so far from dust, he thinks. He feels all the barriers of his mind lift as if he had been living in a tiny bedroom and decided to open the door one day and realised he was in a giant mansion with a million other rooms. He looks down and around the endless corridors of possibility.

They walk the corridors of the hospital with him pulling his wheeled pole stand laden with bags of solution to aid his recovery. The hard, shiny floor under his slippers, a sensation he craves, firm and true. Patients dotted through the corridors standing and talking to family and nurses, some watching television and playing chess.
On a television, on a english news channel; *Panspermia; Origin of life* ticker-taped across the screen.

People speak to him, but hardly any of the hospital staff spoke English and when he's spoken to he just nods until the interaction finishes. She holds his hand on their walk. Her soft velvet skin and her firm grip. The wooden doors and white walls of the corridors, music somewhere, a radio maybe, a ceiling. He needs it all, every single thing. They walk

Caliphate

around for his sake. He watches families greet loved ones in hospital beds, people carrying flowers and foods. He watches the lights beam over the corridor floors and briefly thinks of the stoning grounds. He knows that she watches him while he stares into the floor and that she knows him well enough to know that some part of him has seen something that forced itself deep into his soul, where it will stay for as long as his heart beats. His long stares vacant and lifeless like a derelict building with its remaining windows silent and still, watching the street, as its walls crumble to the ground.

They walk to the hospital garden with him in his robes and her in her dress and they sit on a bench looking out over the car park. Hundreds of cars of every colour and every manufacturer neatly parked in spaces. Motorbikes parked in a row near a curb towards the entrance. He scans the rows looking for the familiar tyres or that stoic headlight of his old horse. After a while he looks away, and never looks back to them.

She lets him stare and ponder at everything without interruption, watches him smell the air, searching for some faint, forgotten aroma that has been trodden and trampled by the decay and destitution of the wastelands. He lifts his head to taste the air as he runs his hand over the rough wooden bench and caresses the tulips in a pot close by.

Caliphate

He watches a small ladybird clamber over the grass and get lodged on its side in a thin crack in the pavement. He bends down and gently nudges it out of the crack with his index finger. It rolls on to its robotic legs and ventures off back on its journey without response, its small sweeping and circling antennae touching and mapping everything in front of it.

He sits up and watches it. A lonely, small freckled red dot meandering through the grass searching for something, struggling, searching maybe for home or a friend, but always hunted. After a moment, he just looks at the empty blue sky on the horizon. The endless blue ceiling as far as the eye can see, and the tiny ladybird.

That's all.

Caliphate